APOLLO'S LIGHTS

Heather H. Baer

APOLLO'S LIGHTS

a novel

Martha~
Your support and friendship are irreplaceable in my life!
Love,
Heather

TATE PUBLISHING & *Enterprises*

Apollo's Light
Copyright © 2011 by Heather H. Baer. All rights reserved.

No part of this publication may be reproduced, stored in a retrieval system or transmitted in any way by any means, electronic, mechanical, photocopy, recording or otherwise without the prior permission of the author except as provided by USA copyright law.

This novel is a work of fiction. Names, descriptions, entities, and incidents included in the story are products of the author's imagination. Any resemblance to actual persons, events, and entities is entirely coincidental.

The opinions expressed by the author are not necessarily those of Tate Publishing, LLC.

Published by Tate Publishing & Enterprises, LLC
127 E. Trade Center Terrace | Mustang, Oklahoma 73064 USA
1.888.361.9473 | www.tatepublishing.com

Tate Publishing is committed to excellence in the publishing industry. The company reflects the philosophy established by the founders, based on Psalm 68:11, *"The Lord gave the word and great was the company of those who published it."*

Book design copyright © 2011 by Tate Publishing, LLC. All rights reserved.
Cover design by Blake Brasor
Interior design by Joel Uber

Published in the United States of America
ISBN: 978-1-61346-321-5
1. Fiction: Romance, General
2. Fiction: Fairy Tales, Folk Tales, Legends & Mythology
11.07.13

In memory of my parents and in thanksgiving to
God for the blessings of family and friends.

THANK YOU

To the St. Charles of Borromeo Catholic School Class of 2009

To Martha Smith, Dana Orwig, Robbie Robertson, and Mary Sine

To Amanda Soderberg for her encouragement and guidance

To my editor, Jaime McNutt Bode

To Tate Publishing for their dedication to the nurture of new authors

To my husband, children, and my beautiful granddaughter

To my late parents, Constantine and Dorothy Haniotis, for encouraging me to explore all aspects of my God-given talents

And finally, to the Lord God for His inestimable blessings

SENIOR YEAR

The darkness creeps upon me stealthily. Chills run down my spine, the hair on my arms stands at attention, and every nerve burns beneath my skin. I turn and run as through water. My body trembles with fear. My legs begin to wobble beneath me. I scream as I stumble into the mist, but the sound is swallowed by the void. The murky figures encircle me; their shapes glide in and out of my consciousness. The blackness closes in on me, crushing my chest. Fear begins to suffocate me as I run into the void calling for him; I call until no voice is left. I am swallowed by the abyss—all is black, all is despair.

I wrenched myself awake. Sweat poured down my face and back. Frantically I sat up, my head spinning, my chest heaving from trying to escape the nothingness. A dream. I pulled my knees up, wrapped my arms around them, and laid my head down. What a way to start my first day of senior year.

The summer had been long and hot, but somehow I wasn't ready for school to begin again. There was something about this year—my senior year—that was unsettling. It wasn't that I was afraid to grow up exactly; Mom and I had been on our own for a long time, and she was gone on business so often that I was fairly independent.

I lay back on my sodden pillow thinking. So why did the beginning of this school year feel so different than all the others? Maybe it was Mom's changed behavior lately; this year was different for her, especially whenever my upcoming eighteenth birthday came up. My friends have told me that their parents can't wait for them to turn eighteen and get out on their own, but not Mom. I could see it in her eyes when she thought I wasn't paying attention, staring at me across the den. Her chestnut eyes would gaze up at me from her book or the work she had brought home, and they were filled with anxiety.

But even without her odd behavior, it *did* seem that many things would change this year, and certainly the year after that. Twelve years of familiar schools, activities, and friends would soon come to an end. All in all, a daunting but exciting future.

I gazed around my room, my childhood reflected within its confines. In the corner sat my treasured stuffed animals; my Winnie the Pooh was almost as big as me when Mom bought it for me! The Beanie Babies were stuffed within the shelves of their multi-level bunk bed, and several teddy bears and rabbits sat on the floor in front of it. On the wall hung several movie posters from the old movies Mom introduced to me at an early age, never knowing what a movie buff I would become. Audrey Hepburn smiled graciously at me from across the room, her hair pulled up into her familiar upsweep. Frames in many shapes and sizes enclosed pictures of my childhood friends, many of whom remain my closest confidantes. Everything was in its place; everything was as it should be. I smiled.

The snooze alarm disturbed my reverie. I couldn't put it off any longer; my senior year awaited. I staggered to the bathroom, took a hot shower, and got dressed. I was dressed in khaki Bermuda shorts (no skimpy shorts allowed); navy, short-sleeved cotton t-shirt with my floral, billowy vest over the top; and Roman sandals that I had laid out the night before. But no outfit was ever complete without my hoodie. It was going to be ninety-eight degrees outside and sixty-five degrees inside the school!

Drying my long brown hair always took awhile, and I was running late, so I skipped the straightener. I lightly lined my eyes with eyeliner the way Jesse taught me last year. She said it accentuated my long lashes. I brushed on a little purple eye shadow and quickly powdered my fair skin. I stared in the mirror. I'd never been very confident about my appearance, but what did it matter? Every boy I'd ever met just wanted to be my "friend." This year was going to be different; I wasn't going to get hurt this year!

I raced down the stairs and skidded into the kitchen. Unusually, Mom was home this morning, sitting at the kitchen table drinking her coffee and checking over last-minute details for a midmorning meeting.

"Morning, Kayla." She smiled, looking up from her work. "Are you all set for your first day?"

"I guess I have to be." I laughed, getting out my bowl and the cereal.

"Baby, I have this morning meeting in town, but I have a plane to catch at two o'clock for Denver." Mom was gathering her papers together and stuffing them into her briefcase. "I'm sorry I won't be here tonight to hear about your day, but I'll call as soon as I can this evening, okay?"

"No problem, Mom. Today's no different than the last twelve 'first days.'"

"Senior year is a big deal. I just want you to know how proud I am of you," she said wistfully. "Sometimes I'm so busy with work and travel that I'm afraid I'm missing your childhood." Her eyes glistened with unshed tears.

"Now don't start that again, Marissa!" I chided, using her given name. She smiled. "You're a great mom, and besides, what would the marketing world do without you?" I grinned, scooping up my cereal.

Mom laughed lightly. "I put my itinerary on the desk in the study, so if you need me, call the office number in Denver if my cell phone is turned off. Have a great day, baby. I'll be back on Friday." She kissed me on the top of my head and swooped out of the room, waving.

"Don't worry, Mom," I shouted after her. "Love you lots!"

"Love you, too, baby." The door slammed shut behind her.

I glanced at the clock. "Oh, crap!" I dumped my cereal down the disposal, put my bowl in the dishwasher, and ran upstairs to finish getting ready.

Ten minutes later, I hopped into my silver Civic, affectionately named "Cindy," and drove toward Enterprise High School. It was already hot at seven thirty in the morning. Starting school in mid-August in Enterprise, Texas, must be someone's idea of a joke. That's probably why every car and building in our Dallas suburb was air-conditioned like a meat locker.

Enterprise High was a large school; twenty-five hundred students attended grades nine through twelve. The brick façade was built in a rectangular shape with a courtyard in the middle, just outside the cafeteria. The courtyard was the grassy area we hung out in during the good weather, which in Enterprise was most of the year.

A long line of cars snaked in front of me toward the student parking lot. Seniors were given a special section of the parking lot close to the door leading to the senior halls where all our lockers were located. I parked in my assigned spot just before my best friend, Amy, pulled in next to me.

"Hey, Kayla! How's it going?" Amy asked brightly. "Ready for our last year?"

I smiled. "Sure, how about you?"

"Yeah, I guess. I'm just a little worried about applying to colleges and ACT tests and AP classes and—"

"Amy!" I scolded. "It's the first day! Just relax and enjoy the moment. Let's just take all that one day at a time." I placed my arm around her shoulder and gave her a little squeeze.

"Thanks. You're right. I worry too much." She grinned. "You know something? You always make me feel better when I get stressed out."

"Years of experience, my friend. Years of experience!" I teased.

I had known Amy since the seventh grade at Harper Middle School. She and I were like corresponding puzzle pieces—kind of shy, smart, musically talented, but not at all athletic. Amy was taller than my five feet, but not by much. Her curly red hair and green eyes squealed, "Kiss me! I'm Irish!" With her shy disposition, it was only in the last year or so that she began to feel really comfortable around boys, especially Rob Bennett.

Rob had hung out with Amy and me ever since the ninth grade. We were all in honors classes and seemed to like the same books, music, and movies. Rob was absolutely charming; he was free spirited and loved life. He loved to tease us but not in a hurtful way.

Amy and I headed toward the school arm-in-arm, smiling and calling out to friends and classmates. Although we weren't members of the popular group, we were comfortable in our familiar surroundings and content with our little group of friends.

"Hey, ladies!" Rob called, running to catch up with us. "Don't you two look ravishing this fine morning!" Rob was always the one to brighten the start of a girl's day.

Amy giggled. "Thanks, Rob! You're sweet."

"You're looking pretty dashing yourself, my friend." I laughed at Rob and winked at Amy. She blushed.

"What AP classes are you guys taking this year?" Rob asked, digging in his backpack. He started every year the same way—

coordinating our schedules. "I'm taking AP chemistry, English, calculus, and advanced ancient history."

"I've got all those, except calculus." I grimaced. "You know me and math. But I bet Amy has all those, don't you?"

"Yup, but I'm worried about calculus." She frowned.

"I'll tutor you, kid." Rob winked. Amy smiled. Maybe this was the year they would finally click.

"Well, there are only a few sections of each of those classes, so we'll probably be together," I reassured them.

"The Three Musketeers together again!" Rob guffawed. "Ms. Richardson will love to see me in her English class again." He was enjoying his own joke; Rob drove Ms. Richardson crazy with his incessant queries about literature and life in general. The tenuous balance of a tightrope artist was much more secure than Richardson's equilibrium.

Since it was the first day, we headed for the commons area to get our schedules. All the familiar cliques were assembled in their regular places: the cheerleaders with the football players, the art students against the back wall, the goths lurking under the stairs like bats.

Rob led us toward a table where Jesse and Rick were already seated with their arms wound around each other. They had been a couple since the tenth grade and were still going strong. Rob cleared his throat jokingly to unglue their eyes from each other.

"Are we interrupting anything?" He smirked. Jesse flashed her blue eyes and smacked him playfully on the arm. "Ow! You wounded me!" he said, feigning agony. Jesse pretended to be offended, flipping her long blonde tresses toward him in mock derision.

Rick laughed and shook Rob's hand. Jesse flashed a grin and said, "You know, you really should be used to us by now." She chortled. "Sit down, girlfriends. I have news!" Rob and Rick rolled their eyes. Jesse was our local information network. Most of her "news" usually had to do with new romances or scandals at school. Jesse was, without a doubt, more bohemian than anyone else at Enterprise High. She did her own thing, wore what she wanted, and was generous to a fault.

"Have you seen the new guy?" Amy and I looked befuddled, so she continued, "Okay, so Mrs. Griffin in the office told my mother that a new boy had enrolled in our class. Can you believe it? New prospects in our senior year!"

"Hey! Do you see me standing right here, girl?" Rick complained, shrugging his wide shoulders at her.

"Just because *my* heart is full to the brim doesn't mean I can't watch out for my friends," Jesse teased, hugging him around the middle.

"Well, all right then," Rick said, bending down to kiss her.

"Okay, really? I think I'm going to be sick!" Rob said, making a face. Jesse reached over to smack him again, but he dodged her.

"I haven't heard a thing about anyone new, have you, Kayla?" Amy asked.

"I don't think I'm on the same network Jesse is." I grinned.

"Well, laugh all you want, but Mrs. Griffin told my mother that his name is Blair Davis. And he's in AP classes like us, so you never know. One of you girls might get lucky!" We laughed, but I noticed that Rob wasn't enjoying the joke.

Mr. Berger, the principal, got up to the microphone then and demanded silence from all of us crammed into the commons. He made his usual painfully boring, repetitive beginning-of-the-year remarks, which we, as seniors, could almost recite word for word. Finally it was time to get our schedules. Each grade had two tables set up with the alphabet split A-K and L-Z. Rob headed for the A-K table, and Amy and I headed for the L-Z.

"Let me see, Makayla Taylor and Amy McDonald. Oh, here you go, girls. Have a great day," Ms. Nape, the counselor, chimed.

"Thanks," we said and headed to find the others.

"I guess I have pre-cal when you and Rob have calculus first period." I frowned. I really hated math, and math without friends was even worse. "I don't have chemistry with you either. Bummer!"

"Don't worry. We have ancient history second period and English before lunch," Amy comforted me. "It's just forty-five minutes, and then The Three Musketeers will ride again!"

I laughed as Rob reached us and hovered until Amy waved me off and headed for calculus with him. As I watched them walk off, I smiled. Rob's body language was so cute. He turned slightly toward her as they walked, sort of in a protective stance. Ah, in my dreams.

BLAIR

I walked to my pre-calculus class smiling, thinking about Rob and Amy. They deserved each other; both were so compassionate and unselfish. They balanced each other perfectly. Rob's melodrama was offset by Amy's shyer ways, but Rob was always good at helping Amy see that most of the things she stressed about were not major crises. I considered both of them two of my best friends. It would be great for them to pair up, wouldn't it? Or would I be the odd woman out?

I wasn't really paying attention to my surroundings, so I was startled out of my trance by Mr. Vincent's voice coming from the front of the room.

"Welcome to Enterprise, Blair. I've reviewed your record, which was very impressive," Mr. Vincent declared.

I looked up to see a tall boy with honey-blond hair that brushed his collar standing confidently next to our teacher. Blair was quite tall, with broad shoulders. He was well built and handsome, but surprisingly that wasn't what caught my attention. When he spoke, Blair's voice resonated with self-assuredness yet with a calm I couldn't quite put my finger on, refreshingly different from the cocky, mouthy personalities of most of the boys at Enterprise.

"Thank you, sir," Blair said politely. He clearly wasn't from Texas, but I couldn't really place his accent; there was no defining dialect.

"Well, I'm glad to have you. Take any seat you would like." Mr. Vincent gestured toward the room as he turned to his desk to start the class.

Blair turned to scan the classroom for an empty seat. As if in slow motion, he turned, and his eyes locked on mine. Heat rushed up my neck as I looked down at my backpack and began to unpack it.

I felt him walk past and settle into the desk behind me. There were murmurings all around as my classmates discussed our newest acquisition. Dan Birch reached across the aisle, introduced himself, and shook Blair's hand. That was polite.

Mr. Vincent handed out the syllabus and began introducing our class objectives and requirements. As the period dragged on, I felt uncharacteristically inattentive; I couldn't sit still. I couldn't stop thinking about how Blair's eyes met mine almost immediately. It was weird! How ridiculous. Surely I could not really feel his eyes on the back of my head. *Snap out of it, Kayla. You're getting weirder by the minute!*

I refocused on Mr. Vincent, and the rest of the class progressed smoothly. I took notes, listened to my classmates' questions, and began my homework when Mr. Vincent assigned it.

The bell rang, signaling the end of first period. I gathered all my stuff and leaned over to put it in my backpack. As I stood up, the world began to spin. I listed toward my desk and sat down hard, shaking my head.

"Are you okay?" a deep but gentle voice asked.

I looked up to see the new boy staring down at me.

"Uh, yeah. I must have stood up too fast or something. Thanks." I smiled timidly.

"No problem. I'm Blair, by the way." He smiled back at me, and I noticed his eyes for the first time. They were hazel, just like mine.

"I'm Makayla, but everyone calls me Kayla."

"It's really nice to meet you, Makayla. Where's your next class?" His eyes glistened in the light.

I made myself stop staring. "I have ancient history with Dr. Fields," I stammered.

"Cool, me too! Would you mind showing me where the classroom is?" Blair smiled, and my heart skipped a beat.

"Sh-sure. It's right around the corner." I got up slowly, to make sure I wouldn't make a fool out of myself again.

When I stood next to Blair, I noticed how tall he really was; he had to be six feet tall. Of course, as anyone who knows me would say, at five feet tall, anyone is tall to me. I am classically vertically challenged! I barely came up to his shoulder.

I decided to try to make him feel welcome. "Where did you move from?" I asked, trying to make small talk.

"I've actually moved around a lot over the years, but the last place I lived was up in Washington DC," Blair explained.

"I hear that it's really beautiful up there. It's a lot hotter down here, though. How's that going for you? It takes a while to get used to." Now that I was talking, I couldn't seem to stop.

"You are full of questions, aren't you?" He laughed.

My face felt hot. "I'm sorry. I didn't mean to be nosy." What had I just told myself about not making a fool of myself?

"No offense taken, but isn't this our classroom?" he inquired. I hadn't even realized where we were. "Maybe we could talk at lunch or something. May I join you, since I don't really know anyone yet?"

"I eat with my friends, but I'm sure you'd be welcome to join us. Two of them, Rob and Amy, will be in this class with us." My hands began to sweat, and butterflies flitted around my stomach.

How was he able to do that to me? I'd never been so flustered around a boy I'd just met.

"Thanks. I'll look forward to it."

It took about two seconds for Amy to notice that I hadn't walked into the classroom alone. Her eyes widened with questions and excitement. I shook my head slightly to tell her to play it cool. She got the message and busied herself with her books.

Amy had saved me a seat next to her; Rob was on her other side. Blair took a seat across the room. As soon as I hit the seat, Amy turned to me and started whispering a mile a minute.

"Is that *him*?" she asked. "Was he in your pre-cal class? How did you start talking? What did he say?"

"Amy, for goodness' sake, I can't answer all those questions before Doc starts class," I hurriedly answered. "But he asked to sit with us at lunch and I told him yes, so I hope that's okay with you." I grinned up at her sheepishly.

"Of course it's okay. Do you think he likes you?" Amy almost squealed.

"Amy!" I whispered. "I just met him!"

Luckily, Dr. Fields began class then, and Amy's attention was diverted. My attention, however, was elsewhere. I doodled idly on my notebook, wondering why I felt so buoyant. Just a few hours ago, I had promised myself that I wouldn't get hurt this year. *No more boy "friends," Kayla!* I really didn't want to put myself out on a limb again, but something about Blair made me...giddy.

When class was over, Amy and Rob headed out the door. I think Amy was hoping that Blair would come over and talk to me again, but he smiled and walked out of the class without another word.

I ran to catch up with Amy. English was going to be a riot this year. I loved Ms. Richardson, but she was quirky and sort of moody. It was absolutely true that Rob drove her bonkers. Amy and I would have to keep a rein on him this year.

Ms. Richardson glided into the classroom moments before the bell rang; she always liked to make a grand entrance. She fluttered around the room greeting all of us, grimacing playfully at Rob, and then advanced to the front of the room.

"This year, my darlings, we will delve into the lives of the classic heroes and heroines of literature. We will explore the deep desires of their hearts and witness the depth of their despair."

Rob rolled his eyes at Amy and me. For the rest of the class, Ms. Richardson kept us so entertained with her eccentric ways that the bell rang before we knew it. She waved us dramatically out of her classroom and wished us, "Fair fortune!"

"Lunch is next!" Amy blurted out excitedly. "Where did you tell him to meet us?"

I grimaced. "I didn't. I forgot to tell him where we sat!"

Rob chimed in then. "I'm sure Price Charming will find you damsels." He smirked.

"You're not jealous, are you, Rob?" Amy teased.

"Do I have reason to be?" he retorted, taking her by surprise.

"Of course not." She blushed, looking at me, eyes wide.

I smiled at Amy, but internally that concern of being left out flickered within me again. If she and Rob paired up, I would be left out. I needed to stop overanalyzing everything! They wouldn't exclude me; they were my best friends. Maybe I wouldn't be left alone.

After going through the food line, we found Jesse and Rick already seated at our usual table.

"Guess what, Jesse?" Amy exclaimed. "Kayla met the new boy!"

Jesse looked like she would burst.

"Okay, don't explode, Jesse," I begged. "He asked if he could sit with us at lunch today, and I said yes, so please behave yourself!"

"I resent that remark, Kayla," she teased. "I will be my delightful, charming, alluring self!"

Rick laughed and picked up his hamburger. I hadn't touched my lunch, but the others were halfway through. I started getting anxious. I was beginning to wonder if Blair had changed his mind, but then I saw him walking toward us.

"Hi, Makayla," he said pleasantly. Jesse and Amy stared unashamedly at Blair's dimpled smile and brilliant eyes. I kicked Jesse in the shin, and she jumped, breaking both of their gazes. "Hey, Blair. These are my friends, Amy, Rob, Jesse, and Rick." I introduced them, pointing to them by name. Blair nodded to them and sat down.

"Thanks for letting me sit with you guys. I hope I'm not intruding," he said.

"The more the merrier," Rob retorted jovially. "Welcome to the quasi-nerd club!"

Blair laughed. "Quasi-nerd? Will you explain that designation please?"

"Well," Rob began, "we don't wear pocket protectors and black-framed glasses taped together in the center or discuss quantum physics at the lunch table, so we can't be full nerds! Therefore, we are quasi-nerds."

Laughing again, Blair picked up his pizza. "I guess I've always been a quasi-nerd too! I just didn't know it." He smiled at me and bit his pizza.

FRIENDS

On the last Saturday of August, Jesse planned for us to go ice skating at the local rink. She was determined that Blair come and determined that somehow we would end up together.

"What's the big deal?" she had said when I questioned her motives. "Blair's new in town, he doesn't have friends, and he's already met our group. If anything else develops, well, that's not my fault!"

I rolled my eyes at her and grinned. "You're impossible! Don't you ever get tired of playing matchmaker for me? It's not like it's worked well in the past," I reminded her.

Jesse had tried unsuccessfully in our sophomore and junior years to match me up with several boys; her circle of friends was wider than Amy's or mine, but her choices never really worked out. It's not like they were mean or anything; they just didn't like the same things as I did, and they surely didn't make me feel giddy. Amy was safe from these attempts because she had shown little or no interest in the boyfriend game, at least not until this year.

My own attempts at the art of "the boyfriend" never worked out. I'd start to like a guy, and we would talk and even go to movies with our group; but in the end, all of them just wanted to be friends. I'd get the feeling that they were calling me to talk to *me* because they liked *me* and wanted to get to know *me*, but the conversations always ended up something like this:

"Hey, Kayla. It's Doug. How's it going?"

"Good. What's up?" Usually my stomach danced a little.

"Not much. I just wanted to ask you something."

"Sure." My stomach now turned somersaults.

"Well…" Doug would pause, deep in thought. "I wanted to ask you, you know, because I really like you and trust you…" I would cross my fingers. "Do you think that Jennifer would go out with me?"

At this point, as my throat tightened and my eyes welled up, I would try to gather myself enough to answer. Doug would continue.

"Are you there, Kayla?"

"Yup."

"Everything okay?"

"Uh-huh."

"Kayla? Did I say something wrong? I thought it would be okay to ask you since we're friends."

Friends. Never would I have thought that such a wonderful concept as friendship could darken my self-esteem.

So it was with some nervousness that I dressed for our skating adventure. Since the rink was always cold, I chose a pair of dark-wash jeans and a long-sleeve purple t-shirt. For extra warmth, I added my long sweater vest. It really was ridiculous to have to dress so warmly in September, but ice rinks are notoriously freezing, and I don't have a lot of meat on my bones, as my mother always says!

I picked up Amy at seven, and we headed for the roller rink. Amy was already stressing about the ACT we would have to take in another couple of months.

"It's really our last chance to improve our scores before we have to apply to colleges. I really need to raise my score a point or two to get some scholarship," Amy worried aloud.

"Look, you already have a good enough score to get into any state university you might want to attend. You're not going to help your test-taking nerves by working yourself up like this."

"I know, I know. Why is it so hard for me to put all these things out of my mind?" Amy reached up and grabbed her head, ruffling her red curls between her fingers.

"I don't know, but I do know that you always do better than you think you will, and then you'll kick yourself for all this!" I grinned as I remembered all the times I'd said this to her. Amy was smart and made good grades, but she came from a family of five children, so scholarship was pretty important. The McDonalds certainly weren't impoverished, but college tuition for five kids is staggering! "It's all going to be fine. You'll review for several weeks before the test, and you'll ace it!"

"Thanks," Amy said. "You know, you really ought to go into counseling or something. You always say the right thing to put things into perspective for me."

"Well, I'm glad. Don't forget that you're going to have to help me with the math section. I really hate that part!"

"So what else is new?" Amy teased. "You've been saying that you hate math since the seventh grade!"

I smirked at her as we pulled into a parking place at the rink. Rick, Rob, and Blair were standing outside waiting for us. I took a deep breath and told myself to relax. Blair looked toward us as we approached.

"Hey, where's Jesse?" I asked, looking around.

"Are you kidding?" Rick replied, rolling his eyes. "If I don't pick her up, she's always late!"

"What time is it? If it's not seven thirty yet, she's not late by her time clock!" I teased.

Rob glanced across the parking lot and spied Jesse's Camaro pulling in. "Here she comes!"

Jesse got out of her car with her normal frazzled expression. "Sorry I'm a little late, but they were having a sale at Carly's, and I had to check it out!"

"Of course you did!" Rick said sarcastically as he kissed her and put his arm around her shoulders. "Let's go skating!"

Rob grabbed Amy's arm and tugged her toward the entrance, leaving Blair and me standing alone. He looked down at me and smiled.

"Are you ready for some skating?"

"I guess so. Just hope I can remain upright more than the last time. I was bruised for a week!" I laughed and walked toward the entrance.

Blair laughed as he reached to open the door for me. "Thanks."

"I wouldn't want you to waste your energy opening the door when you're obviously going to need it to remain upright on the rink!" he teased.

"Ha ha ha. You're a laugh riot!"

As we approached the counter, Blair stepped up and paid for us both.

"You didn't have to do that!"

"It's no problem. What size skates do you need? Two? Three?" He dodged my halfhearted smack toward his arm.

"Okay, okay. Enough with the size jokes! Not everyone can grow to be the Jolly Green Giant!" I smiled in spite of myself.

Blair chortled as we walked to put on our skates. The others were already looping the rink as we got on. Jesse skated by me and winked; I frowned at her and shook my head slightly. Miraculously, I skated pretty steadily as we rounded the first turn.

"Hey, I thought you said you weren't very good at skating," Blair accused lightly. "Looks like you're doing pretty well to me."

"It's early. Don't jinx me!"

We skated awhile in comfortable silence before Blair spoke again.

"Hey, Rob told me that you really like movies. What kind of movies do you like?"

"This may sound kind of corny, but I really like old movies. You know, ones like *Breakfast at Tiffany's* and *Gone With the Wind*." I looked up at Blair to see if he thought that was goofy. He was smiling. "Goofy, right?"

"No, actually I like old movies too. My favorites are old westerns and the original James Bond movies," Blair said. "What about *Star Wars* or *The Lord of the Rings* movies? Do you like those?"

"Actually, I do. Because we've always hung around with Rob and more recently with Rick, we girls have learned to like all sorts of movies. Sometimes we have even dragged them to see some chick flicks—they're really good about it most of the time!"

My insides were feeling a little squirmy. Could it really be possible that Blair had similar interests as me? *Don't get your hopes up, Kayla. Remember, you weren't going to do this!* Even though I tried to talk myself out of it, I was enjoying being with Blair. He was easy to talk to and comfortable to be around.

Just as my mind began wandering, I started to lose my balance. I wobbled and swerved precariously. Amy and Jesse saw me and tried to get to me, but I fell backwards and screamed. Blair caught me under my arms and lifted me up.

"Easy does it!" he said as he steadied me. Amy and Jesse reached us then, and Blair skated past us to catch up with the boys. The girls helped me to the side of the rink.

"You okay, Kayla?" Amy asked.

"Sure." I clung to the wall, trying to catch my breath.

"So how's it going?" Jesse was grinning from ear to ear. She looked like a cat who had just swallowed a bird.

"How is *what* going?"

Jesse frowned. "Don't play coy with me, Makayla Taylor. I saw you two talking. He likes you, girl!"

"Please, Jesse! Don't do this. We just are getting to know each other. Nothing he has said has been out of the ordinary talk that friends have with each other." *He did pay for my ticket though...*

"Let's go get something to drink," Amy suggested. "I'm thirsty."

We skated to the nearest break in the rink wall and headed to the concession stand. With our Diet Cokes in hand, we sat at a nearby table. The boys joined us shortly, drinking sodas and talking about football. Their conversation rose in intensity, and we girls decided to head to the restroom.

"Where are you going?" Rob asked. We just stared at him.

"Haven't you hung around these girls long enough to know where they're going? You know they always go in packs," Rick replied.

"You two are really hilarious!" Jesse snapped as she whipped her long hair around. The sound of the boys' laughter followed us down the hall.

When we returned, the boys were already skating. Halfway around the rink, I noticed that my skate was untied; I stopped and bent down. Blair came up behind me.

"What's up?"

"Oh, my skate is untied, and I can't tie it like this."

"I can fix that." Blair lifted me up onto the wall.

"Hey, hey, hey!"

"What?" Blair asked, confused. "I just made it so you can sit and tie your skate. What's the big deal?"

"Nothing," I muttered. Jesse, Rick, Rob, and Amy skated toward us in a chain; Jesse reached out to grab Blair's arm.

"Hold on, hold on!" he said after they managed to pull him a few feet. "I have to get Short Stuff off the wall!" I instantly took note of the nickname. I liked it.

Blair turned and headed back to me, smiling. He was enjoying himself, and I couldn't help but smile back at him.

"Ready?" he asked.

"Yup! Let's go!"

Blair reached out and lifted me from the wall. I looked up at him; his face was torn as he steadied me. "You okay?"

Blair nodded, let go of me quickly, and skated off. That was really odd. Confusion swelled up within me as I tried to decipher all the different pieces of his personality. He seemed to enjoy talking to me, he bought my ticket, and he even seemed kind of protective of me. And yet, why did he always seem uncomfortable being close to me?

The evening progressed, and I managed to only fall twice. At ten, we decided it was time to head home, so we turned in our skates and headed out to the parking lot.

"Kayla, do you mind if I drive Amy home?" Rob asked.

I looked at Amy, who was smiling shyly. "Sure. Talk to you later!"

Rick and Jesse headed to her car, leaving Blair and me standing on the sidewalk again.

"Well, I better go. See you at school Monday," I said as I headed toward my car.

"Hey, let me walk you to your car. I don't want you to walk by yourself at night."

"Oh, okay. Thanks."

We walked in silence toward my Civic. When I reached my car, I turned and looked up into his face. It wore that same torn expression; it made me uncomfortable.

"I better go," I said, turning back to open my car door. "Glad you could come with us tonight, Blair."

"Yeah, I had a good time." His tone didn't match his words. I turned back around in time to see his face shift into a forced smile. "See you at school," he said as he walked to his car. I watched him, more confused than ever. Years of rejection made it difficult for me to not take his actions personally. It's hard to keep your self-esteem up when every male seems to want to avoid you like the plague! I sighed and got in my car.

As early fall slipped into September and October, life at Enterprise High took on a familiar routine. Blair was in my chemistry class, so that made up for not having Amy and Rob with me. Blair was a regular part of our group now, becoming more and more relaxed with us. Well, at least it seemed like he was comfortable. The only exception was that he still wouldn't tell us much about himself; everything was kind of superficial. Whenever asked, he would divert the questioner by asking a question himself or smile his brilliant smile and answer sarcastically. It was a mystery, but I figured he was entitled to his privacy. Every once in a while, I would catch Blair looking at me with that same bewildered expression, but I decided I just didn't have the energy to figure it out.

Pre-cal was becoming the bane of my existence, and with the ACT rapidly approaching, my frustration grew exponentially.

"Ugh!" I snarled dramatically as I lowered my head on the library table during a pre-cal study period. "I'll never get this!"

Blair was sitting next to me with his book closed; he'd finished his work. "Why don't you let me help you with it?" Blair offered. "You're so stubborn about asking for help."

Actually, that was true, but I hadn't realized I'd demonstrated that around Blair. But then again, he seemed exceptionally perceptive about people. It was not uncommon for Blair to somehow intuitively know when one of our group was upset or discouraged, and often he had the comforting words to make them feel better. I guess that was another thing we actually had in common.

"I hate to saddle you with my mathematical disability," I answered, frustration seeping out of every word.

He laughed to himself, and I looked up. "I really don't mind, and I hate to see you so frustrated."

"It's just with the ACT in a couple of weeks, I'm really stressed out. Math just doesn't make sense to me! It's always been like my teachers were speaking a foreign language. It's starting to give me headaches," I explained, rubbing my temples.

Blair looked nonchalant, but I saw his eyes tightened a bit. "I'm sorry about the headaches. Maybe if you let me help you, they'll get better."

I really did need Blair's help, but it made me nervous to put myself into another position of feeling vulnerable with him. Weighing this against not doing well on the ACT made me push my worries aside.

So every day after school we headed to the library, where I would begrudgingly take out my math book and slam it on the table as if it had personally wounded me, and we would slog through my pre-cal homework. Blair was a patient teacher; he had ways of explaining the concepts differently from my teachers, and it helped. Slowly I began to understand and feel more confident about my chances of doing better on the ACT the second week of October.

I wanted to do something to thank Blair for his help, so I decided to get him a DVD of *Gone With the Wind* because he had told me he didn't have it. On the Friday before the ACT, I met Blair outside our chemistry class.

"Hey, I want to thank you for all your math help over the past few weeks," I said shyly. For some reason I didn't want to look up at him.

"It's no problem. I'm glad I was able to help."

"I wanted to get you something to thank you." I finally looked up into his face and smiled.

"You didn't have to do that, Makayla."

"I know. It's nothing big," I inserted quickly. I didn't want him to think I was making a huge deal out of it or anything. I handed him the wrapped DVD.

Blair smiled at me as he opened it. "It's a new car!" he teased. I rolled my eyes at him; as if his shiny G35 wasn't already one of the best cars in our parking lot. "No, this is great. Thanks. I really appreciate it."

The hall was deserted now, as the other students had headed out to their cars already. An awkward silence filled the space as we looked into each other's eyes. Then it happened again—Blair's face shifted, and although it was still kind, it was not the same—more serious, more distant.

"I'll...see you on Monday. Good luck on the test tomorrow, Makayla. I know you'll do great." He turned and walked away.

I stood in the hallway, frozen on the spot. Confusion and frustration pulsed through me as I watched him walk away. What was it with him? One minute everything was going smoothly, looking like things might progress, and then *bam*! He turned a switch and walked away! Ugh! Men!

GOING CRAZY

The ACT seemed to go well enough, but I was afraid to think so. Most of the time when I think I do well on a math test, I've really blown it! Amy was feeling more relaxed now that the test was behind her. The end of October should have been good; the weather was turning cooler as autumn advanced. The kids at school were looking forward to the championship football game at the end of the month, applications for college were underway, and soon the holidays would be upon us.

Unfortunately, for me, October was not ending so well. I woke most mornings covered in sweat, with my head aching more and more as the day progressed. Mom began to get really worried.

"Kayla, baby, you really need to let me take you to see Dr. Cooper," she complained one evening when we were talking after dinner. Mom was sitting in her overstuffed chair with her feet up on the ottoman, reading her latest mystery. Books were Mom's relaxation after stressful business trips and meetings; in fact, within most of the rooms of our house, books of all genres could be found on the counter, or on an end table, or tipping precariously on her nightstand. "It's not like you to have headaches. Maybe your eyes have changed and you're straining them."

I was lying down on the couch watching some innocuous sitcom, trying to forget the pounding in my head. I turned my head toward her.

"Mom, I just can't miss school for a doctor's appointment right now. The Tylenol takes the edge off. Don't worry, okay?"

"All right, but if this continues, we're going to go no matter what," she pronounced sternly.

"I'm sure they'll get better," I said, secretly promising to never mention my headaches to her again.

"By the way, have you decided what you want to do for your eighteenth birthday?" she asked, trying to look excited.

"Just having a few friends over for a movie night will be great. I don't want you to go to a lot of trouble; we'll order pizza."

"Whatever you want is fine with me," Mom answered quietly.

As my birthday approached—it was just two weeks away—she seemed to be more and more preoccupied. Just a few days ago, I had walked into her study and found Mom staring off, a blank expression on her face, with her book upside down in her hands. There was something in her eyes. Fear? Loneliness? It was unnerving and very unlike my usually confident, loving mother. I was beginning to get worried about her.

So the reason I just wanted to have a relaxed evening for my birthday celebration was to somehow alleviate her anxiety. I couldn't figure out what was really wrong; maybe she was afraid of me going to college, or maybe she thought she was "losing" me. It was awkward because, for the first time in a long time, Mom wouldn't talk to me about it. We usually talked openly about everything—and I mean everything—but whenever I tried to ask her why she seemed worried, she wouldn't give me a serious answer.

"You know how moms are, Kayla," she would say lightly. "It's in our job description to worry." And the conversation would inevitably shift to another topic.

"Hey, Kayla," Amy asked at the lunch table a week before my birthday, "have you decided what you want for your birthday? It's a big one, you know!"

Secretly, I just wanted to feel better. The headaches were not getting better, and I felt dizzy. Truth be told, I thought my headaches *would* get better if the consistently disturbing dreams would stop. It was like entering the same dark space night after night, looking for something or someone, only to end up in the eerily familiar void. This morning, I actually remembered part of the dream, but I didn't understand it.

Standing in the mist, my knees wobbling and skin crawling, I suddenly saw another person—a man, I think—in the distance. I called out to him. The void swallowed my voice as usual, but this time, I heard a frenetic reply. "Help me! I'm waiting for you." I ran toward the man, but he began shimmer and fade into the mist. He disappeared before I could reach him. I was alone again. Alone and afraid.

Maybe I had a brain tumor or something; I was beginning to get scared. I tried to shake off the fear.

"You don't have to get me anything, Amy," I replied. "Just being at the movie night is enough for me."

Jesse chimed in. "Now, now. You know that we're going to get you something, so it might as well be something you want." Rick leaned over and stole a French fry from her plate; she swatted at his hand halfheartedly.

"Just get me a movie on DVD," I suggested, distracted.

"Do you have *Juno*?" Amy asked. I shook my head. "Would you like that? Remember, we thought it was funny when we saw it together."

"That would be great." I sighed. "Other than that, gift certificates would be fabulous; you know how I love to shop." I tried to sound enthusiastic, closing my eyes and rubbing my temples.

Amy's voice came as from a great distance. *I wonder what's wrong with Kayla.*

"I've just got a bad headache, Amy. Don't worry," I answered her.

Everyone looked at me strangely; Blair shifted in his seat.

"How did you know that I was worried, Kayla?" Amy asked, sounding really confused.

"What do you mean how did I know you were worried? You just asked me," I retorted a little sharply; my head throbbed.

When Amy didn't answer, I looked up. Everyone at the table was staring at me, except for Blair, who was casually drinking his soda. That was odd.

"What's wrong, guys?" I was taken aback by their expressions.

Jesse and Rick exchanged worried looks; Rob looked puzzled. Amy placed her hand on mine.

"I didn't ask you, Kayla," she said gently, "but I was thinking it."

"What do you mean, 'thinking it'? I heard you!"

Blair finally spoke. "Amy, it seems to me that Makayla knows you better than you think!" He chuckled, trying to lighten the mood.

I gazed bewildered at my friends sitting around the table. My face grew hot as they stared; I shook my head and bolted for the exit. By the time I reached the courtyard, tears flowed steadily down my face. What was happening to me? Could a brain tumor make you hear things? My head spun.

Finding a little shade under a redbud tree, I slumped to the ground. I laid my head on my knees and wrapped my arms around them. I realized that I was shaking uncontrollably; my insides writhed like serpents.

"May I sit with you, Makayla?" I didn't have to look up to know that it was Blair. I wiped my face on my hoodie but didn't answer him. He sat down anyway.

After several minutes of silence, I looked up. Blair was looking out on the courtyard, waiting patiently for me to get it together. He turned and smiled.

"Are you feeling any better?" he asked.

"Not really. I feel like an idiot!" I blurted out, burying my head again.

"You are far from an idiot, Makayla. In fact, I have found you to be intuitive and exceptionally bright," Blair stated matter-of-factly.

"Thanks, but right now I feel like I'm losing my mind." I couldn't believe I was sharing my deepest fear with this guy who obviously wasn't interested in me, but I couldn't stop myself.

"Let's go back inside. Everyone is worried about you; can you collect yourself for their sakes?"

What an odd way to phrase that.

"I guess," I whispered, trying to stand.

Blair rose and extended his hand to help me. I reached for it and felt a small pulsation when our hands touched. Had he noticed that too? He was looking at me casually, waiting for me to stand.

"Yeah, I don't want them to worry about me," I said as off-handedly as I could manage.

Blair let go of my hand. "Let's go finish lunch, okay?"

"Sure," I responded weakly as we headed back into the cafeteria.

As Blair had foretold, our lunch table crowd looked wary as we approached.

"Sorry, guys," I said, hoping I sounded sane. "I didn't mean to spoil everyone's lunch."

Simultaneously they all reassured me of their unwavering friendship.

"No sweat, kiddo," Rob exclaimed. "We all have bad days!"

"Sure, Kayla, it's okay," Rick stated, smiling and stealing another of Jesse's fries.

Amy and Jesse got up and said, "Three-way hug!" as they reached for me.

For the rest of the day, I tried to act normal, as if I hadn't picked something out of Amy's mind, but I was unfocused. My headache diminished to a dull ache. All day I tried to justify what had happened with a logical explanation, but nothing I came up with was really believable. The more I thought about it, the less sense it made and the more convinced I became that I was really ill.

Coming out of chemistry at the end of the day, I noticed Blair had waited for me just outside the door. I crossed to him feeling self-conscious.

"How are you feeling?" Blair inquired.

"Better, but still embarrassed," I confessed, staring at the floor.

"Why are you embarrassed?"

"You mean, besides sounding like a lunatic and running out of the cafeteria?" I blurted out without thinking.

"Makayla?" Blair said gently. "Look at me."

I looked up; his hazel eyes were filled with compassion.

"You have nothing to be ashamed of. I know what I'm talking about; please try to trust me on this," he implored. "May I walk you to your car?"

"Sure. I just have to stop by my locker first," I responded, feeling a little flushed.

Blair chatted effortlessly as we walked to my locker and then to my car. Gradually I relaxed and began to truly feel better about the afternoon's misadventure.

Suddenly I remembered something Blair said outside my chemistry classroom. "Blair, what did you mean when you told me to trust you because you knew what you were talking about?"

Blair hesitated, and I recognized the faraway look he reserved for those who questioned him. We had reached my car; I turned to face him, waiting patiently. His eyes searched mine unblinkingly, and under his gaze, I felt my face grow red.

I looked down with renewed frustration. "I'm sorry, Blair. I just thought if you wanted me to trust you, maybe you would trust me enough to confide in me." I turned to get into my car. "I'll just see you tomorrow…"

"Makayla, I do want you to trust me, but I don't want to overwhelm you." He looked truly upset.

"I don't understand."

"I know. There are many things that you need to grasp and very little time for me to clarify."

This was beginning to enter the "Kayla zone," that place where I didn't really want to go but had to go from time to time. Butterflies danced in my stomach as I tried to comprehend his words.

"Are you frightened?" he asked.

"I'm not sure," I answered honestly.

"I'm not doing this very well," he muttered, seemingly to himself. "I promise that I'll be with you on this journey, every step of the way."

Blair met my eyes. He smiled, put his hands gently on my shoulders, and the world disappeared around me. My head reeled, the ground came up to meet me, and the shadows closed in.

SECRETS

I was vaguely aware of lying on a soft surface. My eyes weren't cooperating with my attempts to wake up, but I was slowly regaining consciousness. The sounds of an engine and of air flowing alerted me to my surroundings; I was in my car, lying across the backseat.

My eyes fluttered open; I raised my hand to wipe my face. It was moist with sweat, like when a fever breaks. As I focused, I saw Blair leaning over the front seat.

"Welcome back," Blair said.

"What happened?" I asked, trying to sit up. My head felt really light; I shook it gently to try to clear it.

"You fainted."

I was not usually the fainting type. Did I really have a brain tumor? That must be it; I was sure I had a brain tumor! Panic swelled up inside me. My breathing faltered as my heart rate sped up.

Stay calm, Makayla. Breathe slowly.

Blair was looking at me intensely; his hazel eyes shone green.

I stared at him, my mouth agape. "What did you just say? Um…think?"

"What did you hear, Makayla?"

"You told me to stay calm and breathe slowly." I was too stunned to move.

"Why don't we go somewhere to talk?" Blair suggested. "Would that be okay with you? Can we go to your house?"

I nodded.

"I'll follow you home. I want to make sure you get home safely; you look a little ashen." Blair smiled warmly. "Are you able to drive?"

I found my voice. "I think I can drive."

Blair nodded and turned to get out of the car.

My emotions were in turmoil; my stomach churned, but I was very curious. Was it possible that Blair understood what was happening to me or, better yet, that I didn't have a brain tumor? That thought conflicted with the idea that I really *was* hearing voices in my head; no brain tumor, just severe mental illness! Somewhere in the deep recesses of my mind, I hoped that this odd understanding Blair seemed to have would explain his constantly shifting behavior around me.

I climbed out of the backseat gingerly, making sure that my balance was working. It seemed steady. I got behind the wheel and looked at Blair through my open window. He smiled down with understanding, exuding calm.

Deciding it was probably better to distract myself, I turned the radio on softly and pulled out of the student parking lot. My mind overflowed with questions, along with anxiety, but I concentrated on the road, ignoring the sleek sedan following closely behind me. Soon we were in front of my house. Blair parked behind me in the driveway and got out of his car.

"My mother is out of town on business," I told him. I'm not sure why I said it, but I thought he should know.

Blair hesitated, concern in his wary eyes. "Do you feel comfortable being alone with me?"

I thought about that for a minute. Mom would probably freak if she thought I was alone with him in the house, but nothing about Blair had ever unnerved me; confused me, yes, but not unnerved me.

"I'm not worried," I reassured him quietly.

I walked to the door and unlocked it. Blair gestured for me to go ahead of him.

"Make yourself comfortable," I invited. "I'll get us some sodas."

Blair sat down on the couch as I hurried into the kitchen to grab the drinks. Glasses? Cans? Cans, I decided. Relax—keep it casual. I tried to look calm as I handed him his Coke, hoping that my hands weren't shaking as much as my stomach.

"Thanks," Blair said as he took his drink.

I sat down opposite him on the couch. The Diet Coke can shook in my hand, so I hastily put it on the coffee table. I looked at Blair, waiting for him to speak first. The question that came out of his mouth took me by surprise.

"What do you know about your father, Makayla?"

"I… What?" I never knew my father; he died when I was two, and my baby memories had long since faded. Unfortunately, Mom was no help with the reminiscing. Talking about Dad was an unspoken taboo; dark shadows crept into Mom's face whenever I inquired about him. She literally became another person—a haunted soul. I stopped asking about him by the time I was ten. All his pictures were "hidden" in a box under her bed, but I didn't bother to look. It wasn't worth upsetting Mom.

"Your father, what do you know about him?" Blair repeated patiently.

"My dad died when I was a baby. Mom doesn't like to talk about him, so I don't really know too much," I admitted, confused. "What does that have to do with anything that's happening to me now? And how do you know anything about my father?"

He ignored the last question. "Actually, it has everything to do what's happening to you," Blair stated, watching me carefully.

"I don't understand..."

Blair studied my face, probably looking for a lack of control. He put his Coke down.

"Have you ever heard of the phenomenon of clairvoyance?"

"Clair...what?" I seemed obtuse, even to myself.

"Clairvoyance is the ability to see or hear that which is unseen or unheard," Blair clarified.

I gazed at him dumbfounded. "Is that what I am doing?"

Blair took a deep breath and moved closer to me on the couch.

"Makayla, unbeknownst to most people in the world, there are certain people gifted with clairvoyance. We are called Clairvoyants."

"We? Are you talking about you and me or my dad and me?"

"Both," Blair stated plainly. He waited to see what my reaction would be.

For what seemed like a long time, I just stared at him blankly. What was I supposed to think about this? How was I even supposed to believe this? Finally I extricated myself from his gaze. I got up slowly and walked to the window, feeling Blair's eyes follow my every step. Everything looked the same, but everything was different. I wrapped my arms around myself and tried to take a deep breath; it trembled with emotion.

"Explain more, please," I asked quietly. "Are my headaches a 'symptom'"—there wasn't really a better word—"of clairvoyance?"

"Yes, that's very perceptive. Your brain is adjusting to new sensations—specifically, the thoughts of those around you. At first, the brain tries to protect itself from what it perceives as a threat. Even before you actually begin to *hear*, your brain begins blocking the incoming messages. The result is headaches and sometimes fainting." Blair waited for a second before continuing. "Makayla," Blair called softly. When I didn't answer, he walked over to me and stood behind me. Maybe he was afraid that I would lose it again and collapse. "Are you all right?"

"Why don't you just read my thoughts?" Suddenly I was very, very angry; an uncontrolled rage coursed through me. This boy I had known for several months now was springing this thing on me like it was totally normal. Why couldn't he have told me this earlier? It would have saved me a lot of worry and confusion.

"As clairvoyants, we're forbidden to intrude into one another's minds without permission. It's considered discourteous," he explained calmly.

"Oh, I see," I said petulantly. "It's discourteous to read one another's minds, but it's not rude to show up suddenly in someone's life and turn it upside down!" I was almost yelling now, but I didn't turn toward Blair. I was afraid of what I might do.

"I didn't show up to ruin your life, Makayla. I'm here to help you adjust."

I turned to face him with my hands in tight fists at my side. "Why now, Blair? What did I do to deserve this honor? How did you even know to come at all?" I scowled up at him.

"I came now because our powers begin to surface shortly before our eighteenth birthdays. Yours is next week." Blair's face remained composed, which really ticked me off.

I wanted to rail at him. Why did this have to happen? I didn't want to be "special"; I was happy with normal. I crossed the room to put some space between us. Suddenly, something occurred to me, and I faltered.

"Does my mother know about my father?" I was almost afraid to hear his answer.

"Yes, I believe she does."

Now my insides were ready to explode. How could my mother *not* have told me? Did she know about the eighteen thing? Was that why she had been so tense and emotional lately? Abruptly I stopped pacing and sank onto the couch.

"Is my mother afraid of my gift?" I asked timidly. "Does she think it's a bad thing?"

"I don't know the answer to your questions. I've never met your mother personally. You'll have to ask her yourself," he said, joining me on the couch.

"How the… How am I supposed to bring up this subject, Blair?" I was angry again. "'By the way, Mom, nice thoughts you're having today!' Ugh!" I stood up. "Blair, I think you should leave."

"Makayla, there's so much more you need to understand. There are other rules we are bound to obey and so much more you need to be prepared to feel and hear. Please let me help you understand," he implored.

"There's nothing to understand. Please leave my house!" I commanded, walking to the door and opening it.

Blair rose slowly and walked toward me. I didn't know if I could control the tears that were on the verge of overflowing; I didn't meet his gaze.

"I'm sorry, Makayla. Let me know when you're ready to talk again."

"Thanks for the offer, but there will be no need. You're mistaken about me and my father! You must have confused me with someone else more gifted than me!"

Blair sighed; he looked like he wanted to say something else, but the expression on my face changed his mind.

"See you tomorrow at school," he said sadly as he walked out the door.

I slammed it.

A LOVE STORY

I slumped to the floor in utter denial. The weight of Blair's explanation pressed me into the frigid tile of the entry hall. Fear seemed to stalk me. I shuddered; a dull, empty sensation crushed my chest. So much to absorb; too much to believe. I felt the sting of betrayal as the realization of my mother's deception sank into my consciousness. How could she have kept this from me?

I have no idea how long I sat there. Time seemed to be inconsequential, but eventually another thought occurred to me. I got up and headed to my mother's room. Curiosity about my father had waned with the years, but now it was vital for me to understand. The elusive box under my mother's bed held some of the answers I needed. The box and its contents were not actually forbidden for me to look in, but I hadn't bothered in years. Since Mom seemed to think it wasn't a priority, it grew less and less important to me.

Crawling under the bed, I pushed aside long-lost single shoes and dust bunnies. The box was crammed against the wall. I grabbed it and slithered out. As I leaned against my mother's bed, emotion rose in my throat; it tingled. Why? I had no memory my father, so why was my throat constricting? Wiping my eyes, I headed toward the den.

The shrill ring of the phone startled me. I answered it, still clutching my past.

"Hello." My voice sounded lifeless.

"Hi, baby! It's Mom. How's everything going?" she asked brightly.

I wasn't sure how to answer her; she sensed my hesitation.

"What's wrong, Kayla?" Her voice was instantly strained. "Are you okay?"

"It's just been a long day," I mumbled. Now that was the understatement of the century. How should I begin?

"Kayla, please talk to me," she demanded. "What's wrong?"

I answered in one word. "Clairvoyants."

There was a prolonged pause at the other end of the phone.

"I'm catching the next flight home. Please don't leave the house, okay?" She was all business.

"Okay," I answered, but I wasn't sure I wanted to see her just yet.

"I'll see you very soon. I love you. Please remember that," Mom almost begged. The line went dead.

"I love you too," I whispered to no one.

I placed the phone on its base and headed to the den. Dusk was falling; shadows lengthened across the floor. I turned on the light and settled onto the floor. I stared at the unassuming box that now seemed almost threatening; its contents held so many secrets. How many others might I learn in the next few minutes, hours, days? Timidly, I opened the top.

Photographs were thrown haphazardly in it. I took a deep breath and began rummaging through them. In the pictures, I recognized my dark brown hair and hazel eyes in my father's; the smile was a reflection of my own. There were pictures of my dad and mom together, some with inscriptions on the back.

Marissa and Sean in Galveston. Love shone in their faces.

Marissa and Sean in front of our new house. This house.

Some were images of my dad holding me.

Sean holding Makayla at one hour old! Adoration was the only word for his expression; my throat swelled and my eyes burned.

Some were of all three of us, a family.

Marissa, Sean, and Makayla at one month.

I laid the pictures out on the floor in chronological order. These were the images of my dad's life with Mom and me. Tears ran silently down my cheeks and into my lap; I let them fall. Grief washed over me, and I surrendered to it, falling into an exhausted sleep.

"Kayla?" Someone was calling me. I felt a warm hand on my shoulder and was startled into consciousness. My mother was kneeling down beside me, her eyes sweeping the pictures strewn on the floor. I must have slept for several hours.

I looked at my mother, my confidante, my best friend. Her eyes were filled with concern and—could I be imagining it?—fear. Her expression beseeched me to understand and forgive. All anger forgotten, I threw myself into her arms, sobbing.

"Baby, baby. I'm so sorry!" Mom moaned into my hair as she rocked me.

We remained on the floor together until my sobs quieted and my grief abated. Mom held me tight against her chest, stroking my hair to soothe me.

Finally I sat up; Mom watched me warily and then turned to pick up a picture. It was the one of my dad holding me at a month old. She swept her hand gently over my dad's face in a caress.

"I wish you could have known him," she whispered. "He loved you more than anything in the world." She inhaled deeply. "Sean delighted in every new facial expression you made, every sound that came from your lips, especially your first word, 'dada,' your first step…" Her voice broke on the last word.

The question was obvious, but I had to ask. "Why didn't you ever—"

Mom interrupted and finished my question. "…tell you?" In a sudden burst of emotion, she stood and began pacing, waving her arms frantically. I had never seen her like this; it frightened me.

"I don't know, Kayla!" she wailed. "When your dad was… died, I thought my heart would never heal. I got angry with him. How could he leave me alone with a baby? I told myself that maybe you wouldn't inherit his gift and I would never have to deal with it. You would only be 'half' clairvoyant after all. But I always worried—what if I was just fooling myself? What would I do when it was time to explain to you…" Her voice faded.

She stopped pacing and collapsed into a chair. I was speechless, but I wanted to know more. Mom must have sensed that it was time to tell me everything. She worked to slow her breathing; the story unfolded.

"We met in the fall of our senior year of college. Sean was tall with dark brown hair and beautiful hazel eyes. I was so small; he used to tease me and use my shoulder as an armrest." Mom giggled, and I heard her younger self break through the sadness.

"The first week of school, I walked into my philosophy class, and there he sat, waiting for me, or so he always said. It's so cliché, but I really did fall in love with your dad at first sight. It was months later that I learned Sean had fallen in love with me from the depths of my being; he said he fell in love with my soul."

I looked at Mom, and she was staring away, years away. The gentle smile on her face reflected her beautiful soul, the soul my dad loved.

"When did he tell you he was a clairvoyant?" I whispered.

"It was eight months later, after he'd asked me to marry him," she remembered wistfully. "It was a beautiful spring night, and we walked through the campus toward our favorite spot, a small pond behind the chapel. We sat on the grass together, but Sean looked worried.

"When I tried to ask what was wrong, he touched my lips and shook his head sadly. I was scared; I had never seen him so upset. In my insecurity, I thought he had changed his mind about our upcoming marriage." Mom paused to gather her thoughts. I was riveted to her face.

"Sean said, 'How could you think I would ever leave you, Marissa?' Of course I was startled; I hadn't spoken the concerns he addressed aloud. He took my hand gently and began the story of his gift. At first I was overwhelmed; these kinds of phenomenon don't exist except in science fiction!" Mom laughed softly.

"Your dad continued to explain that the gift was passed down from generation to generation. His parents, whom you never met, passed it to him, as did their parents before them.

"That, believe it or not, was not the most difficult aspect for me to accept. Sean continued to explain that, although he wanted me to be a part of his life forever, he could not share all the secrets of clairvoyance with me. The clairvoyants, he said, were bound by strict rules and ethical standards."

Her words reminded me of the words Blair had begged me to hear, "There are other rules we are bound to obey and so much more you need to be prepared to feel and hear." I squirmed guiltily; he really was trying to help me.

Mom continued her story.

"We sat in silence for a long time. My mind was spinning with questions that Sean probably could not and would not explain. I imagine that his pain was doubled—mine and his.

"Kayla, at the end of that long evening, I couldn't imagine life without him. All other concerns soared out of my mind and were replaced by utter devotion. Try to understand, baby. I wasn't thinking with a rational mind but with my heart. All the challenges of our future life seemed negligible; we would deal with them together." She sighed and raised her hand to her eyes wearily.

I got up and moved to sit on the arm of her chair. I wiped a tear rolling down her cheek and smiled at her.

"I didn't consider, at the time, the consequences our union would make to our children. Any trials that arose Sean and I would handle together, so nothing seemed impossible.

"We married after our graduation, in July, and you were born four years later. Looking at your beautiful face, I knew I had made the right decision." She smiled.

I put my arm around her shoulder; she lifted her hand and reached to caress my face. For almost eighteen years Mom had borne the burden of this secret and her fear alone. Now that would change. Nothing else mattered; I knew that we would handle what lay ahead *together*.

APOLOGY

Exhausted, I fell into bed at 1:00 a.m. Mom and I had talked for hours; I explained about Blair as she listened intently. She sat with me until I was asleep, rubbing my back to release my tense muscles. Restlessness surfaced in my dreams, which alternated between the images of my father in our pictures and a much darker place.

In the darkness, I heard voices calling out—voices tinged with fear, people crying out for help—but I could not find them. I struggled to focus on the direction of their cries, hoping to reach them before it was too late. Frustration erupted within me as I frantically groped through the dark. A man's voice…a woman's screams…the panicked cries of a child.

Terrified, I threw my eyes open and wrenched upright, my breathing ragged, my heart racing. It took me a minute to recognize my room. I pulled my knees up and lay my head on them, trying to steady myself. The clock on my bedside table read 4:00 a.m., much too early to get up.

Just a dream, Kayla; just a dream.

As my breathing slowed, I lay back hoping that a peaceful sleep would find me. My brain seemed to be on overload; Blair had used the word *overwhelmed*.

Blair. How was I going to apologize for my deplorable behavior? Since I acted like a maniac, I was sure he wouldn't even want to be friends with me now, and I really enjoyed being with him. He was fun to be with and liked what I liked, and I had really blown it. Nervousness replaced my terror as I contemplated seeing him at school.

School? How was I supposed to explain this to my other friends? Amy was my best friend. What would I be allowed to tell her, if anything? Loneliness swelled in my chest; my eyes stung with renewed tears. For the first time in years, I wanted my dad; I needed him now more than ever.

When soft light finally began streaming into my window, I got dressed without looking in the mirror; I didn't want to know what I looked like after so little sleep. Mom was waiting for me in the kitchen when I staggered down the stairs.

"Oh, Kayla, honey! Didn't you sleep?" Mom asked as she hugged me tight. "I checked on you two times, and you seemed sound asleep."

"I slept for a while, but I had bad dreams," I confessed.

"I think you should stay home today," Mom pleaded. "Let's just stay home together and rest."

I shrugged out of her arms and plopped into a chair.

"I can't stay home, Mom," I explained. "I have to talk to Blair, and I have a test in Richardson's class on *The Great Gatsby*."

Mom started to interrupt, but I raised my hand to stop her.

"It's Friday. I'll rest over the weekend, but if I stay home, I'll just worry about everything. I have to apologize to Blair; I was just awful to him!" I rested my head on the table.

"If Blair is anything like your dad was, he will understand, baby," Mom encouraged. "At least let me drive you today, okay? Humor your old mom." She grimaced, trying to make me laugh.

I agreed and even smiled at the pitiful face she was making. Sleep deprivation was not the best condition for driving anyway.

Mom dropped me off half an hour later, blowing me a kiss like she did when I was five. I wasn't embarrassed; it was rather sweet.

As luck would have it, I didn't run into any of my friends on the way into the school. I headed for the restroom to check my face. Ugh! My eyes were red-rimmed and slightly swollen. My skin was blotchy and ashen. I splashed cool water on my face, wishing that I could wear sunglasses. No wonder Mom wanted me to stay home.

I took a deep steadying breath, lowered my head, and walked to pre-cal. Most of the kids in the classroom were occupied talking about their weekend plans, with one significant exception. Blair sat rigid in his chair watching me walk to my desk, my pain evident on his handsome face. I sat down without speaking. Would he be *listening*?

I'm sorry, Blair, I thought. *Can you forgive me?*

Blair's face broke into a soft smile, and he nodded slightly. I smiled back at him and mouthed, "Thank you."

Leaning closer to me so no one else would hear him, Blair whispered, "Makayla, there's nothing for me to forgive. Maybe I should have waited to tell you—"

I interrupted him. "I doubt that it would have made a difference. As you may have noticed, I can be pretty stubborn and pig-headed."

He laughed softly. "I am saying *nothing*!"

"Smart man." I giggled.

Mr. Vincent began to review for our next test, so we turned our attention to the front of the room. Relief washed over me; I filled my lungs and slowly exhaled, relaxing for the first time since yesterday. Mom was right—Blair was incredibly understanding. I glanced at him sitting next to me, afraid to think about what I was feeling. A sense of peace, of comfort, engulfed me when I thought of Blair now, but I couldn't let those feelings show.

After class, Blair waited next to me while I packed my bag. I stood, a little shakily, and laughed softly, making sure no one else was listening. "I guess sleep deprivation is not very good to an emerging clairvoyant. It's not helping my balance at all!"

"May I?" Blair asked, moving his arm to indicate his desire to help steady me.

"Oh…okay."

Blair carefully placed his hand at the small of my back and guided me to history. At his touch, pleasurable heat coursed through me, but I didn't feel the pulse I had felt the day before.

"Why didn't I feel…" I began but stopped midquestion. I wasn't sure if it was rude to ask such questions.

"You may ask me any questions you want. As your guide, it's my job to help you understand everything about your gift."

"My guide?" I was confused.

We were nearing the ancient history classroom. Blair bent down and spoke in a hurried whisper, "Every emerging clairvoyant is assigned a guide to help them adjust and understand their new gift. I would have explained this to you earlier, but you weren't exactly receptive." He smiled. I grimaced. "If it's okay with you, we'll talk in more depth later where it's more private."

I nodded, and we headed into class. As I expected, Amy's eyes missed nothing—my red eyes or Blair's hand on my back. Her mixed expression was almost amusing. I smiled at her to reassure her that I was okay, but she still looked perplexed. She watched me carefully as I sat down next to her.

Leaning over to her, I whispered, "Mom and I stayed up really late last night talking about my dad. I didn't sleep very well; I'll be fine. I'm just tired."

"Are you sure?" Amy asked, worry creasing her forehead.

"I promise. We'll talk later, okay?" I smiled at her, hoping to reassure her. She nodded and then nodded her head toward Blair across the room with her eyebrows raised. I shrugged. I didn't really know what to say to her about that.

Dr. Fields cleared his throat and began his lecture. I opened my notes and tried to concentrate.

"Today we will begin to explore the ancient Greek city of Delphi. From the fourteenth to the eleventh century BC, a temple was erected at Delphi to Gaia, goddess of the earth. Beginning in the eleventh century and through the ninth century BC, however, Delphi was dedicated to the god Apollo, son of Zeus and the mortal Leto. Apollo is best known as the god of the sun—he is depicted riding his chariot across the sky every day. But Zeus bestowed another great gift on his son, the gift of prophecy. It was to this gift that the temple at Delphi was dedicated.

"To seek this gift, sometimes called 'Apollo's Inner Light,' ancient Greeks traveled to Delphi to hear Apollo's prophecies transmitted through the priestess Pythia, who was said to channel the god's spirit. The oracle, or the spirit of Apollo, was found under the temple at the place where ancient Greeks believed that heaven and earth met. Sometimes the gods also communicated their messages to humans by means of signs. Gifted seers were also blessed with the power to foretell the will of the gods and the future."

I really loved Dr. Fields, but I was so exhausted that I missed half of his lecture. I couldn't even recall any details. After class, Blair walked by and told us he'd see us at lunch. Rob was antsy to get to English, so he hurried on ahead of us.

Amy waited until Rob was on his way. "I'm sorry you had such a bad night. What started all the talk about your dad? I thought your mom didn't like talking about him."

"Well, I guess with my eighteenth birthday coming, she was feeling sentimental." It was hard telling half-truths to Amy. I'd never had to keep anything from her, and it made me uncomfortable. "We both laughed and cried—you know, a real girl night!"

As we headed for English, the other inevitable question burst out of Amy's mouth. "Okay, so what's with the hand-on-the-back thing?"

I felt my face grow hot. "Well, he noticed that I was really tired, and let's face it, I look like death warmed over! Blair was just being sweet."

"I'll say!" Amy exclaimed. "Let me know when he gets sweeter."

"Ha, ha! We're going to be late for Richardson's entrance."

Luckily, the Gatsby test was very straightforward. Even in my semiconscious state, I felt like I did well on it. When the bell rang, Amy and I packed up our bags with Rob hovering, as usual.

"Hey, girls, can you kick it up notch? I'm starving!" Rob whined, rubbing his stomach and pouting.

"Good Lord, Rob, it's not like you didn't sneak a snack under your desk during the test," Amy teased.

"We men need our strength to cope with your alluring ways, you know." Rob put his arm around Amy's waist; she flushed and beamed at him. "Shall we?"

We laughed together and headed out of the classroom. Blair was waiting outside the door.

"What's up, Blair?" Rob asked, punching Blair's shoulder. "Ready for lunch?"

"I was wondering if you and Amy would excuse Makayla and me for lunch today. If that's okay with you, Makayla," he added quickly.

"Sure. Do you mind, Amy?" I asked, turning my back on Blair and smiling at her meaningfully.

"Please tell Jesse and Rick that we'll see them later," Blair said politely.

"No problem; we'll see you later, okay?" Amy nodded. "Let's go, Rob," she said as she tugged him away.

As they left, I heard him ask, "What's that all about?"

Amy nudged him in the ribs and shushed him.

"I thought maybe we could bring our lunch into the courtyard and talk," Blair explained. I nodded my agreement.

We walked through the food line and brought our trays outside to the courtyard. Blair headed for the shade of the redbud tree and held my tray while I sat down. It was a beautiful cloudless day, and a soft breeze cooled the warmth of my skin.

I started to nibble on my sandwich, suddenly feeling self-conscious. My mind was filled with questions, but I didn't know where to start. *I'll just eat and let him start talking*, I thought. Unfortunately, my stomach wasn't cooperating; I just picked at the bread.

Blair was thoughtful. "Aren't you hungry?" he asked, taking a bite of his sandwich. "You really need to keep your physical strength up, especially during the next week or so."

"Why?" I asked, my eyes widening in anxiety. Blair didn't answer at first; I lowered my eyes and fidgeted with the ties of my hoodie. "Is it going to get worse?" I shuddered.

Reaching out as if to lift my face, Blair answered me. "Yes, it is. But I'll be with you every step to help you. Okay?" He dropped his hand, and his hazel eyes shimmered in the light; I couldn't help but feel at ease. All I could do was nod.

"Makayla," he began, "next week will be the most difficult week of your transition." Blair paused to check my face, and probably my mind-set as well. I concentrated on keeping myself calm so he would continue.

"Your birthday is next Wednesday; you should plan to miss school for at least that day and probably the next," he suggested.

"But I can't miss…" I began but broke off when Blair shook his head.

His eyes met mine again, blazing with intensity. "You will not be able to function in public." Blair enunciated every word carefully.

My eyes widened in fear; Blair scooted closer to me. My eyes were blurring, and my hands trembled. The unknown—I'd never been good with being unprepared for anything! It went against my anal tendencies.

"May I?" he asked, suggesting that he wanted to touch me again.

I nodded, really beginning to wonder about his hesitation. He had touched me before, albeit not ever for very long; what was up?

Blair placed his hand ever so gently on my shoulder—again, no pulse—and spoke soothingly, gently, almost melodically into my ear.

"Makayla, if you'll allow it, I won't leave your side during your emergence." His tone was beseeching. "Your mother will not be able to help you process the sensations or manage the inevitable panic that will arise from the onslaught of voices you'll hear."

He waited patiently while I processed his words. I believed him, and that frightened me. But I instinctively knew that I would be able to handle it with Blair at my side. My only concern was for…

"My mom?" My voice was weak with emotion. "She won't want to leave me. What am I going to tell her?" I realized that my voice had risen with every word.

Blair moved his hand down to mine. "I'll talk to her. She knows enough about our gift and the rules we are bound by to accept the truth, although I'm sure she won't be happy with me when I tell her." He smiled, his eyes wary.

"When will you tell her?" I asked, trying to regain control.

"If you want, I'll drive you home this afternoon—I saw your mom drop you off this morning. We can talk this evening and make plans for covering up your absence." Blair was all business now; he had a job to do, and he was going to fulfill it.

He waited patiently until I looked up at him.

"Will you trust me, Makayla? I promise that I'll do everything in my power to make this as easy as possible for you."

There was no way I could doubt his sincerity; his eyes blazed with confidence and compassion. I would be able to do this impossible thing—as long as Blair was with me.

CLEARING THE SCHEDULE

After lunch, I called Mom and told her Blair was bringing me home after school. She agreed hesitantly; I could hear the discomfort in her voice. Mom hadn't known my dad when he'd emerged, but he'd told her that it was the most difficult experience of his life. I guess her job description, as she called it, was on red-alert mother mode.

Blair waited for me outside of chemistry; on the way out, we met Amy and Rob going to the parking lot.

"Hey, Kayla." Amy sparkled, seeing me with Blair by my side. "Do you have plans for the weekend?"

"Nah. Mom's home, so I'm planning to spend some time with her and catch up on some studying. What about you?" I asked, smiling, noticing that Rob's arm was around Amy's waist again.

"Amy and I are going to the movies tonight," Rob answered, rather proudly, I thought. "Do you guys want to go?"

Before I could answer, Blair said, "Unfortunately, I have a family commitment this weekend. How about another time?"

"Sure, that would be great!" Amy chimed in excitedly. "Talk to you later, Kayla." She looked like she might burst.

"Sure, Amy," I answered, wondering how much I would be able to say to her. "You guys have fun at the movies."

Rob steered Amy toward their cars as I watched wistfully. My emotions were so close to the surface; my eyes welled up. I wiped them away quickly, hoping that Blair hadn't noticed.

"How are you holding up, Makayla?" he asked softly.

I was becoming accustomed to the fact that Blair noticed everything. I just shrugged.

The ride home was quiet. Soft rain began to fall, splattering the windshield with its drops; the sound was soothing to my frayed nerves. As I stared out the window, I began to worry about the time Blair and I would soon be spending together. What if I really lost control and made a fool out of myself? I really was trying to keep my burgeoning feelings for Blair hidden for the time being, but what if under the strain…?

"What are you thinking?" Blair asked softly.

I laughed incredulously and rolled my eyes.

"What's so funny?"

"I keep forgetting that you don't just read my thoughts automatically," I replied, remembering and feeling very grateful for that right now.

"It's a courtesy we attempt to extend to each other, but it doesn't always work that well, to be honest," he explained apologetically. "Sometimes it's more difficult than at other times." Blair smiled sheepishly and looked away.

"I don't understand. I thought that was like the number one rule or something."

"It is, among clairvoyants we don't know well. The closer we get to each other, the harder it becomes to keep our thoughts private."

Now *that* was frightening! Suddenly, although I instinctively trusted Blair, I didn't know whether I wanted him to know—everything. All the protection normal human minds were given, all the thoughtless things we think but luckily don't say, all the emotions we try to keep to ourselves until it's safe—these would not exist for me, for us. Fear, or was it embarrassment, flooded me; I felt the heat rising in my face.

"Makayla?"

I couldn't meet his eyes; I stared at the floorboards of his Infiniti.

"You're afraid." It wasn't a question. Blair continued gently, "I would never do anything to hurt you."

Blair pulled into my driveway and waited for me to look at him—to say something.

"Makayla, may I?" he asked, reaching for my hand.

"Why do you always ask me before you touch me, Blair?" I sort of blurted it out, but I was dying to know.

He laughed; I frowned, well, really scowled at him. It wasn't my fault I didn't have all the stupid clairvoyancy etiquette down!

"I'm sorry. I forgot to tell you that. No wonder you look confused. I ask you so that my touch doesn't startle you. The closer to emergence you become, the more susceptible you become to the extra currents, for lack of a better word, that come from another clairvoyant. I'm more careful now because I caused you to faint yesterday. I'm sorry; that was careless of me. I'm not here to add to your stress." He still had his hand raised to touch mine.

"Oh." I sighed with relief. "You may," I answered and smiled. He took my hand. "Will that always be necessary?"

"No, as you become more in touch with your gift, it won't be necessary to ask all the time, but…" Now it was his turn to look embarrassed.

"What?" I asked, worried, immediately feeling self-conscious.

"Well, I don't want to assume that you want me to touch you, if you don't." He looked at me almost shyly.

I realized that this was the first time since he told me about our gift that Blair had ever really sounded like an eighteen-year-old boy. It comforted me to know that I was not the only one insecure about this relationship.

"I'll let you know if that becomes a problem," I teased.

Blair laughed and then suddenly turned toward my house.

"What's wrong, Blair?" I looked but didn't notice anything out of place.

"Your mom's getting anxious; we should probably go in," he explained, letting go of my hand and getting out of the car.

My body froze; I couldn't get my legs to move. Blair saw me through the windshield and came around to the passenger side. He opened the door.

"Makayla, aren't you coming?" His face was patient, but I heard his intended directive—I had to get out of the car and face what lay ahead. Part of me was still resentful. It kind of sucked that I had no choice but to let my mind lead me in whatever direction it was taking me. But what other choice did I have?

I got out of the car and headed for the door, which opened before I touched the doorknob.

"Kayla!" Mom cried out, hugging me. "I've been so worried. How are you feeling? Is everything okay?" She looked over my shoulder and saw Blair for the first time. I heard her gasp.

"What's wrong, Mom?" I asked, pulling away from her death grip. I looked between her face and Blair's; his face was tranquil and composed. Her eyes were far away.

Mom recovered herself and extended her hand to him. "It's very nice to meet you, Blair," she said formally.

He took her hand and shook it. "It's nice to meet you too, Mrs. Taylor."

"Please, call me Marissa," Mom said, trying to be a good hostess. Secretly I wondered how long she would feel this friendly toward Blair. Something was off about Mom's voice, but I couldn't put my finger on it.

"Come on in and sit down," she invited, still holding on to one of my hands and pulling me onto the couch next to her. "How was your English test, Kayla?"

"It was fine. What'd you do today?" I asked, trying to make small talk.

"Mostly I worked on clearing my schedule for next week," she announced proudly. "I want to be here for your birthday…" Her mind drifted for a second; then she recovered. "I want to… celebrate with you."

Mom never could hide how she really felt. Her blatant message was that she wasn't going to leave my side. How had she figured that out already?

I shifted uncomfortably and glanced at Blair. He looked at ease, but I doubted he had any idea how stubborn she… Oh, duh! Of course he had!

"Marissa," Blair began, "how much did your husband ever tell you about his emergence?"

Nothing like plowing right into the wall, Blair! I thought. The corner of his mouth twitched.

Mom looked from his face to mine and then back again. "Not very much, just that it was very difficult," she murmured, stroking my hand nervously.

"That's right; it *is* difficult, but not impossible and not dangerous. Makayla will be perfectly safe." Blair was obviously reassuring her thoughts.

Mom took a deep breath. "How can I help her?" she asked, her eyes glazed with oncoming tears. I stiffened unconsciously; she turned to me. "Kayla?"

"Mom…I…don't…you…" I stumbled over my tongue. She gripped my hand more firmly. I couldn't look at her.

"Marissa…" Blair began.

I totally chickened out; I couldn't sit here and watch this. "I'll go get us some drinks!" I shouted and headed for the kitchen without waiting for anyone to respond.

Taking a firm grip of the kitchen counter, I tried to steady myself. It was one thing that I didn't have a choice in this mess, but why did it have to hurt my mother? All my life we had been a team, supporting each other, helping each other through the rough times. Now that wouldn't be possible. How would she react?

My mother's raised voice broke through my panic. Blair's voice was soothing and businesslike as he tried to explain this horrible ordeal my mother couldn't share with me. Her voice, strident with emotion, was rising and then broke. I couldn't hear either of them—nothing.

Muscles tense, I tiptoed to the hall and peeked into the den. Blair was sitting next to my mother, his hands on either side of her head as she rested it on his shoulder. What was he doing to her?

As I entered the den, Blair's eyes focused on me, and he shook his head slightly. I froze. Slowly, he lowered his hands from my mother; she took a steadying breath and opened her eyes. Blair's compassionate eyes met hers; he smiled and nodded his head.

"Kayla," my mom called softly.

I hurried to her side. "I'm right here, Mom. Are you going to be okay?" Tears were falling silently down her face. She looked so vulnerable; I swallowed hard.

Mom held out her hand to me, and I hurried around to take it. "I'm going to go away for a few days next week, okay? I don't think I can concentrate on work, so I'll go visit your Aunt Julie in Austin. Tell your friends that I'm taking you on a birthday trip… tell them that you'll be with me." She sighed. "I'm going to call my sister now," she announced, and without waiting for me to respond, she headed upstairs to her room.

I stared after her in silent astonishment. After a moment or two, I turned to face Blair.

"What…how…why?" I stammered like a fool. "What happened?"

"It was obvious that your mother's emotions were getting in the way of her rational thought, which is very understandable under the circumstances. I just calmed her down and showed her what needed to happen for you to be as comfortable as possible next week."

"Is that what you were doing when you held her head?" I asked. I realized that my mouth was gaping; I shut it.

"Yes, as clairvoyants we're able to calm another's mental state by focusing our own positive thoughts into their minds," he continued without a pause. "In this case, I was able to refocus your mom on what is really important to her."

I must have looked confused.

Blair grinned. "You, Makayla, are the most important thing in the world to your mother. Underneath her fears and her protective instincts, she wants to do what's best for you."

"Will she be able to hold it together until next Wednesday is over?" I whispered. "You won't be with her to calm her down then."

"The effects will last long enough. When she returns Thursday afternoon, she'll be able to see for herself that all is well."

He sounded so certain of that. I wished I was that confident.

EMERGENCE

Spending the weekend with Mom was a good thing for us both. We slept in late, spending the days pampering ourselves with manicures, pedicures, and facials, and baking cookies and eating them hot out of the oven. At night we rented movies and ate popcorn in our pajamas. Neither of us spoke of my birthday; it seemed that nothing was left to say.

Tuesday at school I told my friends, with as much enthusiasm as I could muster, of my birthday "trip" with Mom to Austin. I told them I wasn't sure when I would get back, just in case my emergence didn't go well. Amy and Jesse were really disappointed that I was going to miss school on my birthday; they had hoped we would do something special together.

"Don't worry," I implored, "we still have our movie night on Saturday, and we'll all be together."

Finally they agreed and even sounded excited about my trip.

"Hey, make sure you hit the outlet mall for some shopping!" Jesse called out as I headed to my car Tuesday after school.

"I will!" I said, waving. My stomach was really uneasy; my nerves were definitely starting to get to me. Once again the fear of what the next day would bring welled up in me. I leaned against my car to steady myself. My head was beginning to ache, and it was making me a little dizzy.

Makayla… a soft voice called.

Lifting my head from my arms, I looked around to see who had called me. There was no one around me. Panic began to creep up me; my breathing accelerated and my heart pounded. I had to get into my car before it got any worse.

Fumbling for my keys, I dropped my bag on the ground. I bent down to retrieve it, and I heard it again.

Makayla…

I stood up too fast and had to grab the car door.

Suddenly a louder, clearer voice sounded, startling me.

"Makayla? Are you okay?" Blair's resonant voice rang out a few feet away; he was hurrying toward me. I turned toward his voice and lost my balance. His hands grabbed me before I hit the ground. A strong pulse shot through me, making me wince.

"I'm sorry. I didn't have time to warn you."

"It's o-okay, I think." My voice was shaking. "I'm fine."

Blair leaned down, picked up my bag, and opened the car door for me, all the while keeping one hand on me. Sitting me down in the seat, he continued his apology.

"Senora Rodriguez stopped me in the hall; I couldn't get to you sooner." He squatted down in front of me. "What happened?"

"I'm not sure. Jesse called out to me, I waved, and then I started to feel, I don't know…weird." Blair nodded but didn't interrupt. "Someone was calling my name, but it sounded far away. I turned to see who it was and got really dizzy."

"It's beginning earlier than I thought. We need to get you home. Let me help you get around to the passenger's seat; I better drive."

My head was still woozy as I stood with Blair's assistance. He walked me around the car and opened the door for me. I guess he buckled the seat belt, but I didn't remember him doing it.

Leaning my head back against the headrest seemed to make the dizziness better.

Blair started the car and pulled out of the parking lot.

"What about your car?" I remembered, closing my eyes.

"Don't worry. We'll get it later; nothing will happen to it in the school lot for a day or two. I'll just tell people it broke down."

When the car stopped and Blair turned off the engine, I opened my eyes. We were in my driveway, and Mom's car was gone. Moisture swelled in my eyes, and a sense of loneliness enveloped me. Blair was with me, I knew that, but I was scared, and to be honest…I wanted my mother.

Blair opened my door. "Can you walk, Makayla?" he asked.

"I think so," I said automatically, but as I swung my leg out the door, I felt myself listing with it. I grabbed the door to stop the forward motion.

"May I carry you?" Blair asked softly with his arms outstretched.

"No!" I responded too loudly out of habit. Blair was taken aback, and I was a little ashamed. Being carried was one of my pet peeves; I hated it! All my life, people, thinking I was so cute and small, had picked me up without asking. Kids at school did it because they could; they thought it was hilarious. Actually, it was humiliating, and by the fourth grade I was openly aggressive if someone even looked like they might pick me up.

"I'm kind of weird about being carried, Blair," I explained ruefully. "It comes from being small. It's kind of a complex, you know, 'I'm a big girl now.' I get cranky when someone tries to pick me up." I tried to smile to cover my behavior.

Blair burst out laughing, which really got my back up. I glared at him, and he tried to contain himself; he wasn't too successful.

"It's not funny!"

"I'm really…sorry." He snorted. "I just had this image of you, tiny as you are—no offense intended," he said quickly, hands up, "stamping your foot at someone trying to pick you up."

"Well, I'm glad you're amused," I said sardonically as I tried to get up again. Actually, the anger made the dizziness dissipate—I'd have to remember that. I stomped off toward the house with Blair trailing behind me; I opened the door.

"Makayla…" I ignored him. "Makayla," Blair implored, "I really am sorry. Don't be mad at me; I didn't mean to upset you."

Looking back at his striking face disarmed me, and I smiled. "It's fine. I overreacted, as usual." I laughed to myself. "Actually, I have been known to stomp my foot when I'm mad."

Blair smiled but didn't dare laugh. I turned toward the table in the den where Mom and I left messages for each other. An envelope lay on the table with my name on it. I opened it and read.

> Kayla,
> I couldn't bear to say good-bye in person; I'm on my way to Austin. I hope you can forgive my cowardice. I love you more than you will ever know, Kayla. I pray that your dad will be with you and give you strength.
> Love,
> Mom XXOO

I placed her note back in its envelope and clutched it to my heart. My mother was no coward; it took great strength for her to leave me. I would draw on her courage, rely on it, along with her love, to see me through the next twenty-four to forty-eight hours.

My eyes, brimming with tears, sought Blair's. I was losing control, apprehension overwhelming me. My shoulders shook as the ragged sobs overtook me. Blair reached out to me, wordlessly warning me of his touch; I crumpled into his arms.

"Everything's going to be fine, Makayla," Blair assured me, seating me next to him on the couch. He leaned me against his shoulder, keeping his arm around me; he seemed more comfortable than usual being close to me. Slowly I regained my composure.

"Sorry," I whispered. "I'm just scared."

"That's totally understandable."

My breathing slowed down as I relaxed, but my heart was thudding wildly—enjoying its close proximity to Blair much more than it should. Blair pulled away gently. Had he noticed?

"Are there questions I can answer to help you be less afraid?" he asked.

"Only a million or two." I sniffed, trying to clear my throat. "I don't even know where to start."

"Well, let's just take it a step at a time," Blair suggested. "With each new sensation, your body will react differently. For instance, the dizziness may get worse before it gets better, so I'll be staying close to you. I probably won't have time to warn you, but I'll try to make eye contact with you before I touch you. Eventually, probably by tomorrow morning, you will have become used to my touch, and it won't affect you so much."

I wouldn't count on that, I thought, hoping Blair was obeying the rules, but I just nodded. "I'll go get us something to drink and a snack," I said, leaving the room before he could notice my blush or read my thoughts.

I opened the fridge and scrounged for some food, noticing that Mom had filled it for the next few days. That was thoughtful. I took out some cheese, grapes, and sodas, went to the cabinet and got out the Wheat Thins, and placed them all on the counter. As I reached for a plate in the overhead cabinet, a wave of dizziness struck. The plate slipped out of my hand and fell to the floor, but I never heard it shatter.

How was your day, Sarah?

Apollo's Lights

If you do that again, Tony, I'll scream!
What's for dinner, Mom?
Then she said that she never heard my questions! Yeah, right!
Can you tell me how to get, how to get to Sesame Street?

Suddenly I felt myself being lifted off the floor; someone was carrying me. *Put me down!* I thought. As I regained full consciousness, I realized that my arm was stinging.

"Ow," I moaned. I was placed gently on the couch; I opened my eyes. Blair was standing over me. "What happened?" I asked, wincing.

"You fell and cut your arm on the shattered plate," Blair explained. "Where do you keep your first-aid stuff?"

"In the kitchen cabinet next to the fridge," I muttered, dazed.

Blair hurried into the kitchen. I examined my arm. Blood was dripping down my arm from several small lacerations. Blair came back carrying the first-aid kit and some paper towels. I turned away as he wiped the blood from my arm, carefully looking to make sure there were no fragments in the cuts.

"What happened?" he asked while still tending to my arm.

"I was just getting us a snack, and then all these different voices filled my head. I guess I got dizzy again." My head was feeling a little yucky, but I wasn't sure if it was because of the voices or the blood. As a child I had fainted at the sight of blood; even now, it made me woozy.

"You were probably hearing voices from the neighborhood," he explained while bandaging my arm. "I'll clean up the broken china and get the snack; you stay put, okay?"

Without waiting for my response, Blair headed to the kitchen. This was ridiculous! How many times was I going to hit the floor? My bottom lip jutted out into a pout; I didn't even bother to hide it.

Blair came back carrying a new plate with the cheese, crackers, and grapes in one hand and our sodas in the other. When he saw me, he stopped short. I looked up and caught him smiling at me.

"What?" Even to myself, I sounded like a six-year-old.

"Nothing." Blair smirked. "You're pretty cute when you're mad, that's all." He put the food on the coffee table and handed me a Diet Coke.

"I'm not used to being helpless or weak. Believe it or not, even last week, I could have walked into the kitchen and gotten a snack without landing on the floor!" I was definitely pouting; at least Blair was amused.

"No one thinks you are incapable of taking care of yourself, Makayla. You just need to be patient for a day or two and let me take care of you, okay?" He grinned so sweetly at me that I had to smile back.

"Blair, what do your parents think about you staying with me? Aren't they concerned about that? You know, most parents might worry that…" My face flushed, and I took a sip of soda to cover my embarrassment.

"My parents are in Florida, so they won't worry about anything. Don't worry; your virtue is safe with me!" he teased.

"Are they on vacation or something?" I pushed for the answers that had been nagging me for a while. Blair never talked about his family at all. In fact, none of us knew where he lived.

"They're on business near Tampa; we talk every night or so. Every month, they travel to Florida for a week or two. I've become used to being on my own," he explained casually. "Anyway, enough about them. How are you feeling?"

"Pretty good right now, kind of hungry." I reached out and grabbed some cheese and a couple of crackers.

"That's good. You need to eat a lot of protein to keep your strength up. For some reason, our blood sugar fluctuates a lot during emergence; I don't want you fainting from low blood sugar. In fact," he hesitated, "I need to tell you that there'll be times when you don't feel like eating and I'm probably going to have to insist on it." His emphasis on *insist* got my attention right away.

Oh no. My stubborn streak normally flared up when someone ordered me to do something I didn't want to do. I could only imagine how bad that was going to get under pressure.

"Blair." I grimaced. "Remember what I told you about being picked up?" He nodded. "Well, I'm not too good at being ordered around either…" My voice trailed off, and I squirmed.

"This is going to be an interesting experience for both of us, isn't it?" Blair smirked. "Don't worry; I can take it."

I smiled at his jest. So many questions were swirling in my head, and I really didn't know where to begin. Blair sensed my preoccupation.

"What is it? Ask me; if anything is worrying you, you need to ask. That's part of being a guide—being able to answer questions that are natural concerns for an emergent."

One question popped into my head and out of my mouth before I could stop myself.

"Blair, why do you always call me 'Makayla' instead of 'Kayla'?" This was something that had been bothering me for months, and although it wasn't as important as some of my other questions, I really wanted to know.

Blair looked a little surprised, probably by the triviality of my question, but he answered anyway.

"Do you know what your name means?"

"It's the feminine of Michael, right?"

"That's right, but do you know what 'Michael' means?" When I shook my head, he continued. "Your name means 'gifted by God.'" Blair waited while I processed his words.

"I never knew that," I admitted.

"From the first time I heard your name and knew its meaning, I felt it was more appropriate to call you 'Makayla.' You *are* gifted, and your name was chosen for a reason."

"Does every clairvoyant's name have a special meaning?"

Blair laughed. "I hope not, because if my name was chosen for a reason, I should be a farmer! My name means 'from the fields'!" I giggled and moved on to a more pressing question.

"I guess I better hear the rules before I break one of them," I joked lightly. "I wouldn't want to blow this gig on my first day!"

"Well, you already know that you shouldn't read another clairvoyant's mind without their permission." I nodded. "We may not tell anyone, other than our family and partners, that we are clairvoyant; we use our gifts subtly to help those around us. There are three very important rules that must be obeyed at all times."

I sat up straighter to pay better attention.

"We cannot use our gifts for immoral or illicit purposes, we cannot put ourselves in danger to help someone, and we must never use our gifts to force someone to do our will. God does not give us these gifts to make us powerful or controlling; our gifts are always to be used to help people."

Blair finished and sat patiently while I absorbed his words. For the most part, the rules made perfect sense to me, but I certainly didn't understand why some people are clairvoyant and others aren't. I figured that even Blair didn't know the answer to that one! Even "normal" people are gifted differently; some are musical, some are athletic, some are brilliant, and so forth.

"Anything else?" Blair asked. I hesitated, and he pressed me further. "Makayla, ask."

"What will happen to me during emergence?"

I waited for Blair to answer, my hand going to my hair and twirling it out of nervous habit. Blair seemed to be considering his words carefully, and that made me more nervous. Maybe I really didn't want to know what was going to happen after all.

"Everyone's emergence is different, but there are some commonalities. As I said before, you will begin to hear the thoughts of people close by more and more, such as your neighbors or even cars driving by the house. Some emergent clairvoyants have dreams and visions, which can be overwhelming at times."

The more I heard, the more frightened I became. Blair stopped talking. feeling my tension.

"Look, it's my job to help you when things get rough. I promise you'll be okay." He looked at me and smiled. "The problem is that because everyone's emergence is different, it's not really possible for me to tell you everything that will happen, but I will be able to calm you down when you get overwhelmed."

"How?"

"Remember the currents I told you about?"

"Uh-huh."

"Well, they can also be used to refocus some of your distress onto me."

"That doesn't seem fair," I admitted, worried about him.

"It's all in the job description! We'll deal with it together, okay?"

"Okay," I answered softly. *Together…huh?*

NIGHTMARES

The faces were all in shadow, the voices getting more strident with each word. My heart pounded in my chest. "This has gone far enough," *a calm voice spoke.* "It stops here." *Shifting dark figures oozed away from the wall.* "I don't think so, my friend," *another man's cold voice retorted. I shivered. The shadows crept toward him.* "You'll never get away with this!" *The man's slow, agonized moans pierced the night. Someone screamed...*

The scream was mine.

"Easy, Makayla." I heard Blair's soothing voice and felt a cool, moist cloth brush against my face. "You're safe. I'm right here with you. Slow down your breathing."

I opened my eyes and tried to concentrate on calming myself. It was fairly dark in the den; the soft light of a lamp across the room threw shadows across Blair's face as he sat on the floor next to the couch.

"What time is it?" My halting voice was raspy.

"It's three in the morning. Was it the same nightmare again?" he asked softly.

I winced, remembering the dream. "Yes," I whispered. "Someone, a man, needs help. Someone or something is hurting him,

I think." My voice rose in panic as I recalled the scene. "What does it mean, Blair? I don't understand what it means!"

Blair wiped the tears from my cheeks. "I don't know, but sometimes when we're emerging, we have nightmares brought on by underlying fears. It's our responsibility to use our gift to help those in need, as I told you before, and maybe you're just realizing that and it frightens you subconsciously."

"How can our gift help others? I don't really understand that aspect of it."

"Sometimes it's possible to foresee a danger to someone, either by hearing the fears of that person—as in preventing a suicide or other self-inflicted harm—or…" Blair hesitated, looking uncomfortable.

"Go on," I encouraged him.

"Some of us can see future events through the ill intentions of others." Blair paused but continued when he saw that I was confused. "Makayla, if someone around us is planning to hurt someone, or even kill them, sometimes it's possible for us to prevent that crime." He still looked unsettled.

"What is it, Blair?"

He sighed. "The hardest part of that is when we can't prevent it." Sadness shrouded his face. I reached out to touch his hand—the pulsing was long gone with the hours we had spent together.

Taking a deep breath, Blair continued, "We're not gods, Makayla, only blessed to be gifted. Sometimes that's hard to accept." He smiled, but it didn't touch his eyes.

I contemplated his words as best I could, but comprehension still eluded me. It was going to take a long time for me to understand all the dimensions of my gift.

"Aren't you tired?" I asked. "You haven't slept at all."

"I'm okay. Time for something to eat," he announced, rising to his feet and stretching.

"Get something for yourself; I'm not hungry," I said, lying back down and closing my eyes.

"Makayla…" His voice was reproachful. "How about some peanut butter crackers or something?"

"Blair, I've eaten more food since we got home from school than I've eaten in the past week! I'm a little person. There's no more room in here," I said, pointing to my stomach.

"All right, maybe just some orange juice," he announced, leaving the room.

"Were you somebody's little old grandma in another life?" I asked sarcastically.

I heard Blair laugh from the kitchen, but he returned and held out the glass for me. I rolled my eyes, pouted, and whined some more, but he didn't budge.

"Okay, okay. I'll drink the orange juice! I've never noticed before just how pushy you are."

"I'm hurt," he teased, sitting down on the couch by my feet and yawning.

"Blair, please lay down for a while. I can sit in the recliner," I said, trying to get up. He pushed me back gently.

"Just stay where you are, Short Stuff," he teasingly threatened. "I'll just lean back here."

"Hey, enough of the snide 'vertically challenged' comments," I snapped, throwing a pillow at him. Inside, my heart skipped a beat at his endearment. The short breaks during which my mind was free of pain were becoming a joy to me. My hopes were cautiously rising in spite of myself.

Blair held me tight while I struggled.

"Let me go! I can't take it anymore," I cried. Chaos roiled inside my head, wave after wave of emotions drowning me. The seething fear…loathing…pain…hate buffeted against me like surging waves. Again and again they slammed into me, drenching me in sweat and tears.

"Please!" I implored. "Just let me go!"

"Makayla, focus—look at me!" Blair ordered, holding my face between his hands. I strained against his grasp, wanting nothing but escape from the torture. But his strength overpowered me, and I finally met his gaze.

Relief washed over me. I gasped, trying to control my sobs. I felt my body relax as he guided my head to his shoulder. Slowly other feelings overtook the nightmare—peace, tenderness, joy, love.

Blair removed his hands from my face and lay back into the couch with me cradled in his lap. I heard his heart and breathing slow along with mine. Exhaustion replaced anxiety, and I fell into a dreamless sleep.

When I woke, sunlight was streaming through the window. Blair was sleeping next to me on the couch. Hoping not to wake him, I sat up slowly and looked at the clock on the wall—ten o'clock. I needed to use the bathroom and brush my teeth; my mouth felt like parched desert sand.

I got up carefully, checking for dizziness; Blair would be furious if I fell while he was sleeping. Softly, I crept upstairs to my bathroom. I looked in the mirror and gasped. Dark patches circled my eyes, my face was pale, and my hair—well, there was no describing it. Brushing my teeth felt great, so I washed my face and brushed through my tangled hair. I really needed a shower, but I didn't want to risk getting dizzy in there. I just changed into clean yoga pants and a t-shirt instead.

I decided to get something to eat in the kitchen. How could I possibly be hungry after all that food Blair stuffed down me yesterday? Blair was still sleeping, so I headed for the kitchen. I poured a glass of orange juice and sat down at the table. In the light of day, last night seemed a distant but disturbing dream, all except for the memories of Blair.

I remembered his face, his gorgeous eyes, his tender touch, his chiding and teasing—even his stern expression when I refused to eat. My heart had never been so full, and yet I was worried. What would our relationship be like after tomorrow? Would we go back to "normal" and forget what we shared together? I was lost in thought when I heard Blair call out to me.

"Makayla, where are you?" he called anxiously.

"I'm in the kitchen."

Blair entered the kitchen, rubbing his hands through his golden hair, looking like a little boy. I giggled.

"What's so funny?" he asked, smiling.

"Your hair looks about as bad as mine did this morning! Are you hungry?" I asked, laughing.

"Yeah, I am," he answered, heading for the fridge.

"Hey! This one's on me," I said, pushing him into a chair. "Do you like eggs and bacon?"

"Sure. Are you sure you're feeling up to it?"

"I'm fine, for the moment. Why don't you help yourself to the bathroom upstairs, and I'll fix breakfast." I smiled at him shyly and turned to get out the ingredients.

"Okay, if you're sure," he replied. I watched as he grabbed his backpack and headed up the stairs.

Ten minutes later, Blair returned in clean sweatpants and a t-shirt and plopped himself down at the table. I got him some juice and set his plate of eggs, bacon, and toast in front of him.

"And she can cook too! What a woman!" he teased.

"It's the least I can do after what I put you through last night." I stared down at the table, embarrassed.

I felt Blair's hand reach out for mine; I looked up. He smiled and teased, "All in the line of duty, ma'am. Oh, and by the way… happy birthday!"

"Stay away from me!" I screamed, running to the corner and crouching into a ball. "It's everywhere…in my head…my heart… I can't get away from it!" I rocked back and forth sobbing. I was hyperventilating; the room was beginning to spin. And still the pictures ran through my mind.

You don't deserve me! I'm leaving! she screamed at him as she stormed out the door, slamming it.

Why don't you just go to hell! I hate you! The boy glared at his stunned father then stalked away.

Get out of the way, moron! Can't you see the green light? the driver of the red Camaro yelled out the window.

Please stop! Stop, it hurts! The little boy cringed, watching his father's belt fall again.

I hate you!

Blair crouched down next to me but didn't touch me. His face was tortured; for the first time, he didn't know what was going on.

"Makayla, please!" he begged, reaching out to me. "Let me help you! Let me touch you!"

"No! Don't touch me! Can't you feel it?" I stared at him, my frenzied eyes wide with terror. "Fear is everywhere. It's in the walls. Can't you hear it?" I rocked some more. "Yelling…fighting…hate," I growled the words. "I can see it; it's everywhere!

"Falling…I'm falling! I can't breathe, Blair! It hurts!" My sobs were nearing hysteria.

Faster than I would have imagined possible, Blair grabbed me and pulled me into his arms.

"No…" I struggled to free myself, but then there was nothing but silence.

I was still moving back and forth, but it was not the frenzied rocking of the past hour. Blair was gently rocking me, crooning comforting words in my ear.

"I'm sorry, Makayla. Push the feelings away; block them from your mind. I didn't know… Don't cry now. I'm here." His words, meant to be comforting, were cut by the pain in his voice. "Try to find goodness, Makayla. It's out there too. Find the happiness, the joy." Blair's voice broke on the last word.

I reached for his face without looking up; he lay his cheek in my hand. Moisture…his face was wet. Was he crying too? No, this wasn't right! Blair shouldn't have to suffer with me. *Focus on the good, Kayla,* I thought. *Focus…*and they flowed into me with a rush.

I love you, Mommy! The blonde, curly-headed child ran to her mother's outstretched arms.

You are so special to me, Sammy; I'm so proud of you! A mother embraced her soldier son.

Let me help you with that, Mrs. Jeffrey. The teenage boy rushed to the woman's side as she tried to pick up her groceries.

How nice of you to come see me, dear! An elderly woman's face beamed at the sight of her young visitor.

I will love you forever…

A giggle escaped me; I hiccupped. Blair released me slightly and looked down at me, confused and apprehensive.

"It is out there, isn't it?" I whispered, my voice hoarse from screaming.

"What is?" Blair asked, anxious.

"Goodness…happiness…love." I smiled weakly.

"Yes, it is." Blair sighed with relief. His eyes glistened, but his face was tense.

"Are you all right, Blair?"

"Don't go worrying about me, Short Stuff," he admonished. "You have enough to be dealing with without worrying about me." He smiled gently.

"Blair?" I couldn't ask, afraid of his response. I looked down at my hands.

"What is it, Makayla?" Blair asked, his tone serious again.

"Nothing…never mind."

He reached down and pulled my face up; I still couldn't look at him. I pushed myself up out of his lap. He let me go but held on to me until I was standing.

It was just past six in the evening; low sunbeams streamed into the front windows where I stood. Dusk was just falling. Blair came and stood behind me, but I didn't turn to him.

"Makayla, your gift is stronger than the average clairvoyant. What you are struggling with now is an empathic ability."

"What does *that* mean? I don't understand…" I broke off, too exhausted to comprehend anything else. How many times had I asked that question today? I leaned my arms against the window and rested my head on them.

"It means that beyond your ability to hear the thoughts of those around you, you are able to feel and see them as well. You'll learn to channel that gift and relate to others in ways impossible for most humans." Blair sounded awestruck.

"What do you mean, 'relate to others in ways impossible for most humans'?" I asked, turning to face him at last.

"You'll be able to offer an inner peace, a feeling of self-worth, to those in need of it; you'll be able to help people help themselves and those around them. You'll even be able to fill their hearts with love when they are devoid of that most precious gift." Blair crossed to the couch and sat down; he put his face in his hands, exhausted.

You'll be able to see through me.

ANOTHER RULE

I stood stock-still; my feet refused to carry me forward. My overwhelming desire to comfort him battled with his last thought. What had he meant, "...see through me"? I had worried about what this time together would do to our relationship, or if we even had one. Now it seemed that Blair's feelings were not the same as mine. Was he afraid to be honest with me...to hurt me?

Afraid that this would put me over the edge I was so precariously dangling from, I said softly, "I'm going upstairs to take a shower. I...just...can't..." I couldn't look at him. That would crush me, bury me deeper into despair. I willed myself to move forward, crossing in front of the couch to get to the stairs.

Blair reached for my hand and stopped me. "Please, Makayla, wait. Let me explain," he begged.

I tried to pull away from him, but he refused to let me go. "Let me go, Blair," I implored softly. "I can't do this right now."

"Not until you've heard me out. Please..." His voice was filled with misery. "Please sit down, just for a minute."

Without looking at him, I turned and sat at the opposite end of the couch. He let go of my hand. I stared at the floor, fighting to hold back the tears welling in my eyes. I had never felt so vulnerable in my life...transparent. Was this a gift or a curse?

"Makayla, I…" He hesitated. "I need to explain something to you that I should have told you long before now."

I don't think I want to hear this. My heart pounded so loudly that I was sure Blair could hear it. I pulled my knees up and wrapped my arms around them hoping, literally, to keep myself together.

"One of the rules that we are bound to follow has become very difficult for me." He paused. Blair took a deep breath and continued, "Guides are not supposed to get involved with their emerging clairvoyants."

Not supposed to get involved… I glanced at him; he was looking at me, his eyes hopeless and beseeching at the same time. What was he trying to tell me? That he couldn't or wouldn't get involved because of the rules? Why hadn't he told me this before? Or… I looked back down at the floor, preparing myself for the ultimate rejection.

Whoever made the rules, or whatever they are, must have forgotten what it was like to go through emergence. How could any clairvoyant expect that the shared experience would not bind the participants? My soul had been ripped apart bit by bit over the past twenty-four hours, with only Blair to keep me together. I was laid bare, helpless, hopeless. What kind of person could share that and walk away? Could Blair?

"Okay. I understand. I'm going upstairs now," I said, unwinding my arms and hoping that my heart would not fall on the floor.

Blair reached for me again, forcing me to remain on the couch. Then he continued, "You don't understand, Makayla." He paused. "I don't think…I can…leave and go back to being friends." He stared down at the floor, despairing. "I was raised to follow the rules; they have been ingrained in me since I was a little boy. It is physically painful to think of breaking the codes, like deserting my faith, the foundation of my world." Blair lowered his head into his hands; his body trembled.

My attention was focused on his pain, and then my mind caught up as well. I moaned, rolling my head around to release the pain—his pain. Afraid to cry out, I clenched my teeth together. It only took a few seconds for Blair to realize what was happening. He wrapped his arms around me and pulled me close into his chest.

"Oh no, Makayla. Block out my pain; close your mind to it. Please...I'm sorry...release it!" he pleaded. "Find peace; find it!"

Without thinking, I raised my hands to his face and pulled it down toward my shoulder. With my eyes closed, I focused on finding inner peace, but more than that, I wanted to share.

Blair gasped, closed his eyes, and took in a slow breath. He raised his head and gazed at me. "How did you do that?" he whispered softly, obviously utterly astounded.

"Do what?" I asked, not quite sure if my intention succeeded; still, I smiled shyly.

"How did you transfer your peace, your tranquility to me? You're not supposed to be able to do that for...years, if ever." Blair was mesmerized.

"I don't know exactly," I admitted. "I sort of reacted instinctively." My face grew warm. "I couldn't stand for you to be in pain."

"This is amazing!" Blair rejoiced. "You shouldn't even be able to control your gift, let alone channel it!" He pulled me onto his lap and hugged me tight. "You are something special, Short Stuff!"

I laughed but then sighed. Blair pulled away to look into my face. "What?" he asked, still smiling gently.

"Blair..." I had to free him, even if it wounded me beyond repair. "You need to do what's right for you. I don't think you should give up everything you believe in just for...me." I swallowed hard; I had to finish. "Nothing is hidden between us, so you know how I feel, but I'm not sure it's worth it—that I'm worth it," I said, my voice breaking.

Blair's strong arms turned me toward him. He took my face in his hands. "You *are* worth it." He drew my face to his, haltingly, hesitating for just a moment, then kissing me gently. My body tingled with sensations I had only dreamed of as he leaned me back onto the couch. "If you will have me…" he said softly, moving his mouth to mine again.

I wrapped my arms tightly around his neck and wound my hands into his hair, pulling him even closer to me. His tongue caressed my lips, and I gasped for breath. Blair laughed gently and moved his lips to my ear.

"Is that a yes?" he whispered.

I don't know what made me say it. "I'll think about it," I retorted, teasing.

"You're a mess!" he chided, pulling himself up to look at me, amused. "Has anyone ever told you that?"

"Hmm…let me think." I paused, bringing my forefinger to my chin. "I may have heard that once or twice!"

Blair hugged me again. "I tried to keep myself from falling in love with you," he admitted seriously. "Every time we were together, at the skating rink or at the movies, or even studying math together, I felt pulled in two directions. One part of me always kept my job as your guide in my mind, but the other part…well, the other part just wanted to be with you."

I lay on his chest and soaked in his words. He really did like me for me.

"I wondered sometimes why you always got so serious and pulled away just as we started to get along and enjoy each other," I admitted.

"I bet you thought I was crazy!"

"No." I hesitated, and Blair drew back to look at me.

"Go on."

I looked down at my hands. "I just assumed that you didn't, you know, like me."

"I'm so sorry, especially since the exact opposite has been true all along. From the moment I saw you, I was attracted to you. What's not to like? You're beautiful, smart, witty, compassionate, a little on the sarcastic side…"

"Who, me?" I laughed. *Beautiful? Compassionate?* My heart fluttered wildly in my chest.

Blair laughed and kissed me. "Time for something to eat!" Blair stood and put me gently on my feet.

"Are men always so guided by their stomachs?" I asked grumpily. "I can think of better ways to spend some time." I smirked, climbing onto the couch to reach around his neck and kiss him.

"Food first," he commanded, pulling his face away gently. I pouted. "You can pout all you want, but I'm still responsible for your emergence, and it's time for you to eat."

I didn't let go and tried to smile coyly.

"That's not going to work either." Blair smirked. "And if you don't let go, you are liable to end up being carried to the kitchen," he threatened, smiling broadly.

"You wouldn't dare!"

"You asked for it!" Blair threw me over his shoulder, carrying me into the kitchen. I yelled and beat on his back with my hands. He set me down on the counter.

"You can't just sling me around like a sack of potatoes!" I chided. "I love you, but that doesn't give you the right…" The expression on Blair's face stopped me mid-rant.

His smile widened; his hazel eyes were radiant.

"What?" I asked, lowering my eyes, feeling suddenly bashful.

"That's the first time you said you loved me…well, out loud at least," he explained, grinning from ear to ear.

I threw my arms around him, drawing him closer to me, and wrapped my legs around him. "Are you sure you still want to eat first?" I teased.

"Ugh! You are impossible!" Blair moaned, kissing me lightly. He disentangled himself from me and headed to the fridge. "We'll eat something first; then we'll see what opportunities arise…" He chuckled, but then his voice grew serious for a minute. Turning to look at me, he said, "It's not quite over, Makayla. There may be more flare-ups before tomorrow morning. You really do need your strength."

He moved to the refrigerator and pulled out the lasagna Mom made for us before she left, placing it in the microwave to heat. I hopped down from the counter, grumbling under my breath, and pulled out the plates. We worked in silence, but the kitchen was charged with the energy emanating from us.

I smiled to myself and wondered how we would ever be able to control this in public. School was going to be interesting, to say the least, and how were we going to explain to our friends the sudden shift in our relationship?

Suddenly, I froze with the plates still in my hands. If this was against the rules, what would the repercussions be for Blair? Was there a ruling authority over clairvoyants? What would happen if they, whoever *they* might be, found out?

I felt Blair take the plates from my hands carefully; he pulled me close to him.

"Why are you worrying about that?" he asked, uneasiness coloring his tone.

"I was just wondering…" I hesitated, and Blair pushed me away slightly to see my face.

Our eyes met, and he answered my question. "You don't have to be concerned about that. I'll take care of everything. I promise."

"Blair," I whispered softly, picking the word out of his head, "who are the Ileesia?"

THE ILEESIA

Blair's body became rigid; he closed his eyes and took a deep breath. As I waited, horrified by his reaction, something shifted; my head became quiet. For the first time in the last hour, I could not *hear* Blair. The silence was more frightening to me than the avalanche of sounds had ever been.

Pulling away from him, I reached up and covered my ears; the silence was deafening. I doubled over, pained by its absence. All at once, his voice returned to me, and I relaxed a little. I slowly pulled my hands from my ears and stared up into Blair's face in confusion.

"I'm sorry, Makayla," Blair apologized sheepishly. "It's a natural defense mechanism that you have also; it's called blocking." He reached out to me, but I backed away from him.

"Why did you block me?" I asked, frowning. What did all his words about love mean if he didn't trust me with his thoughts?

"I didn't mean to, consciously; it's just…well, I wasn't ready to talk about the Ileesia just yet. Please forgive me," he begged, reaching out to me again. "I'm not accustomed to allowing anyone to hear all my thoughts. It may take me a while to get out of the habit of blocking."

Slowly I moved back into his embrace. "Thanks," Blair said, kissing the top of my head. The microwave buzzed, and he headed to retrieve our dinner. "Let's eat, okay?"

"Will you explain it to me while we eat?" I asked, getting our glasses. He didn't answer at first. "Please, Blair…I need to understand."

I poured our drinks and returned to the table. Blair put our plates down silently and sat down. I stood behind my chair, waiting for his response.

"I can stand here all night," I threatened. "I guess I'm not the only stubborn person in the room, am I?"

"No one ever said that you were; you're just the cutest stubborn person in the room." He smirked.

"Okay, here's the deal: if you want me to eat, you better start talking!" I crossed my arms and glared at him. I could hear all his comebacks. "That won't work…nope, that one either…you wouldn't dare!" I took a step backward.

Blair groaned. "Okay, you win. I give up; you're way too much for me to handle," he conceded, throwing up his hands. "Yup, all five feet of you!" He scooped me up before I could say a word and threw me over his shoulder again.

"Hey…hey…hey! Put me down you, big bully!" I laughed. Blair plopped me into my chair, grinning evilly.

"You eat, and then we'll talk." He kissed my forehead and sat back down. "No more bargaining. Take it or leave it!" he said as he stuffed his mouth full of lasagna.

I stuck my tongue out at him, sniffed haughtily, and dug into my lasagna.

We ate in silence for a while. The lasagna tasted good; I was actually hungry. The highs and lows of the last hours had really worn me down. I started to get sleepy as I finished eating, but I was determined to get the answers I needed.

I forced myself to get up and walk to the sink, where I rinsed my plate and opened the dishwasher. Blair came up behind me and kissed the back of my neck. I shrugged and giggled as his breath tickled my neck.

"Stop it, Blair. I'm going to break another plate!" I squealed, squirming away. "Now give me your plate and bring me the glasses."

"As you wish, madam." He smirked, headed to the table, handed me the dishes, then went to wrap up the leftover lasagna.

When the dishes were all cleared away and put into the dishwasher, I turned and bumped right into Blair. He laughed and picked me up into his arms.

"You're sleepy," Blair said, heading for the couch. "You should rest for a while." He lowered me onto the couch, but I held on around his neck.

"I don't want to sleep," I cooed. "I want you to tell me about the Ileesia." I batted my eyelashes at him, making him laugh.

"You do have a one-track mind, Short Stuff."

"And you are trying to distract me so that you won't have to keep your end of the bargain. I ate; now you talk!" I bellowed.

"Ugh! You certainly are a demanding little thing," he said, rolling his eyes at me.

"Thank you. It's a gift." I kissed him lightly. "Please tell me, Blair," I asked more seriously. "If you don't, I'll only think it's somehow worse than it probably is."

He sat up, pulling me with him, until we were sitting next to each other on the couch. I leaned my head against his shoulder and waited.

"The Ileesia is a group of powerful clairvoyants who are chosen as the governing authority over all of us." He paused. "Each month, they meet to hear reports of the successes, and the rare failures, of our world. They are the elders, the blessed, those whose gifts are the strongest of us all. It's their mission to guide us to use our gifts for righteous causes, especially for the betterment of humankind.

"Each of us is given different gifts; the majority of us are only able to lead people in the right direction by hearing their thoughts. Some are given strength to be guides to emerging clairvoyants."

I smiled up at him. "Like you."

Blair caressed my face and nodded. "Okay, so some clairvoyants are empathic, some have the power of telekinesis—you know, moving things with their minds—some can sporadically get notions about the future, and the rarest of us can receive messages in our dreams."

"Messages?" I asked, confused.

"You know, like dream interpretation."

"Oh. Go on. Tell me more about the Ileesia."

"The word *Ileesia* comes from the Greek, meaning 'the home of the blessed.' Our gifts date back to the ancient Greeks. Do you remember when Dr. Fields lectured on the oracle at Delphi?" he asked, looking down at me.

I nodded. "I remember."

"The priestess Pythia was the first clairvoyant, that we know of, at least. I'm sure there were others before her, but history has not recorded any others. The Ileesia has been around ever since the ninth century BC; it has been passed down through the generations."

I yawned. "Okay, time for some sleep," Blair announced. "Do you want to sleep here on the couch or up in your bed? I think that you'll sleep better tonight, so you may want to be more comfortable."

"Wait, I'm not finished asking questions," I complained. Blair frowned at me, but I held up my hand. "Just a few more…please?"

"Just a couple more; then it's off to bed. Deal?" He looked down at me sternly.

I nodded. "Where is the Ileesia? Do they have an office or something?" I asked, thinking that the question sounded kind of dumb.

"Here in the US, the Ileesia is located in Florida, but believe it or not, there is still an Ileesia at Delphi. It is located in a sophisticated underground complex under the ruins of Apollo's temple. I've never been there myself, but I'd like to visit it someday." Blair stared off across the room.

My eyes were getting really heavy; I was having trouble fighting the fatigue. "Who…are…the members…of…" I yawned again, and this time, there were no deals to be made.

Blair picked me up in his arms and carried me upstairs to my room. I was even too tired to argue about being carried, so I just put my arms around his neck and enjoyed the ride. He lay me on my bed, but I clung on to him.

"Will you stay with me, please?" I mumbled. "I don't want to be alone."

I felt him lower himself and lay beside me. "Sleep now, Short Stuff. I love you," he said, kissing me gently.

I rolled over, relishing the words he had never spoken aloud before, and nestled into his chest. "Love…you…too…"

No, you can't give up everything; I won't allow it! After all we have done for you… You will lose everything! Think about what you are doing, son. The powers of pure clairvoyants run in your blood. Your future—your destiny—lies without her!

Gasping, choking, unable to breathe, I was suffocating. The darkness was burying me further and further into the pit. I struggled, pushing myself out of its grasp. My body felt weighted. Please let me go; let me wake up…wake up!

"No!" I shrieked. I bolted upright and flailed to escape my blanket.

"Makayla! What is it?" Blair's arms encircled me. I struggled to get away. "No, honey. It's me; it's Blair." He took my face in his hands. "Focus, Makayla. Look at me!"

My panicked eyes found his. I was gasping for breath. My body trembled violently; my heart thudded uncontrollably. "Blair!" I screamed. "I'm scared! Hold me…please hold me tight!"

As his arms drew me closer to him, irrepressible sobs swept through me. My chest hurt from the unrelenting grief. Blair held me, stroked my hair, and kissed my forehead. "It'll be all right, Makayla. Calm down; it was just a dream." He rocked me, as he had during the past night, until my sobs broke off into short gasps; my breathing was still too shallow to speak.

"What did you dream? Was it the same nightmare as last night?" he asked, continuing to rock me gently.

"No," I gasped. "It was different… It was… Oh, Blair!" I turned my tear-streaked face to him and reached up to find his lips. Climbing further into his lap, I pushed him back on the bed, kissing him fiercely. His kiss was hesitant, confused. I moved down to kiss his neck and chest, wanting nothing but to bury myself in him. *It couldn't be about us!*

Blair's muscles tightened, and his arms clamped me to his chest; I couldn't move to kiss him. My renewed tears fell onto his t-shirt, soaking it. "Makayla," he said softly, "tell me about your dream." My mind had forsaken me. I shook my head slowly against his chest. "I need to know what you dreamed; maybe I can help interpret it for you."

"I don't want a dream interpreter!" I tried to free myself so I could reach his mouth again, but he wouldn't release me.

"No," he whispered. "Not until you calm down."

His rebuff tore into me; tears stung my eyes. I looked away and tried to wriggle free of his grasp, this time to flee from him, but again, he wouldn't let me go. "Makayla, honey, it's not like that," he assured me, obviously hearing my insecurity. "I want to be with you too, but not because you're upset. Please tell me. I only got small bits of it. What did you hear?"

Blair waited patiently while I tried to gather my thoughts and courage together. I didn't know what to say or how to say it. "I'm not sure who was talking or to whom she was talking. It was a woman speaking." I paused, hoping that would be enough to satisfy him.

"Go on," he encouraged.

"The woman was talking to her son, telling him that he was making some kind of mistake..." I couldn't continue speaking; my heart burned from the painful memory. *She said that her son's destiny lies without someone, but I'm not sure who,* I thought.

Blair was very quiet as he heard my thoughts. Finally he spoke. "I don't think it means anything particular. It was probably just a random, emotion-filled dream like the ones you had last night," he tried to reassure me. "It's late, and your mother will be home later today. Let's try to get some more sleep, okay?"

He was probably right; I was just overreacting to a nightmare. Blair reached down and pulled my face to his. "I love you, Makayla. Nothing can change that." And without hesitation, he pulled me on top of him and kissed me with enough passion to extinguish any nightmare.

I rolled over reaching for Blair; he wasn't there. I opened my eyes and found him standing by my window, sunlight cresting over the sill. He looked over at me and smiled.

"Good morning, Short Stuff. How are you feeling?"

I sorted through the sounds and emotions in my head, but none of them were overpowering. Actually, I felt more rested than I had in a while. "Pretty good, I think. My head doesn't hurt even though there are soft sounds swimming around in it."

"That's a good thing," Blair said, moving to sit on the side of my bed. "You're already learning to filter the sounds. Soon you'll be able to hear only the voices you concentrate on, the ones you want to hear. Not being an empath myself, I don't really know how that will develop, but we'll handle it as it comes." He opened his arms to me, inviting me in. I sat up and hugged him around his waist.

"I feel like there's so much more I need to understand; it's a little overwhelming," I admitted. "For one thing, I'm not sure how I will handle being at school with all those voices around me."

Blair leaned away from me. "Hopefully, by the end of today, you will have learned to filter enough to be comfortable. It's not going to be easy, but I have faith in you. You've already shown abilities far above the abilities of most emergent clairvoyants."

I nodded, but that wasn't the only thing worrying me. "What is it, Makayla?" Blair asked.

"How are we going to explain our relationship to Amy and the others? And how will you explain that you were absent the same two days as me? Amy is far from stupid; she's going to be suspicious." I bit my lip.

"Well, let's talk about the easy one first," Blair suggested. "They'll just assume that we have been dating on the sly and we've decided to 'come out,' as they say. Amy's been wondering about us for a long time anyway. Like you said, she's not stupid. And Jesse's been trying to hook us up since I got here!" He laughed, leaned down, and kissed me lightly.

"To explain the question of my absence, I'll just say that my family had an emergency and we went out of town for a couple of days. They don't know much about my family, so hopefully they won't question my explanation." He looked at me to see if I agreed.

They're not the only ones who don't know about... I stopped myself mid-thought, but Blair had already noticed. I looked down at the floor, embarrassed.

"Makayla?" His voice was reproving as he raised my face to his. "Didn't you get upset yesterday when I blocked you?" He raised his eyebrows. "Finish your thought, please."

I took a deep breath. "Will you tell me about your family, Blair?" I looked up at him, hopeful.

Blair sighed. Why wouldn't he just tell me? Doubts swirled in my head; my insecurities rose to the surface again. I got up and moved to the window. His hesitation was making me nervous, almost frightened. I shivered and wrapped my arms around myself. Closing my eyes, I concentrated on staying calm.

Blair's arms wound around me from behind; he laid his chin on my head.

"I have an older brother, twenty-six, and a sister, twenty-three, both married and both clairvoyants. Benjamin and his wife, Holly, live in Austin; they have a two-year-old daughter named Leila. Briana and her husband, Jonah, live in Denver. My parents are Blake and Bethany..." He laughed softly. "They like *b* names!"

"That wasn't so hard, was it?" I asked, turning around to face him. "What do your parents do for a living?"

It was almost imperceptible, but Blair's eyes tightened just a bit. I frowned, not understanding his distress. "Um, they're lawyers..." He hesitated.

"And..." I said, shrugging.

"And...they are members of the Ileesia."

I swallowed hard and swayed on the spot. Blair steadied me and hugged me tight. "It's going to be all right, Makayla. I promise. Trust me," he begged.

Could this get any worse? Breaking the rules was one thing, but breaking the rules when his parents were in the Ileesia! I trembled, remembering my nightmare; it was *his* mother, and she was talking about me.

EMPATH

It took Blair about half an hour to calm me down enough for me to function. I took a hot shower, letting the water relax my aching muscles. My body felt like it did after recovering from the flu—weak, achy, unstable. As I washed my hair, I tried to believe Blair's reassurances that all would be well with us.

"We're meant to be together, Makayla," he had said. "Nothing will keep me from you, not rules or other people's opinions."

I finished showering, brushed my teeth, and dried my hair. With my towel still wrapped around me, I stood in front of my closet, boggled. This was going to be my first normal day with Blair since we had pledged our love to each other. I wanted to look nice for him. After choosing my skinny jeans, a striped tunic, and my Toms, I skipped down the stairs.

Blair was in the kitchen; he had used my mom's shower to clean up and get dressed. He wore a clean pair of jeans and a green v-necked t-shirt, which clung to his frame and accented his eyes. His back was to me as I approached, but he turned, finding me leaning in the doorframe.

"Hey there, beautiful!" He grinned. "What are you doing?"

"Just admiring the view," I teased. He held his arms out to me, and I ran to him, reaching for his shoulders to pull myself up. Blair lifted me off my feet and pressed his lips to mine. I giggled.

Kissing me between each word, he asked, "What's…so…funny?"

"To think, I didn't like being picked up just a few days ago." I wrapped my arms around his neck. "I don't seem to mind as much when you do it."

"I'm glad," he said, giving me a squeeze and putting me down gently. "Are you hungry?"

"Not for food," I teased, reaching up for him. Actually, I was a little surprised by my *appetite*, having never experienced love before.

"You do seem to be insatiable lately." He laughed, bending down to kiss me. "But you still need to eat food too. Woman does not live by kissing alone!"

"Dang it!" I stomped my foot for emphasis, and Blair roared with laughter. "Okay, if you insist," I said, rolling my eyes, letting go of him, and heading to the refrigerator. "What do you want to eat this morning?" I opened the door.

"Let's go out to breakfast," he suggested. "How about Panera? They have great bagels and pastries."

That stopped me in my tracks; I stood like an idiot staring into the fridge. I loved Panera for breakfast, but the thought of leaving the house so soon scared me. Stepping back, I closed the door but didn't turn to face Blair.

His long arms wove themselves around me. "Why are you afraid? I wouldn't take you out if I thought you couldn't handle it."

"I know," I whispered, holding on to his arms around my waist. "What if someone sees us, like a parent of our friends or something? That might be hard to explain." I knew I was grasping at straws and that Blair wouldn't buy it. He didn't.

"We'll go up to the Vista Ridge Mall in Lewisville. No one will see us there." Slowly, he turned me around to face him. "It's important that we practice your filtering skills today before your mom gets home this evening and certainly before we go back to school."

He was right and I knew it, but I couldn't quite shake all my doubts. *What if I lose it while we're out?* I thought.

"You won't; I'll help you. If you become agitated, I'll help you filter."

"How can you do that?" I asked, curious.

"All I have to do is make eye contact with you, like we did the other night. I won't let it get out of hand, so I won't have to touch your face," he explained. "No one will even notice anything out of the ordinary. They'll just think we can't keep our eyes off each other." Blair flashed his gorgeous smile, and I couldn't help but feel better. I smiled back at him.

"Let's go then, okay?" He seemed really happy to be getting out of the house, and if I was honest, I'd have to agree with him.

As we headed out to the car, I grabbed my purse. "Where the heck are my keys?" I muttered to myself as I rummaged around in it.

A jangling sound caught my attention; Blair was dangling my keys in the air above my head, grinning.

"Okay, very funny. Hand them over, big guy." I smirked. "Don't make me come over there!"

Blair shivered in mock fear, which made me laugh. "Seriously," he said, lowering the keys. "I think I better drive just to be careful."

"This better have to do with my emergence and not some testosterone crap!"

"No, ma'am. No testosterone crap." He shook his head, grinning. "Safety first, Short Stuff; safety first!"

I couldn't help but laugh at the goofy face he was making. "Just as long as you don't keep using that 'safety' line as an excuse forever. Let's go. I'm starving."

"After you, my lady. Your chariot awaits!"

Blair's buoyant mood was infectious; I had never seen him so totally elated. We drove the ten miles to Panera, chatting merrily about school, friends, and life in general. His hand never left mine as he drove—so much for "safety first."

As we pulled into the mall, I took in a long, slow breath. Blair squeezed my hand, got out of the car, and came around to open my door for me. I took his hand and concentrated on breathing steadily in and out. Walking into the restaurant, I paused, closing my eyes for a moment, trying to get a grip on all the voices competing for my attention.

Blair looked down at me. "How's it going down there?"

I raised my eyes to his and smirked. "Fine. How's it up there? I hear the air is thinner the higher up you are!" I lifted my nose in mock offense and pulled him toward the counter while he chortled softly.

We ordered lattes and bagels with cream cheese. Blair carried them to a table in the corner, which was separated a little from the nearest people. I spread my sesame bagel with cream cheese and dug in. It was delicious, and the latte was excellent. Blair ate his cinnamon crunch bagel and watched me surreptitiously across the table.

My head definitely sensed all the people in the restaurant, but it wasn't unmanageable. At least, not at first. Suddenly, a woman's frightened voice exploded in my head: *Timmy! Where are you? Oh my God! Where's my baby?*

I gasped and closed my eyes. Blair reached across the table. "Makayla, what is it? I didn't hear anything alarming. You look terrified," he whispered frenetically.

Opening my eyes, I frantically searched the restaurant for the mother and her son. Everything was normal; no one was panicked or distressed at all. My eyes fell upon a table across the restaurant. A young mother sat with a toddler in a booster seat, but she was laughing and playing with him as the baby giggled with delight.

"Makayla, look at me please!"

I refocused on Blair and tried to explain what I had heard. After relaying the experience to him, I said, "I don't understand. The only mother and baby in the restaurant are across the room, and they're just fine."

Suddenly another image entered my mind; the force of it jerked me back. Blair moved next to me and put his arm around me. "Makayla, talk to me. Please!"

I opened my eyes and found his. "I saw a toddler running into the parking lot in front of a car!" I paused and looked across the restaurant. "Blair," I hesitated, taking a breath, "it was that little guy sitting with his mom."

Blair stared across the room and then back to me. "Do you think it could be an emotional reaction or something?" He seemed unsure of himself. "I still don't sense any panic."

"Maybe," I said, not really believing it. "Look, he's fine; let's just eat." I tried to smile and picked up my bagel again.

The rest of our breakfast went well. I was able to filter the voices so that I could concentrate on my conversation with Blair and enjoy my bagel. This revelation boosted my confidence significantly, which was probably Blair's goal.

We finished our breakfast and stood to throw away our trash and put up the tray. Blair put his arm around my shoulder and beamed. "I'm really proud of you, Short Stuff! You did better than I did on my first outing after emergence. It took me two or three days to be able to filter the way you do."

"Well, thank you kindly, sir." I smiled and did a little curtsy. He laughed and steered me toward the exit.

Just as suddenly as before, the vision flashed through my mind. This time, though, I knew what I had to do. I broke away from Blair and ran to the parking lot, turning right and heading to the corner. From behind me, I heard the woman's cries, "Timmy! Where are you? Oh my God! Where's my baby?"

I darted between two parked cars and scooped the little boy up just as a red sedan sped around the corner. I moved aside and shielded him in my arms. The driver slammed on his brakes, shouted an expletive, and the car screeched to a stop, exactly where the baby had been standing.

The little boy started crying. "It's okay now, Timmy. You're safe. I'm going to take you to your mommy." I bounced him up and down, trying to calm him, which was difficult since I was shaking like a leaf.

The man burst out of his car. "Is he okay? Oh my God! I didn't see him!" He leaned against the car, trying to catch his breath.

"He's fine. Just slow down next time in the parking lot, okay?" I said, hoping he heard the reproach in my voice.

Looking up, I saw Blair leading Timmy's despondent mom toward us. Her face was frantic, a frozen mask of horror. I met them on the curb and placed the baby in her arms.

"Oh, Timmy, my sweet boy! Mommy is so sorry. I love you!" Tears were streaming down her face. "I don't know how to thank you," she cried, looking at me and reaching for my hand. "I just turned my back for a minute; I don't know how he got out the door!" She hugged Timmy tightly to her.

I took her hand and gave it a little squeeze. "I'm glad to have been in the right place at the right time. You're a good mother; don't beat yourself up," I consoled her. "Bye, Timmy. Be a good boy and stay by Mommy next time, okay?"

The little boy peeked out from his mother's chest and reached his arms out toward me. His mother leaned him toward me so he could give me a hug. I hugged him and his mother. "Thank you," she whispered, her voice breaking.

I pulled away from them and smiled, turning back toward Blair. He stood against the building, his mouth split in a wide grin. I smiled up at him and leaned into his open arms. He kissed the top of my head and said, "Life with you is really going to be an adventure!"

"Are you up for the challenge?" I asked, tilting my head up to him.

"I think I can handle it." He smirked.

"Can we go back home now?" I asked. "I'm feeling a little hungry."

"You just ate…" Blair said, confused. I rolled my eyes at him. "Oh…*hungry*. Let's go!" He ran toward the car, pulling me behind him, laughing hysterically.

As I sat snuggled next to Blair on the couch, I started thinking about what had just happened. Was this something that was going to happen on a regular basis? That thought left me frightened and confused. Blair heard my concern.

"Talk to me, Makayla."

"I don't know what to say. It's all so confusing. First of all, it's enough of a challenge to hear and feel people's thoughts and emotions, but to see the future… Is that what happened?"

Blair shifted so he could look into my face. "Yes, I think that is what happened, and although it is a rare gift, it is not unheard of. You remember, I told you about it yesterday."

I nodded. "Will it always be as scary and life-threatening as that?" Fear began to burn through my adrenaline. "Look at me! I'm just a tiny, normal girl. How can I deal with things like that all the time?" I felt myself slipping into panic mode. Blair reached up and cradled my face against his chest with his hand; immediately I felt the distress fade.

"It won't happen all the time, and certainly the situations won't always be life-threatening. As for you being 'normal'…

well, I'm not so sure about that!" He was teasing me; I rolled my eyes at him.

"Thanks a bunch!"

Blair kissed my forehead and laughed. "You know what? We'll just have to deal with what comes together, okay?"

Together...what a wonderful word. I reached up and wrapped my arms around his neck as he lay me back onto the couch. Thoughts swirled like whirlpools in my mind, thoughts of all the possibilities of what "together" might mean for us. Then I thought of another question that I had been wondering about.

"Blair, this is going to sound like a stupid question, but how old are you?" He raised his eyebrows at me. "I guess what I really mean is, how long did it take for you to fully adjust to your gift?"

"That's not a stupid question, actually. I turned eighteen last February," he explained. "Everyone is different; some take a whole year, some a few months, or in extraordinary cases, a few days." He smiled down at me lying across his chest. "Why do you ask?"

"I was just curious, and I was wondering if it was common for a guide to be so young." This had occurred to me last night when I was thinking about the bond between a guide and emergent. If it was against the rules for us to be involved, as Blair had said, why would they partner me with someone so close to my age and of the opposite sex?

"Well, actually that's not really common. Most guides are several years older," Blair admitted.

"How did you become a guide so young? Not that I'm objecting, of course!" I added hastily, reaching up to kiss his cheek lightly.

Blair hesitated, and I raised my head off his chest to look at him. "You're not going to do your 'standoffish' routine again, are you?" I tried to look stern, but he just laughed.

"No, I'm just trying to figure out a way to say this without sounding like a pretentious ass," he admitted.

That piqued my curiosity. "I think I know you well enough now to know that you aren't a pretentious ass, Blair. A bossy son-of-a-gun, maybe, but not a pretentious ass!" I teased.

He scowled. "Are you finished?" I nodded. "My gift surfaced early, Makayla. I emerged at sixteen."

"Wow!" I lay my head back on his chest. "Do you know why you emerged at such a young age?"

"There are only hypotheses. It's an extremely rare occurrence; even my brother and sister emerged at the normal age."

"What are the hypotheses?"

"Do you really want to talk hypotheses, or…" He pulled me up to his face. "…might I interest you in something a little more entertaining?"

Before I could answer, Blair pressed his lips urgently to mine, rolling onto his side, his tongue tracing my lips. His hand slid down my spine and pressed me into him. I wound my hands into his hair and eagerly responded to his desire. He moved his lips down my neck.

His lips returned softly to mine and then pulled away. "What's wrong?" I asked, reaching for his face again. He held me away, gently but persistently.

"Makayla, there's something important you need to know."

"Right now?" I asked incredulously.

"Yes, right now." He sighed. "Intimate love between clairvoyants is…different than it is for normal people." When I continued to look confused, he continued. "The intimate bond between a man and a woman unites them physically and, in our case, mentally in very powerful ways. It is…dangerous for an emerging clairvoyant. It can overpower, or *overload* may be a better word, your emerging mental capabilities."

Blair paused to let his words sink in. I had never given much thought to intimate relations with anyone; I'd never had the desire or opportunity. Like many, I had been taught the importance of waiting until after marriage, but even if I thought that was a little too old-fashioned, I always knew I would wait for my life partner, my soul mate.

Suddenly uncomfortable, I wondered if Blair thought I was… well…something I'm not. "I didn't mean to…give you the wrong impression." I was embarrassed; my face flushed with heat. "I'm not expecting you to…or even wanting to…" I didn't know how to continue.

"No, honey, of course you're not," Blair reassured me, kissing my forehead. "That's not what I meant at all. It's just that even this kind of intimacy can be hard on an emergent. There's a reason you have such a voracious 'appetite' right now!" He laughed softly. "Emergence seems to awaken our desires, as well as our gift."

Oh great! Now my gift is turning me into a brazen hussy!

"I heard that!" Blair laughed. "Don't be ridiculous. It's not that I'm not *enjoying* your appetite; I just want us to be careful. Do you understand?"

"I think so. I suppose I'm the weak link in this scenario, aren't I?" I pouted.

Blair kissed my pouty lip. "Well, you are the emerging one here! But it doesn't mean that I'm a perfect example of restraint." He laughed and hugged me tight.

"Blair, can I ask you a question?"

"You already know you can. Go ahead."

Feeling embarrassed again, I buried my face in his chest. I couldn't say it aloud. *Have you ever…?* My thoughts trailed off.

No, Makayla. I have never been intimate with anyone. I was waiting for my one true love, the one I would be bonded to forever. Blair reached to lift my lips to his; his eyes were exultant.

FIRST NIGHT ALONE

Mom came home around six in the evening. I ran up to her and hugged her, telling her how glad I was that she was home, how much I had missed her. She held me tight and started telling me every detail about her visit with her sister: how my cousins were doing with their jobs, kids, anything to keep from talking about what she was really thinking.

So afraid and yet dying to know what had happened over the last two days, Mom babbled on and on about trivialities. Blair and I both knew the conflict and fear in her mind. Several times the pain of her anxiety shook my focus, and I had to close my eyes and breathe deeply; then I could open them and be the relaxed, happy daughter she needed me to be.

We drove Blair to the school parking lot to pick up his car. The car ride was awkward; I sat in the front seat with Mom driving while Blair sat in the backseat. Mom continued to chatter nonstop the entire way. As we approached the school, it became harder to control my growing panic.

Tonight, Blair would not be with me to soothe away the nightmares and focus the insanity that still threatened. With my hands clenched in fists, I tried to push the choking fear away. It was more than fear—it was longing. He would not be there to hold me, to rock me—to kiss me.

Makayla, I won't be far.

I know. I'm just scared.

Call me anytime you need me. I love you.

I love you too.

"Well, here we are, Blair," Mom announced, pulling into the almost empty lot. "Thanks so much for all you've done for Makayla." She was dismissing him.

"Thanks for the ride, Marissa," Blair said, opening his door. He closed it and turned toward my window. I opened it.

"See you tomorrow, Makayla. Have a good night." His smile radiated his intended message.

"Oh, we're going to have a great time," Mom exclaimed. "How about ordering Chinese food and watching some chick flick?"

"Sounds good, Mom," I said, hoping that my smile covered up my ambivalent attitude. Turning back to Blair, I added, "See you tomorrow." *I'll miss you!*

Me too, Short Stuff. More than you know. He waved and turned toward his car without another word.

The Chinese food tasted good, and we watched *Moulin Rouge*. The tears flowed like rain, and tissues littered the floor of the den. It was a good night, and Mom seemed to relax, becoming more like herself as the evening progressed.

Around ten, I decided I better try to get some sleep if I was going to handle school in the morning. I put on my pjs, washed my face, and brushed my teeth. It had been a very long couple of days; my bed felt warm and comfortable. Mom came in to say goodnight and tuck me in.

"Mom, I'm eighteen years old, for heaven's sake. You don't have to tuck me in anymore!"

"Don't ruin the moment with all that grown-up stuff," she teased. Caressing my cheek, her face turned serious. "I love you,

Kayla." She was worried; her thoughts were filled with fears of losing me to this phenomenon, this lifestyle, to which she did not belong and could not share with me.

"Love you too, Mom," I reassured her. I had to say something to soothe her fears. "Mom, things don't have to change just because my birthday has passed." I couldn't seem to say *just because I have emerged*. "For the most part, nothing is going to be different between you and me. You will always be my best friend."

Mom leaned down and hugged me. "We'll just have to handle the future the way we have always handled things—together." She kissed my forehead and left the room, turning off the light.

Turning on my side, I tried to find a comfortable position. Moonlight was streaming through my window, creating a kaleidoscope on the floor. I focused on closing my mind and breathing steadily. Before long, the exhaustion of the past two days compelled me to sleep.

The faces were still in shadow, but occasionally the fog cleared and I made out some details. The voices were getting more strident with each word. My heart pounded in my chest. "This has gone far enough," a calm voice spoke. "It stops here." Shifting dark figures oozed away from the wall. What were they? Animals…or people? "I don't think so, my friend," another man's cold voice retorted. The mist cleared, and I saw the man's back. I shivered. The shadows crept toward the first man. "You'll never get away with this!" The man's slow, agonized moans pierced the night. He looked up as the picture cleared. I stared into the terrified face of my father.

I muffled my scream in the pillow; my body shuddered. Raising my trembling hands, I felt the clammy moisture dewed on my face. My pajama top was adhered to my back from the sweat dripping down it. *Breathe, Kayla*, I told myself. *Slow down your breathing.* I tried to remember Blair's words of comfort; what had he said? *You're safe. I'm right here with you.* If only that were true. Should I call? No, it would just upset him that he couldn't come to me. Eventually I was going to have to cope with this on my own.

As my pulse and breathing decelerated, my mind spun with the vision of my father. What could it mean? Surely the connection between his face and the nightmare was simply a product of my emergence or perhaps just dream imagery. It would be expected that his face would enter into my consciousness more now that I had emerged; that had to be it.

The clock read 12:00. I got out of bed quietly and opened my dresser drawer, looking for a dry top. Somehow I would have to find a way to get back to sleep if I was going to function at school at all. I turned on my ceiling fan to circulate the air and got back into bed.

I had to find a better vision, a happier, safer dream. Blair… Blair holding me, teasing me, throwing me over his shoulder… I laughed softly. Blair touching my face and kissing my lips… telling me he loved me…

The alarm clock went off at 6:00 a.m., waking me from what had turned out to be a very good dream. I sat up and stretched, feeling pretty rested considering my nightmare. I swung my legs off the side of my bed and listened for my mom. All was quiet, even in her dreams. She didn't have to go to work today, so she would be sleeping in.

I crossed by my window, heading to my closet to get my clothes. Something caught my attention, just out of the corner of my eye. Blair's car was parked in front of my house. What the heck was he doing? I hurried to my closet and grabbed my hoodie, throwing it over my head as I ran as softly as I could down the stairs and out the front door. The early November morning was brisk; I shivered.

The driver's seat of Blair's G35 was reclined; he was sound asleep. I knocked gently on his window, trying not to startle him. "Blair," I called softly, and then a little louder, "Wake up!" With a start, Blair opened his eyes and sat up. I stood outside his door with my arms crossed and face stern. He opened the window.

"What are you doing, Blair? Have you lost your mind?" I smirked at the pun. "You could have caught pneumonia; a crazy person could have killed you in the night or something!" I yelled.

Blair smiled sheepishly. "I couldn't sleep. I was worried about you, so I decided if I was just outside your house, I might hear you if you needed me."

"That is the craziest, most insane, sweetest thing anyone has ever said to me." I smiled and leaned in to kiss him. "Get out of that car right now and get inside for breakfast!"

"Yes, ma'am! Bossy, bossy, bossy." He closed the window and opened the door.

I threw my arms up around him, and he lifted me off the ground and kissed me again. "We better go inside." He laughed. "What will the neighbors say?" As he led me toward the house, his most urgent question spilled out. "How are you, Makayla? Did last night go all right?" Evidently he had arrived after my nightmare. His eyes were so apprehensive that I couldn't tell him about it.

"It was okay," I said, smiling slightly. "Don't worry, big guy; I can handle it." I consciously filled my head with the visions of my dreams about Blair, hoping that those dreams would be the ones he would pick up. "I've got to take a shower. Wait for me down here; get yourself something to drink."

"Hey," Blair whispered, "what about your mom?"

"She's sound asleep; she isn't going to work today. We'll probably be gone before she wakes up, and if she does wake up…" I paused, thinking.

"I'll just say that I stopped over to check on you and we decided to go to school together," Blair pronounced proudly.

"Nice one. See you in a bit!"

I took the fastest shower in known history—well, at least in my history of extremely long showers. I bounded down to the kitchen twenty minutes later, dressed in my jeans, sweater, and boots, with my hair dried and straightened. Blair was asleep with his head on the table. *What an idiot!* I thought. Blair woke with a start.

"Hey." He scowled. "That's not a very nice way to wake someone up!"

I crossed to him and put my arms around him. "I'm sorry, but you really can't camp out in front of my house every night. First of all, people would definitely talk; second, I'm still worried about crazy people hurting you; and last of all, I won't be able to sleep if I think you're out there," I explained. "So no more sleeping in the car, deal?"

"Okay, it's a deal. I guess I have to let you 'grow up' sometime," he teased.

"Thanks a heap." I frowned.

We decided to keep breakfast simple, just cereal and juice. As I was loading the dishwasher and putting the cereal away, I heard Mom shuffling around upstairs.

Makayla...

I'm on it!

I rushed up the stairs to intercept her.

"Good morning, baby," Mom said, yawning.

"Hi. Why'd you get up so early? I thought you didn't have to go to work today."

"Just woke up out of habit, I guess," she said, heading for the stairs.

"Mom," I blurted out too loudly, "I need to tell you something before you go downstairs."

"Okay."

"Blair is here." She looked confused. "He was worried about me."

"Are you okay, Kayla?" Mom looked a little distressed; she came back to me and put her hands on my shoulders.

"Yes, I'm just fine," I assured her, "but like I said, Blair was worried, so he's here…" My words trailed off. I shrugged nonchalantly, hoping she would buy our cover story.

"Well, that was very nice of him," Mom finally answered. "I'll just go say good morning to him while you finish getting ready." She smiled as she turned and headed down the stairs.

I brushed my teeth quickly, ran the brush through my hair again, and put on my lip gloss before bolting to my room and grabbing my backpack and hoodie. As I ran down the stairs, I heard Mom and Blair talking.

"So you're sure that Kayla will be okay at school?" Mom was asking him.

"Yes, I'm sure," he reassured her. "If she has any trouble, I won't be far away."

I entered the kitchen to see Mom with that all-knowing look in her eye. It wouldn't be long until she figured out our relationship. She smiled at Blair and then turned to me.

"So, since I'm off today," she began matter-of-factly, "is there anything special you want me to pick up at the grocery store for your movie night with your friends?"

"Just pick up some of our favorite junk food," I said, smiling at her. "Will you have time make your famous brownies?"

"You bet! It wouldn't be your birthday without brownies."

As I turned to leave, Blair's question stopped me.

"Do you just want to ride with me today, Makayla?" He looked at my mom and added quickly, "If that's okay with you, Marissa."

I didn't give her a chance to object. "Sure. I'll see you after school, Mom," I said, crossing to kiss her good-bye. "Love you lots!"

"Love you too," Mom answered, smiling. *I wonder…*

Blair and I smiled at each other. Nope, it wouldn't be long at all.

SCHOOL

I rode to school with my hand in Blair's. It wasn't until we were turning into the school that the subtle din of voices that were always present in my head now began to grow in intensity.

"Makayla…" Blair said softly, feeling my emotions rise.

I pulled my hand out of his and brought it to my temple. "I've got it," I said, holding up one finger. "Give me a minute." The tumult of voices, not to mention the raging teenage emotions, were difficult to block. There were so many of them—too many. My heart sped up.

"Makayla," Blair called more loudly. "Look at me, please."

"No, I can do this. Just give me…a…minute." I grimaced as the noise ebbed and flowed. *Push it back; push the wave back*, I thought, concentrating hard.

"Don't be stubborn, Makayla," Blair scolded. "Let me help you."

"No!" I shouted. "I have to be able to do this myself."

Blair sighed, shaking his head and smirking as he pulled into his parking space. With all the concentration I could muster, I finally lowered the volume in my head. I took a deep breath and lowered my hands.

I looked over at Blair; he was staring at me incredulously. "Has anyone ever told you that your temper is much too big for such a little body?" he asked, grinning.

Heat flooded my face, and I looked down. "As a matter of fact," I whispered, "I have been told that once…or maybe twice." I glanced up at him; his eyes smiled. "I'm sorry. I'll try to be better about accepting your help."

Blair leaned over and kissed me. "You're forgiven. Now when we enter the building, the noise will increase again," he explained. I nodded. "I think that if you are holding my hand, I can assist your blocking."

I snorted. "What?" he asked.

"That's the cheesiest pickup line I've ever heard!" I raised my eyebrows at him and smiled.

"Pickup line or not," he replied, grinning, "it will help."

"I think I can deal with that," I said, leaning over to peck him on the cheek.

Walking across the grounds to the senior entrance holding hands with this amazing guy was almost surreal. Having never had a real boyfriend—not counting the two middle school "romances" of course—this was all new to me. It seemed too good to be true to have been gifted with clairvoyance and my soul mate all at the same time. Blair squeezed my hand, acknowledging my thoughts.

Blair was right, of course; as we walked closer to the building, the burgeoning sounds blasted me.

And then she said that he said that I was hot! Can you believe it?
Oh crap! We had math homework last night…
Faculty meeting today after school…great way to end a week.
If you don't know, then I'm not telling you!
I wonder when Kayla will get back.

The last voice was familiar; I focused on it, trying to filter all the others away. Blair lifted our hands to kiss the back of mine.

"You okay?"

"I think I heard Amy's voice. Is it possible to filter enough to just hear one particular voice in a crowd this big?" I asked, inquisitive.

"It is possible; in fact, with a little more time and practice, you will be able to do that all the time. You'll be able to search, for lack of a better word, for the thoughts of specific people."

"Wow...that's cool!"

Blair hesitated and drew me to the side of the hall. "Look, let's try something. If you have trouble blocking the noise in any of the classes that I'm not in, search through the sounds for me. I'll be searching for your voice during the day also, so hopefully we will be able to communicate."

"Do you think that will work?" I asked, unsure of my abilities.

"The farther away we are from each other, the harder it will be. Most of our classes are just a few doors away from each other, so it should work. Well, it will work with practice anyway."

The bell rang for first period, so we headed to pre-cal. I hadn't had a chance to see Amy or anyone yet, but I would see them soon enough. Amy was going to burst when Blair and I entered ancient history hand in hand!

Walking into the room, Blair let go of my hand and headed for his seat. I approached Mr. Vincent to ask about my makeup work for the past two days. Grumpily, he told me what assignments I had missed and informed me that I still had to take the scheduled test today.

"But Mr. Vincent..." I stammered. "I forgot about the test, and I didn't study." It's hard enough for me to pass my math courses, for heaven's sake.

"I'm sorry, Miss Taylor," he snapped, not sounding at all sorry. "The test was scheduled, so you have to take it! Sometimes life isn't fair!" As he turned his back on me, I reeled from his thoughts. *I don't have the energy to cope with these kids today.*

Budget cutbacks... I've taught here for ten years! I closed my eyes, willing myself to block out his angst.

Makayla, snap out of it! Blair's voice cut through Mr. Vincent's like a knife. My eyes shot open; I took a deep breath and headed for my seat.

Sorry, Short Stuff. I didn't mean to yell at you, but I needed to get your attention fast.

I know; it's okay. It sucks hearing everyone's pain!

Blair nodded slightly and smiled. Mr. Vincent was handing out the tests to the class. As he passed my desk, I looked up at him and smiled. He hesitated and then smiled a little, nodding his head. *Nice kid...I wish I hadn't snapped at her.*

Well, that was the last time I smiled during pre-cal. The test was hard, and I was having trouble concentrating. I looked over at Blair, who was diligently writing his equations.

Hey, Blair?

What?

What's the answer to number twelve?

He turned his head ever so slightly to me and scowled severely; I flinched. I had never seen him look quite that stern.

Makayla... His tone was filled with seething reproach.

I was just kidding! He shook his head and looked down at his paper. *Just trying a little clairvoyance humor! Sheesh!*

Let's keep the comedy routines out of class, okay? Blair's tone relaxed; he smiled just a little, shaking his head again.

I managed to write an answer to each question, but I didn't have any idea how accurate they might be. Hopefully one failed test would not crush my grade too much. As I packed up my bag, Mr. Vincent called me to his desk.

"Yes, sir."

"Makayla, I know that math is not your strongest subject." He sighed. "It was wrong of me to make you take the test when

I knew you hadn't studied. Please study over the weekend and retake it on Monday during your study hall."

"Thanks, Mr. Vincent. That'll be great!" I beamed at him, and the corners of his mouth turned up into a smile. "Hope you have a good weekend," I said as I joined Blair, who was waiting by the door.

The hallways of Enterprise High were always chaotic while classes were changing. There was no avoiding the tumultuous noise both inside my head and outside it. Blair grasped my hand tightly, and I looked up at him; his face was serene and composed, and he was able to take the edge off of the racket.

"Kayla! You're back," Amy's voice called from behind us. "I missed you so much. How was your…" Her voice broke off as she noticed our hands. *Well, well, someone has been busy!* she thought wryly. "Hi, Blair."

Blair smiled at her. "Hi, Amy."

"I missed you too, Amy." I smiled, winking at her. "How's everything going around here? Were you able to hold the place together without me?" I laughed.

Just then Rob came around the corner with a disgruntled look on his face, carrying a paper. "Why does calculus exist?" he bellowed.

"What's wrong, Rob?" I asked, concerned.

He frowned and held up his test paper. "I got a B! A B…can you believe it? I may have to go into hiding for a while." Rob's flair for the dramatic had only grown with the years.

Amy put her arm around his waist and hugged him. "It's not the end of the world, Rob," she declared. "The world will continue to spin on its axis even though you got a B on a test!"

Rob stuffed his paper into his bag with malignant force then sighed, putting his arm around Amy's shoulder. "Easy for you to say, smartie pants! You got an A!" He leaned down and kissed her lightly on the cheek. Amy blushed. *She is so beautiful when she blushes. Wow, I really wish I could get up the nerve to…* Rob's thoughts broke off and shifted to less important concerns.

Last weekend's movie date obviously had gone well for Amy and Rob. They certainly were more attached to each other than they were when I left them Monday afternoon! But, of course, who would know anything about becoming that attached to another human being in just two days? *Not me, certainly…* I giggled.

"Lots of people kind of hit a wall in calculus, they tell me," Blair said, offhanded. "I bet one test won't bring your grade down that much; don't worry about it."

"Yeah, I just blew my pre-cal test right out of the water," I joked, not including that Mr. Vincent was letting me retake it, "and I'm still standing!"

"With a little help, I noticed," Rob jested.

"Hey," I retorted. "Pot? Have you met Kettle?" Everyone laughed as we headed into the classroom.

As the end of the hour approached, dread began to creep up my spine; sweat dewed on my forehead, and my hands became cold. English would be my first class without Blair, like swinging on a trapeze without a net. What if I lost it in Richardson's class? She would flip out and want to call the marines in or something similarly theatrical!

Easy, Makayla. Take a deep breath.

I obeyed him automatically, breathing in slowly and focusing on establishing a respiratory rate below hyperventilation.

That's it, honey. Focus—you can do it.

The bell rang, startling me. Amy heard my quick intake of breath.

"Are you okay, Kayla?" she asked, leaning toward me across the aisle.

"Yeah…I'm fine," I stammered. "I must have been day-dreaming and the bell surprised me." She looked dubious. Blair waited for me as I gathered my books and packed them into my backpack.

"We'll see you in Richardson's class, Kayla!" Rob called as he pulled Amy along with him. She looked back and rolled her eyes at me.

Blair held my hand and walked me toward English. "Makayla, I'll be two doors down from you in Mrs. White's room. I'll be listening for you, so call me if you need me; I can meet you in the hall or something."

I was still concentrating on regulating my breathing, which made it difficult to focus on blocking the mayhem in the hall. Leaning my head against Blair's arm, I closed my eyes, allowing him to guide me. My eyes opened as I felt him slow down; we were outside Ms. Richardson's classroom.

I was jittery, shaking like I was loaded with caffeine. "Why can't I seem to calm down, Blair?" I leaned my head against his chest. Tears were beginning to fall from the corners of my eyes; I wiped them, frustrated. "This is freaking ridiculous! I'm afraid to go into English class!"

Blair snickered but stifled it when I glared up at him. "Go to class, Blair!" I commanded, heading for the door.

He caught me from behind and whispered, "You are one fiery little fiend!" I swatted at him; he dodged me and laughed as he headed for his class.

Stay angry, Short Stuff; it will help you focus! I love you…
Me too.

As with most situations, the fear of something is often worse than the reality. How could I concentrate on all those other annoying sounds with Ms. Richardson flitting across the room, striking poses as she explained literary terms? Demonstrating the concept of "catharsis," she disappeared behind her desk and crawled, agonizingly slowly, up the desk like it was Mt. Everest. I was laughing so hard that tears were streaming down my face.

The bell rang, and everyone filed out of the classroom wiping the tears from their faces. Blair was waiting outside the door for us.

"What's so funny?" he asked, grinning. "Everyone looks like they just left a comedy club."

Rob snorted. "Ms. Richardson would make a fortune working the comedy circuit. Let's eat. I'm starving!"

"Does it seem to you, Kayla, that boys are always hungry?" Amy asked.

"Their stomachs do tend to run their lives!" I agreed. *Even when there are more entertaining things to do…*

The corners of Blair's mouth turned up into a grin. *You're embarrassing me, Makayla. I'm shocked.*

We walked to the cafeteria together and headed for our regular table. Jesse and Rick were ensconced in deep eye contact as usual. As we approached the table, Rob blurted out, "Earth to Jesse and Rick! Houston, we have a problem!"

Jesse wrenched her eyes from Rick's and scowled at Rob. "Rob, your timing absolutely sucks," she growled. Then her eyes moved to Blair and me. "Well, well, well, look at you! Hm, hm, hm… I knew it! I told you, Rick; didn't I tell you Blair and Kayla were made for each other?"

Rick shook his head knowingly. "Yes, Jesse, you are a regular matchmaker in training." He laughed and turned to the guys. "Let's eat!"

The boys walked off together and left us girls by ourselves.

"Spill it, girl!" Jesse exclaimed, bouncing up and down on her chair. Amy laughed but looked to me for an answer.

"What do you want to know?" Jesse stopped bouncing and screwed up her face. "Okay, I'm just kidding." I laughed. "I don't really know when it started, but it really took off when I… returned from Austin yesterday." I hated to fib to my friends, but at least the important facts were correct.

"That's so cool, Kayla!" Amy sighed.

"Yeah, it is," Jesse agreed. "Now all three of us have our man—at least, I think we all do…" She broke off and raised her eyebrows at Amy. "We do, don't we?"

"I think so," Amy replied shyly. "Rob seems to want to be with me… I mean, he calls me and obviously hangs on me, but…"

"But what?" Jesse and I asked together.

Amy flushed and looked at the ground, embarrassed. "He hasn't kissed me yet. You know, really kissed me. Is that weird?" She looked up at us sheepishly.

"No, Amy," I reassured her. "You and Rob have been friends for a long time, and sometimes it takes longer for friendships to evolve into…more than that." I wished I could tell her what Rob thought when she was near him; he was crazy about her, but underneath all his bravado, Rob was shy.

"He'll come around," Jesse agreed. "Just give it a little time, girlfriend!"

"Are you girls going to eat during this lunch period?" Rob called as he crossed to us.

"Hold on to your drawers, there, Junior!" Jesse grumbled. "We're going."

The day turned out to be a good one. I was relieved to have it behind me, though. Now I felt confident that I was going to be able to function like a normal person. I was sure that challenges would still arise, but it was great to get through that first day back to school.

At the end of the day, I was exhausted from the effort it had taken me to block everything. My head kind of ached, but Blair assured me that he thought it was just fatigue. We gathered our homework and books and headed for his car.

"Will you come in the house for a while?" I asked, hopeful.

"Your mom is already suspicious; does that bother you?" Blair asked, opening my door for me.

"No, Mom will be cool with it," I reassured him. "She'll just be happy that I'm happy." I sighed, remembering the dream of the mother and her son. I closed my eyes and leaned my head against the headrest, trying to think of something else.

"Makayla…" Blair said softly. "Do you want to talk about it?"

I kept my eyes closed, hoping against hope that Blair would think I'd fallen asleep.

Nice try, but I'm not buying it.

Opening my eyes slowly, I glanced over at Blair, who was waiting to pull out of his parking space. "I can wait all afternoon if that's what it takes," he scolded me. "As you have pointed out, you are not the only stubborn one." He raised his eyebrows at me.

"Well…I'm just worried…" I looked down, and heat rose up my neck.

Blair reached over and took my hand. "What exactly are you worried about?"

Suddenly it all flooded out. "Your parents are coming home Sunday, and…they're in the Ileesia…and you weren't supposed to…get involved with me!" Tears of frustration and exhaustion spilled over my face. "What if they're so angry that they forbid you…"

"Makayla." Blair stopped me and picked up my hand to kiss it tenderly. "I've already told you that nothing is going to break up our relationship." He reached up and wiped my tears with his fingertips.

"But what if they hold it against me?" My voice faded to a whisper.

"Short Stuff, look at me," he commanded. When I didn't respond, he reached over and lifted my chin. "When your parents are clairvoyants, it's impossible to keep secrets, and that can be a real pain while you're growing up. Imagine not being able to hide anything from your mother." I grinned, remembering some of my youthful misadventures and my ability to keep them from Mom.

Blair continued, smiling. "On the flip side of that, because of who they are, they'll be able to see my deep commitment to you and understand. They're my parents first and members of the Ileesia second."

"Are you sure? I mean…is it worth it?"

"How can you ask me that?" I looked at him, surprised to see him almost angry.

"I…didn't…mean…" I stammered softly, my breath catching in my throat.

"We are of one mind, Makayla." He softened his tone and took a deep breath. "You know how much I love you." His eyes glistened with emotion as he took my face in his hands and kissed me gently.

Blair released my face; I was stunned into silence. The reality was that I did know how much he loved me, but a small part of me—the insecure, vulnerable part—still could not believe that he was mine.

"Let's go home," he said. "You're tired and need to rest. Then we'll tackle studying for your makeup pre-cal test." I groaned; he grinned.

MOVIE NIGHT

I slept in late on Saturday morning, probably making up for the lack of sleep a couple of days ago. Mom and I spent the rest of the day cleaning the house and making snacks for the party that night. We made a huge bowl of puppy chow, that chocolate, peanut butter-coated cereal mix drowning in powdered sugar. Mom made her famous triple-chocolate espresso brownies, which were my favorite. Since we were going to overdose on chocolate and sugar, Mom suggested that we cut up some veggies to have with ranch dressing. "At least I can pretend I'm offering something healthy for you all to eat!" she teased.

Amy, Rob, Jesse, and Rick were arriving around six. We planned to order our pizzas from the great little family-owned pizzeria, Torentino's, not too far from our house. Their crust was hand tossed, crispy on the edges, and not too thin. The boys all wanted conventional meat pizzas—pepperoni and sausage—but we girls liked some of Torentino's specialty pizzas—chicken alfredo and veggie delight.

Blair showed up around five, offering to help us in any way he could. Mom sent him out for the soda we'd forgotten, and before he left the store, we called him to get ice as well.

"Blair's really a good kid, Kayla," Mom commented after calling him again; we forgot paper plates.

"I think so." I smiled and she laughed.

"So how long were you going to wait to tell me that you two were an item?" Mom asked, grinning.

"I was counting on your keen eye to notice for yourself," I teased while setting out the snacks on the table. "I wasn't keeping it a secret exactly."

"It's sort of funny," she said, bringing over the veggies. "Blair reminds me of your father in some ways."

"Really?" I asked, looking up at her. "How?"

"Well, he's tall like Sean was, and he has the same hazel eyes." Mom paused and then continued. "The first time I saw him, the resemblance sort of startled me." I remembered her reaction; she had gasped and stared off, obviously seeing my dad in her mind.

"There's more to it than that, though. It's the way he looks at you, Kayla." She took my hands in hers. "It looks like he sees all the way to your soul. Sean looked at me that way too." She smiled wistfully, tears welling at the memory. I threw my arms around her and squeezed.

"So you approve?"

Mom laughed and pulled away from me. "Do I have a choice? If you're happy, then I'm happy, Kayla." But her face became serious. I started to ask what was wrong, but she stopped me. "Kayla, just remember that this is your first really serious relationship—I know that you know how to be responsible and safe…"

"Mom! Please…"

"Okay, okay," she said, holding her hand up. "I'm not naïve, Kayla. I just want you to protect your future. One mistake can totally alter your plans."

"I know," I insisted, frowning.

"I know that you know that in your head, but the closer you and Blair become, the more temptations there will be." She was so calm and businesslike; it kind of freaked me out. "Just know that you can talk to me about anything and come to me about everything, okay?"

"Okay, can you find something else to fill your mind before Blair gets back? Talk about embarrassing!"

Blair came back shortly after our discussion, but luckily Mom was talking to Aunt Julie on the phone, so her mind was occupied. We set out the soda and paper plates and then put the ice in a cooler.

Around 5:45, Mom hung up the phone and left to pick up the pizzas. Blair whirled around and swept me off my feet, kissing me fiercely. He started laughing before our lips parted.

"What's so funny?" I asked, pulling my face away to look into his eyes. They were blazing.

You didn't do a very good job blocking your conversation with your mother," he teased, putting me down.

I blushed and buried my head against his chest. "How freaking embarrassing! And I warned her to fill *her* mind before you came home."

"At least you know she doesn't mind me being around!" He smiled an impish grin. "That's a good thing, isn't it?"

"That's a very good thing!" I reached up to kiss him again. Blair scooped me into his arms and carried me to the couch.

Now it was my turn to laugh. *Your mind isn't too hard to hear either, big guy!* He lowered me onto the couch and jumped on top of me, holding his weight off me with his arms.

I wrapped my arms around his neck and stared into his fiery eyes. "You *do* know that we don't really have time for this now, don't you?" I giggled.

Blair sighed and rolled off the couch. "You're killing me, Short Stuff!"

Just then the doorbell rang. I jumped up and ran to get the door. *You might want to calm your expression just a tad, Blair.* I heard him laughing behind me as I opened it. Amy and Rob were there, with Jesse and Rick pulling in the driveway just behind them.

"Happy late birthday, Kayla!" Amy squealed, throwing her arms around me. "Hi, Blair," she called over my shoulder. She carried a gift bag in her hand.

"Hey there, birthday girl," Rob said. "Can I have a hug too?" He stuck his bottom lip out in a pout and forced a frown.

"Sure, Rob." I laughed. "I wouldn't want you to feel deprived!" I hugged him quickly and waved down the driveway to Jesse and Rick.

"How's it going, Blair?" Rob asked, shaking his hand.

"Pretty good. Have you recovered from your earth-shaking experience after calculus yesterday?" he asked, smiling.

"Uh, yeah. Thanks for brightening my evening!" Rob scowled. Blair punched him on the shoulder, and they laughed.

Jesse and Rick walked in with their arms full of presents. "What the heck is all that? Did you buy the store out, Jesse?" I asked, frowning.

"No, I didn't buy the store out." She sneered, teasing. "But I did have a great time shopping!"

"And shopping…and shopping…and shopping." Rick moaned, rolling his eyes.

"You have the patience of Job, my friend," Rob said to Rick in an exaggerated whisper.

The boys all laughed at Rick's resigned expression as we moved into the den. Blair showed them where the drinks were as we girls arranged the presents on the side table.

"Really, Jesse." I grimaced. "I think you overdid it."

"You're only eighteen once, Kayla," she reminded me. "You might as well enjoy the moment!"

"Hey, what do you girls want to drink?" Rick hollered from the kitchen.

"Diet Coke," all three of us chimed together.

"What a surprise!" Rob retorted.

Just then Mom came back from Torentino's with the pizzas. Blair immediately offered to carry them to the kitchen. Mom thanked him, handing them over, smiling. She winked at me; Jesse and Amy snickered. I rolled my eyes at Mom and nodded my head toward her study, subtly, I hoped.

"Come and get it, ladies," Blair called. "Before it's all gone!"

"Not much to worry about there, Blair," Amy replied, rolling her eyes. "Rob won't touch any pizza without greasy meat on it."

"Hey!" Rob complained with a mouth full of pepperoni pizza.

"Ew! Gross, Rob," we called in unison.

Blair had opened the boxes on the counter, ripping off the box tops so they would fit. He handed Amy and Jesse plates, shoving Rick and Rob out of the way. They griped but slid over so the girls could get to the alfredo and veggie pies.

Blair! My thoughts screamed at him.

He was at my side quickly, turning his back on the others to shield me from their eyes. *What is it, Makayla?* His voice was concerned at the sudden shift in my demeanor.

Get me out of here. Hurry! My head was beginning to spin as images flashed through my mind.

"Excuse us just for a second," Blair told the others as he guided me carefully out of their sight.

"Hurry back, birthday girl!" Jesse called after us.

Turning into the hallway, I grabbed the wall for support. Blair turned me gently toward him and held on to my shoulders. Suddenly, the images became clear, and their impact whipped my head back. Blair pulled me safely away from the wall and held me close.

"Tell me," he ordered in a whisper so that Mom wouldn't hear him in her study.

"Jesse…" I panted.

"What about her?"

"She fell…lots of blood…"

"Can you tell where or when?" Blair asked, rubbing my back, soothing my tension.

"Here, Blair…tonight!" I stared into his bewildered face.

"Any details?"

I closed my eyes and tried to bring the images back; this was critical. "She tripped and hit her head," I recalled. "There was lots of blood…a gash over her eye." I winced.

"What did she trip on?" Blair asked, encouraging me to continue. When I didn't answer at first, he shook me gently. "Makayla, concentrate. This is important!"

"Don't you think I know that?" I fumed, opening my eyes and glaring at him. Taking a deep breath, I closed them again.

Jesse stepped over Rick's legs to reach the puppy chow. They sat on the floor in front of the couch with Amy and Rob while we sat on the couch. As she lifted her left leg, it caught on the leg of the coffee table. Jesse screamed as she fell, hitting her head on the corner of the entertainment center. Blood gushed down her face as Rick rushed to her side and Amy ran for the phone…

I opened my eyes. "Did you get it all?" I asked quietly.

"Yeah," Blair answered guiltily. "Sorry. I know you're doing your best. I lost my focus." He leaned down to kiss me softly. "Are you okay?"

"I'm fine." I smiled. "Let's just watch out for Jesse tonight. I don't want to call 911 for my birthday!"

We walked back to the kitchen where everyone was enjoying their food.

"Is everything all right?" Amy asked, concerned.

"You bet," Blair assured her. "I just couldn't wait any longer to get her alone!" Everyone laughed; I flushed.

"What movie do you guys want to watch tonight?" I asked, reaching for a slice of pizza.

"It's your birthday," Jesse responded lightly. "You choose!"

"Well, did I get any new movies for my birthday?" I asked, coyly batting my eyelashes.

Amy giggled. "As a matter of fact, if you open the yellow bag with the green ribbons on it, you might find something you like!"

They all followed me, carrying their pizza into the den. I reached for the yellow bag and sat on the couch. Amy sat next to me as I opened it. Sure enough, *Juno* was tucked inside there.

"What a surprise!" I teased. "Just what I wanted!"

Amy smiled. "There's something else in the bag. It's just from me." Her face flushed a little as I put my hand into the gift bag and retrieved a square jewelry box. I hastily untied the ribbon she had placed around it.

Inside the box, nestled in folds of blue velvet, was a pendant—actually two pendants. "It's called a Mizpah Pendant," Amy whispered. "It's from Genesis 31:49, 'The Lord watch between me and thee while we are absent from each other.'" My eyes were brimming with tears. "See, the two charms fit together like a puzzle, two parts of a whole. You wear one half, and I wear the other so that when we are away at college, we will still be close."

Everyone was very quiet, even the boys. Jesse was smiling softly, her eyes glistening, holding Rick's hand. Rob put his hand on Amy's shoulder. I was speechless. Tears spilled over as I drew Amy close to me.

"Thank you. It's the best gift ever."

"Okay, is this a party or *what*?" Jesse bellowed, wiping the tears from her eyes. "Let's watch *Juno*, and then Kayla can open our presents."

I laughed through my tears and put my half of the pendent on while Amy put hers around her neck. "Let's bring the snacks in here on the coffee table so we can eat while we're watching." I sniffled. I smiled at Amy and grabbed her hand, squeezing it gently.

We gathered up the veggies, dip, and the puppy chow and spread them out on the coffee table. Rick opened the DVD package for me as I carried in some more drinks.

"Is everyone ready?" he asked jovially.

Everyone sat down, in the exact places my vision had predicted. I caught Blair's eye; he smiled and winked at me, reassuring me that everything was going to be fine. I wedged myself next to him under his arm and relaxed a little.

The movie was hilarious. Even the boys seemed to enjoy it. We snacked and laughed for over an hour. About that time, my head started to feel weird again, and this time, I knew what was happening.

Blair! My head is spinning. He held me tighter to him and stroked my face gently. *No! Forget about me!* I shouted. *Catch her!*

At that exact moment, Jesse stood up and stepped over Rick's legs. Her foot caught on the coffee table leg, and she began to tumble. She screamed. Rick grabbed for her and missed. The coffee table trembled, and Blair caught Jesse by the waist. I sighed and closed my eyes for a second.

"Easy there, kiddo!" Blair cried out, easing Jesse back onto her feet.

Soda and food had flown all over the table and the floor. "Oh, Kayla!" Jesse cried. "I'm so sorry! Look at the mess I made!" She grimaced. "I'm so freaking clumsy!"

"Jesse, it's fine. No harm done. I'm just glad you didn't get hurt." *Thanks, Blair. I owe you one!* Getting up to get some paper towels, I heard Blair's response. *I'll have to think of something good.* I laughed out loud, forgetting the others.

"What's so funny?" Rob asked, grinning.

"Just thinking about the movie," I answered.

Rick paused the movie after checking to see that Jesse was unhurt. Everyone helped pick up the mess. Mom must have heard the commotion; she called from the hallway, "Is everything okay, Kayla?"

"Yeah. We just had a little spill."

"Do you need help cleaning it up?"

"Nope. We got it," I answered, picking up the last bits of puppy chow from the floor. Blair was working on the soda spill; I was just grateful that it was soda and not blood.

"Dang it," Jesse complained, "I really wanted some puppy chow!" She whined, and Rick kissed her pouty lips.

"I've got more, Jesse," I called from the kitchen. I was bouncing around elated; it felt good to be able to keep my friend from getting hurt. Maybe this gift was not so bad after all.

I carried the puppy chow and the brownies into the den. Rick and Rob pounced on the brownies; they'd had them before. "Everyone ready to watch again?" Rick asked, looking around the room.

"Yup!" was the general consensus. He picked up the remote, and we picked up, happily where we had left off. I snuggled back into Blair's side and wrapped my arm across him. He kissed the top of my head.

Just in case you were wondering, Blair thought, *I'm waiting to give you my present until everyone is gone.*

I looked at him and raised my eyebrows. *I am intrigued! Can I have a hint?*

No way, Short Stuff. You'll just have to be patient! He squeezed me and tweaked my nose.

Yeah, because I'm so good at the patience thing!

Blair laughed but began thinking about other things to keep me guessing. The movie was over around nine thirty, so it was time to open Jesse and Rick's presents.

"You better not have spent a lot of money, Jesse!" I scolded, knowing her overly generous streak.

"It's just money, Kayla," she scoffed. "You know what they say, 'You can't take it with you'!"

The first present was a beautiful striped, long scarf accented with gold threads in muted tones. I slipped it around my neck and looped it. Then there was a set of bronze bangle bracelets, a new wallet, and a gift certificate to my favorite store in the mall.

"You shouldn't have, Jesse! But I'm glad you did!" I squealed, throwing myself into her arms.

"Hey, what am I?" Rick complained. "Chopped liver?"

"Thanks, Rick!" I said, hugging him too. "You guys are all the best!"

Around eleven, everyone headed home, except for Blair. We gathered up all the trash and dirty glasses and headed for the kitchen. Mom came in behind us.

"You don't have to do that, baby. I'll get it in the morning," she said, yawning and stretching.

"Blair will help me, Mom. It won't take long at all," I said, rinsing the glasses and putting them in the dishwasher.

"Did everyone enjoy the party?"

"Yeah, we had a great time. Thanks!" I replied.

"Well, I'm going to head off to bed. Not too much later, Kayla," she chided. "Tomorrow's another day."

"Goodnight, Marissa," Blair said politely.

"Goodnight, honey." She smiled. "See you tomorrow, I'm sure." We heard her laugh as she headed toward the stairs.

Blair bagged up all the trash in the den and kitchen and carried it out while I finished wiping down the counters and started the dishwasher. Its hum covered up Blair's approaching footsteps. He wrapped his arms around me, and I jumped.

"I've never seen a clairvoyant startled before!" Blair laughed, kissing my neck. I raised my hand to my chest; my heart pounded like a bass drum.

"I'm glad you're amused, but you almost gave me a heart attack!" I panted.

"Sorry," he said, picking me up and kissing me. I wrapped my arms and legs around him, molding myself to his body. He carried me back to the couch, his eyes never leaving mine.

Lowering me gently onto the couch, he said, "So do you want your birthday present now?" His eyes were excited as he lowered himself next to me. "Or…" He pressed his lips to mine again with more intensity; my body tingled with pleasure. *Who needs birthday presents anyway?* I mused as Blair's hand traced down my spine. I shivered, and my yearning for him increased in intensity. I pressed my body closer and felt every line of his against me.

I traced his lips with my tongue; he sighed and pulled away. Blair rolled under me and held me to him while our breathing slowed down. "I could get used to this," I whispered against his chest. He laughed softly, and our bodies shook as one.

"Blair?"

"Hmm," he muttered, rubbing his lips against my cheek.

"Can I have my present now?" I turned my face to him and found his lips.

"I'll think about it," he teased, moving his lips to my neck. I giggled as his breath tickled it.

I sat up a little and put on my most pitiful face, pout and all. "Please, Blair?"

"You ought to know by now that pouting will get you nowhere with me."

I smacked his chest playfully. "You don't play fair!" He laughed and sat up, moving me beside him.

"Wait right here, Short Stuff," he commanded as he got up and moved to his jacket hanging on the back of the recliner.

"Whatever you say!" I beamed, saluting him.

Blair paused for a moment behind the chair looking at me. He took a deep breath and smiled. Moving to sit beside me, he said, "Makayla, I've never felt the way I feel when I'm with you." He paused, and I looked down shyly. Blair lifted my face to his as he placed a small box in my hand.

My hands shook slightly as I opened the box. Inside was a beautiful sterling silver ring, filigreed to look like lace. Blair removed it from the box when I didn't move to retrieve it. "Read the inscription inside, Makayla."

I took the ring from his hand and read, "Today…tomorrow… forever." The ring blurred from my sight as my eyes overflowed. I looked up into Blair's face; he was euphoric. He took the ring from me and placed it on my left ring finger.

We are of one mind, one soul, and someday, of one body, he thought. *I love you.*

I moved into his lap and sat within his embrace. *As I love you…*

SHOCK

Blair left around two o'clock, both of us unwilling to part sooner. Lying in bed, I gazed at my promise ring shimmering in the moonlight. My mind whirled thinking about how my life had changed over the past week. I'd never even considered that I would fall so deeply in love at such a young age, and yet, the intensity of my love for Blair—the eternal strength of it—made it impossible to think of a life without him.

The clichés of first love paled next to the overwhelming, all-consuming passion of the bond I now shared with Blair. Being separated from him now would rip my soul asunder; this in itself led to our discussions late into the night. There were many things that we had never discussed, and those topics occupied us long into the night. The future held many possibilities, some of which were so life-changing that I didn't want to consider them yet. The bond between us seemed so strong, but could something change that?

Throughout our conversations, there was one subject I dared not broach: his parents' reaction to our relationship. Although I was still worried, Blair was adamant that they would be understanding and accept our future together. The nightmare of the mother pleading with her son to abandon his love hovered just under the surface of my consciousness.

I woke late in the morning, around eleven, and found my mother sitting in her study drinking coffee and reading the *Sunday Dallas Morning News*. She looked up, hearing me shuffling in.

"Good morning, sleepy head!" Mom grinned as I plopped down into a chair. "What time did you get to bed?"

"Blair left around two," I answered, yawning. Mom frowned. "We lost track of time." I grinned, and she shook her head, smiling.

"So what did you get for your birthday?"

"Lots of stuff—the DVD of *Juno*, a scarf, bracelets, a wallet, a gift certificate, and a beautiful necklace from Amy."

"What did Blair get you?" Mom asked, glancing at my left hand.

"Oh, I forgot." I smirked at her. "This ring." I held my hand out so she could examine it closely.

"It's lovely, Kayla." She squeezed my hand lightly and picked up the paper again.

"Mom," I said hesitantly, "can I ask you something?"

"Sure, baby," she said, looking over the top of her paper. "What's on your mind?"

"Well…I wanted to know about the first time you met Dad's parents."

"What brought that up?" Mom asked, confused.

"Blair's parents are coming home today, and I'm kind of… worried about meeting them," I admitted, looking down at the parquet floor.

"Why are you worried?"

I hesitated, not sure if I was allowed to tell her. Surely I could confide in my mother without breaking some stupid clairvoyant code. "Okay, here's the deal," I blurted out, talking fast to get it over with sooner. "Blair was not supposed to…get involved with me."

"Why not?" Mom asked, furrowing her brow.

"Because the 'rules'"—I made quotation marks in the air—"say that a person who assists with someone's emergence is not supposed to…" My voice broke and I sighed.

"Get involved." It was not a question. I looked up to see my mother's face; she was irritated. She crossed to me, sat on the arm of my chair, and put her arm around me.

"When your father told your grandmother that he was marrying someone without clairvoyance, she threw a fit, and I'm not talking about a small fit. She screamed that his blood was pure, meaning both of his parents had the gift, and that his destiny, as she put it, lay without me."

I stared at her with my mouth agape. Could it be true? Was it possible that my nightmare was not about me and Blair but about my mom and dad? I shook my head. "Dad told you?" I asked, incredulous. "Why? I mean, didn't he know that it would hurt your feelings?"

"Your dad was so mad that there was no way he could keep it from me." Mom paused, lost in memory for a moment. "We shared everything, Kayla, the good and the bad. That's what love and marriage are about."

"What did Dad say to her?"

Mom smiled. "He told her in no uncertain terms that we were bonded and that nothing would change that."

"Did my grandmother ever get over it?" I really needed this answer.

"Oh, yes, baby," Mom assured me. "By the time we got married, she and I had come to an agreement of sorts." When I looked confused, she continued. "We both loved your dad, so we had to grow up and get over ourselves!" She laughed. "Mother Taylor didn't live to see you, Makayla. She would have loved you so much." She squeezed my shoulders.

"Now I have a question for you," she began, looking down at me. I looked up at her, waiting. "What does the ring signify for you, Kayla?" Mom smiled at me with that meaningful look in her eyes. I looked down, not sure how much to tell her.

The night my mother returned from her trip to Austin, I had promised her that my emergence would not change our relationship. As I learned more about my gift, I would only be able to share bits and pieces with her, and she knew that. Determined to keep my mother, my best friend, a part of my life, I decided on the truth.

I took a slow, deep breath and removed the ring from my finger. Handing it to her, I said, "Read the inscription, Mom. That should tell you everything you want to know."

Mom took the ring and brought it up closer to her face. "Today…tomorrow…forever," she read softly. I realized that I was holding my breath, anxious to hear her response.

Mom handed me the ring, rose quietly, and walked to the window. I focused on her thoughts, trying to get a sense of her reaction. *Just like Sean… I'll lose her, just like Sean.*

"No!" I shouted. She turned at the sound of my outcry. I crossed to her quickly and threw my arms around her. Tears brimmed from her eyes and mine. "Why do you think you'll lose me?" I cried. "I won't let anything happen to keep us apart. Blair wouldn't want that either."

Wiping the tears from my face, Mom whispered, "I want you to be happy, Kayla." She paused. "But I'm worried about your future with the clairvoyants."

"I don't understand."

Mom surveyed my face, deciding something instantaneously. "Makayla," she whispered; her breath shuddered. "Just before Sean left on his last business trip to Florida, he seemed preoccupied, worried, and tense. He wouldn't tell me anything about it, which could only mean one thing." My eyebrows furrowed together. She continued, almost in a whisper. "Sean *had* to be involved in something, something he couldn't share, something dealing with his clairvoyance, maybe even something for the Ileesia. It couldn't have been an accident…" Her voice choked off; she raised her hand to her mouth.

The words struck me with blunt force. How did she even know about the Ileesia? I staggered back from her, my breath escaping in short gasps. Mom moved toward me cautiously, but I held my hand up to stop her. Sitting down, I lowered my head into my hands, trying desperately to control the spinning.

With my eyes closed, the nightmare of my father flew across my mind like a film. His calm voice, trying to stop someone from doing something wrong. The cold answering voice, chillingly unconcerned, as the dark shadows converged on his enemy. My father collapsing under the weight of some unseen force.

"No…" I moaned softly. "It can't be!" Blair's parents were members of the Ileesia; what might they know about my father's death…his murder? I shivered.

"Kayla. What can I do?" Mom fluttered nervously. "Should I call Blair?" She was beginning to panic, not knowing how to help me.

I nodded shakily; I couldn't deal with this alone. She ran to get my cell phone off the coffee table in the den. I heard her speaking in a frenzy, her tone wary and afraid. Listening to her thoughts, I felt her guilt.

"He'll be here in ten minutes, Kayla," she reassured me. "I'm so sorry, baby! I didn't mean to upset you." I heard her approaching me with caution in her step.

I looked up; her face was grieved and lined with angst. I couldn't find my voice. What could I say? She had no idea that I had been witnessing my dad's death—his murder—in my dreams. Mom knelt down next to me and laid her hand on my arm. I lay my head back and closed my eyes again, trying to block the emotions, hers and mine.

The doorbell rang, and Mom ran to get the door. Blair was at my side within seconds, kneeling down in front of me. The floodgates opened as I released the pain in my heart, in my soul. My pulse raced, my breathing quickened, and my head grew dizzier. I gasped for breath as the sobs tore through me.

"Makayla, look at me," Blair ordered, putting his hands on my shoulders. But I could not find his face through the tears. "Focus, Makayla. Now!" His voice was sharp, demanding my attention; his hands grasped my face to steady it.

I opened my eyes and slowly, through the haze of shock, found his. Gradually my body relaxed; the tension washed away by Blair's gift. My arms felt weighted as I reached around his neck. He picked me up and sat down, rocking me in his lap.

"Easy, honey," Blair crooned. "I'm right here. Calm down and breathe." He held me close against his chest. My despair had sapped me of all my strength; I slipped into unconsciousness.

When I woke, I was lying on the couch with my head in Blair's lap and my mother seated anxiously at my feet. I looked down at my mom and tried to smile. She rubbed my legs softly and smiled back, unsure of what to say or do. In her thoughts, she blamed herself for my collapse; the pain on her face could be read easily.

Raising a shaking hand to my damp face and looking up at Blair, I asked, "What happened?"

"Your brain overloaded with sensations and shut itself down," he explained calmly. "How are you feeling now?"

"Tired."

"Kayla," Mom whispered, "I'm so sorry, baby. I should never have…I didn't know it would affect you like that…" Her voice broke on the last words.

"No, Mom; don't." I paused, thinking of how to word what I wanted to say without upsetting her more. "You didn't do anything wrong. I just…was surprised. Please don't upset yourself," I begged. "We're in this together, right?" I reached down, and she took my hand.

I moved to sit up with Blair's help. My head was definitely still woozy, but it was getting better. I leaned into Blair's side as he wrapped his arm around me.

"Did Mom tell you…?" I began, not making eye contact with him.

"Yes, she did." Blair's voice was tight; he was worried. "We'll talk about it later, honey, when you feel stronger. Okay?"

I nodded. He kissed the top of my head. "Have you eaten anything today, Makayla?" I groaned.

"No, she hasn't," my mother answered. "I'll go get her something right now." She bustled into the kitchen, glad of something productive to do for me.

Blair, we need to talk alone.

I know, but right now we have to make sure your mother is satisfied that you're okay or she won't let you out of her sight for a week.

I nodded my understanding.

When do your parents get home?

Around four. I'll take you to see them this evening. He paused and sighed. *I didn't know…*

I know…

Mom came in carrying a tray with orange juice and toast with peanut butter spread on it. I was feeling kind of nauseated, but I knew neither Blair or my mother would accept no for an answer. I ate quietly while she and Blair made small talk about his family—with some important details conveniently left out—his plans for college, and his career interests.

It was obvious that Mom was grateful for Blair's presence. It was going to take a while to convince her that I wasn't a ticking time bomb. To be honest, it was going to take some time for me to get my confidence back. Friday and Saturday had gone so well; I guess I hoped that my setbacks were past me.

I felt better after eating and finally convinced my mother that I was strong enough to take a shower and get dressed. Blair assured her that he would stay downstairs to make sure I was okay before he left to go home and see his parents. Rejuvenated by my shower, I dried my hair and straightened it to perfection. I chose my clothes carefully, wanting to look respectable for Blair's parents. Finally I dressed in my black dress pants, white shirt, and gray sweater, deciding to err on the side of dressy versus casual.

As I made my way downstairs, I heard Mom and Blair talking about the coming week.

"I'm just worried," Mom was saying, "because I have to go out of town again on Monday and won't get back until Thursday evening. What if Kayla has a problem while I'm gone, especially during the night?"

Blair's voice was calm and reassuring. "I'm sure that Makayla would be welcome to stay at our house while you're gone. We have plenty of room, and my parents certainly understand the stress of emergence after going through it with all three of their kids!" He chuckled. "And most parents think they have trouble with their teenagers."

"I hate to impose, but that would make me feel more comfortable," Mom admitted with a wan smile.

"Then it's all set," Blair responded confidently. "As long as Makayla agrees, of course."

I was glad I got some say in the decision. I felt my infamous obstinacy rear its ugly head as I approached the kitchen. I might not have been able to control what my mind was doing, but I wasn't going to be pushed around otherwise. They both looked up when I entered, Mom looking wary and Blair confident and relaxed.

Thanks for letting me in on the decision, Blair! I blasted petulantly.

Don't start, Makayla, he warned. *We* will *do whatever makes your mother comfortable.* His face was uncompromising. I glared back at him.

"Blair and I were just talking about the upcoming week, baby," Mom said hesitantly. "I have to be out of town Monday through Thursday, and I would feel better if you stayed at Blair's house while I'm gone."

I took a cleansing breath and tried to smile. "We'll work something out, Mom," I assured her. "Don't worry. I'll be fine."

Mom looked cautious; she knew that I hadn't agreed to their plan, but she didn't know about Blair's power of persuasion. As ticked off as I might get, he would win this battle. She looked from Blair's face to mine and quickly decided to skirt the mine field and do some work in her study.

"Why are you so upset about staying at my house while your mom is gone?" Blair asked indignantly. "I think it's a great idea."

"I haven't even met your parents yet, and you have me living with them for almost a week!"

Blair frowned and looked into my face intently. I shied away from his gaze, straightening a wrinkle in my sweater. Blair's arms encircled me and held me to him.

"This doesn't have anything to do with that stupid dream, does it?" he asked, miffed.

"No, not really." I was almost sure of that. "I'm just nervous about meeting them and…"

"And what?"

"Blair, I'm so confused and conflicted right now. I don't know what to think!" I broke away from him and sat down, putting my head on the table. Too much information and yet too little. How much more could I take?

Blair knelt down next to me and lifted my chin with his fingertips. "I don't know what all this means, Makayla, but I do know this," he said tenderly. "Whatever it is, we will deal with it together." His lips brushed mine softly, and he smiled. "You know that, don't you?"

"Yes," I replied, smiling weakly.

Today…tomorrow…forever.

BLAIR'S PARENTS

Blair left around three o'clock to meet his parents when they got home at four. At the door, he wrapped me into his embrace and kissed me. "I'll pick you up at six," he said gently. "Don't worry about anything, deal?" He pulled away from me slightly and made a grumpy face, probably mirroring mine.

"Okay, okay." I smirked. "I'll try not to worry, but you might as well accept the fact that I inherited the talent of excessively worrying from my mother."

"We'll just have to work on that, won't we?" He smiled. "Worrying is a waste of valuable time that might have been spent more enjoyably." I smacked his arm playfully; he laughed. "I'll see you soon, Short Stuff. Love you!"

"Love you too!" I waved as he walked to his car. Only three more hours left. It felt like I was going to walk the "long green mile." I sighed. Surely, as was usually the case with me, things would go better than I expected tonight. After all, how bad could it be?

My legs danced nervously; my stomach churned with each bounce. Blair shook his head, grinning at my jumpiness, but knew better than to try to stop the momentum. I twisted a strand of my hair around my finger and sighed. Blair had tried to tell me everything was all right with his parents; they weren't even surprised by his news. Still, I couldn't get the nightmare totally out of my psyche.

Blair's voice cut through my reverie. "Makayla, you're not going to face a firing squad. Relax." He took my hand and kissed it. "I've already told you that they're just fine with us, as I knew they would be," he inserted smugly.

"I know," I retorted, still bouncing. Blair muffled a snicker.

"I can't take you into the house bouncing like a ping pong ball for heaven's sake. You've got to calm down."

"I'm trying!"

"Yeah, I can see that." Sarcasm dripped from his words.

We turned into a neighborhood just a few miles from mine. I stopped bouncing, petrified with dread. Blair squeezed my hand again and smiled. The car slowed and turned into a long driveway just past a hedgerow of evergreens. In front of us was a large, two-story home built in the French country style. The various roof lines and gables added a special charm to it, almost like a gingerbread house. The mixed stone and brick work was warm and inviting.

"It's beautiful," I mused.

"I'm glad you like it."

I grimaced and looked down. Feeling absolutely ridiculous, I finally blurted out the question that had been driving me crazy all afternoon.

"This is going to sound really lame," I warned him, my voice harried. "But…um…"

"What is it?" Blair asked, concerned and confused.

"Does your family…you know…talk out loud or always in your heads?" I shrugged, embarrassed by my ignorance.

Blair's face transformed from concern to hilarity in a split second; I had never seen him laugh so hard. I drew in a breath through my nose and glared at him.

I'm glad you find me so entertaining! I snapped.

"I'm really…sorry…" he choked out, trying to control his laughter. My glare must have convinced him of my tenuous mood because he reached out and put his hand on my arm. "Really, I'm sorry, Short Stuff. It's a logical question—it just caught me off guard." His lips turned up into his beautiful smile, which melted away some of my frustration. "Of course we talk out loud, honey. The quiet would drive us crazy!"

Blair parked the car behind a four-door red BMW sedan and got out. He came around to my door and opened it, holding his hand out for me. I took it, noticing that it trembled slightly, and stood next to him. With his free hand, Blair stroked down my face and raised my chin up.

"I love you," he said wistfully, "and they're going to love you too."

"Okay," I huffed, "let's get this show on the road!" Blair leaned down and kissed me before leading the way to the front door. He opened it and stood back for me to enter first.

The inside reflected the same warmth and hominess as the outside. The dark wooden floors and soft ecru walls were accented by an eclectic mix of antiques and traditional furniture. This was a house that was lived in; somehow that was comforting to me. It diminished the insecurity I felt meeting Blair's clairvoyant parents.

"Mom, Dad," Blair called, "we're here."

Blair's mother came around the corner with a dishtowel over her shoulder. She was tall, probably around five foot eight, with

Blair's honey blonde hair and hazel eyes. She wore a bright yellow apron over a pair of tailored dark-wash jeans and a fitted blouse. An immediate feeling of calm washed over me at her warm smile. "Well, it's about time, Blair," she scolded, teasing. "I've been so anxious to meet you, Makayla." She beamed at me and extended her arms.

With Blair's nodded encouragement, I moved to embrace her. "It's very nice to meet you, Mrs. Davis."

"Please call me Bethany, sweetie," she said, holding me at arm's length to look at me. "You're so beautiful. I can see why my son loves you so deeply."

I blushed. "Mom," Blair chastised, "do you have to embarrass me before we even get out of the foyer?" He turned to me. "I should have warned you that my mother has a tendency to say exactly what's on her mind." He rolled his eyes, and I giggled.

"That's okay, Bethany." I grinned. "I have that same problem!" She hugged me again and led me into the large family room.

Blair's father entered from a hallway across the room. "Sorry, Blair. Judge Holloway called, and you know how much she likes to talk." Blair's father was tall, but his hair was a darker hue and slightly receding off his forehead. His face was handsome, but in a more rugged way than Blair's; Blair obviously looked much more like his mom. I noticed quickly that he wore the same familiar smile, but he definitely exuded an air of authority; therefore, his warm greeting took me by surprise. "Welcome, Makayla!" he exclaimed, shaking my hand. "It's so nice to meet you at last."

I was slightly confused about his wording; "at last" usually indicated a long period of anticipation. Blair and I had only be seriously together for less than a week. "I'm happy to meet you as well, Mr. Davis," I replied, not wanting to assume his desire to be on a first-name basis.

"Oh, Makayla." He smiled. "Please call me Blake—or Dad is fine with me too." He winked; I smiled back at his warm endearment.

"As you can see, Makayla," Blair inserted, "both of my parents are painfully introverted and soft-spoken." Everyone laughed, but I was more than relieved by their welcome.

"I hope you're hungry," Bethany said. "I'm making spaghetti and meatballs. I thought something simple and familiar would be comforting tonight."

"May I help you with something?" I asked.

"That would be great. Come on in and we'll finish up."

Blair's mom put her arm around my shoulder and led me into her beautiful kitchen. The cabinets were dark oak, with a black marbled granite countertop. I didn't even recognize some of the appliances. Obviously, cooking was very important to Bethany.

"Wow!" I exclaimed. "This kitchen is fabulous!"

"You're sweet. Cooking is my way of unwinding after a difficult day in court or at the office. I sort of splurged on the kitchen." She winked and leaned in conspiratorially.

"I'll say," came Blake's voice from the doorway. "How many home kitchens do you know, Makayla, that have a regular oven, a convection oven, an eight-burner gas stove, three warming drawers, and a commercial refrigerator/freezer unit in them?"

I laughed at his bemused expression. "Not too many," I admitted, "but it sure looks like fun to me!"

"I notice you boys don't complain too much once the food hits the table!" Bethany teased.

"She's got you there, Dad," Blair admitted, thumping his dad on the back. Blair met my eyes with obvious pleasure at the comfortable banter between us all.

Blair and I set the kitchen table while Blake tossed the salad and Bethany dished up our plates of spaghetti and meatballs. It smelled amazingly delicious, and I realized that my appetite had finally returned after the morning's turmoil. After retrieving the garlic bread from a warming drawer—I'd never even heard of those before—we sat down together to eat.

The conversation continued, flowing freely and easily across many subjects. Bethany enjoyed telling me stories about Blair as a child, several of which embarrassed him greatly. Blake asked about my mother and our lives together, seemingly sincerely interested in every aspect of our lives.

After helping to clear the table and load the dishwasher, Blair and I joined his parents in the family room for coffee. I was so stuffed that I was beginning to feel sleepy. Blair put his arm around my shoulder, and I leaned into his side, watching the fire crackling in the fireplace.

Blair's parents sat quietly, sipping their coffee and winding down from their day of travel. I was just closing my eyes when Blake cleared his throat and spoke gently.

"Makayla," he began cautiously, "Blair told us about your conversation with your mother this morning." He waited, gauging my reaction; Blair tightened his arm around me. I didn't answer; there was no need for words.

Blake rubbed his hand over his mouth, almost nervously, then continued, "What Blair doesn't know is that your father and I were friends." Blair stared at his dad, stunned, while I sat up to listen more intently. Bethany moved to sit on the other side of me on the couch, obviously concerned that she might need to be closer if my mood shifted.

"Sean and I actually grew up together in Kansas City, living just a few houses down from each other. Neither of us knew growing up that either of our families were clairvoyants until we emerged." Blake had my rapt attention; no one had ever told me anything about my dad's childhood. Blair was rubbing my shoulder soothingly, but he too was silent.

"All through our senior year, we were inseparable. We both played basketball on the school team during the season and played every day off season as well. When it came time for college, we ended up at different schools and lost touch. I heard about his marriage to Marissa but was unable to attend.

"For several years, I heard nothing about Sean; it wasn't until five and a half years after their marriage that I heard from him again." Blake paused, taking a sip of coffee and contemplating his next words. Bethany placed her hand on my arm and smiled at me.

"You were about a year and a half old when Sean appeared in front of the Ileesia." I flinched involuntarily, and both Blair and Bethany patted me softly. "He was preoccupied, not his usual even disposition; it concerned me. Sean seemed to be concerned about the misuse of our gifts by an unnamed clairvoyant, but he wouldn't be specific. Zandria, the leader of the Ileesia, told him that he had to be absolutely positive about his facts before bringing any charges against another.

"You have to understand, Makayla, charging another clairvoyant with the misuse of our gift is the most serious accusation in our community. Sean said he was not ready to divulge the circumstances of his concerns, so the council had no choice but to adjourn.

"I invited Sean to have dinner with me. He sat in the restaurant with me for several hours, talking about Marissa, their life together, and most importantly about you, his most precious daughter. All throughout the meal, Sean was restless, almost distracted. When we left each other that night, I was uneasy, but I didn't know exactly what to do." Blake took at deep breath and moved to kneel in front of me on the couch.

His hazel eyes glistened with emotion as he met mine. "Six months later, Sean was found dead at the base of a twelve-story building. The reports said he must have fallen from the rooftop garden. No one knew what he was doing there or who he might have met there." Tears flowed unabated down my cheeks, but my eyes never left Blake's. The obvious pain he felt, the loss, the guilt was etched deeply into his face. "I should have read his thoughts…" Blake's voice broke with regret.

We all sat in stunned silence for a while. Blair laid his cheek against my head and kissed my hair. Bethany reached for her husband's hand and smiled gently through her tears. In all the years since my father's death, my mother had never gone into any details; the shock took a while to seep into my mind. Meeting Blair and his parents might finally put all of the missing pieces together.

"Thank you for telling me, Blake," I said sincerely. "I really want to know as much as you can tell me about my dad." I reached forward and hugged him around his neck, trying to assuage some of his guilt.

"There's one more thing, Makayla," Blake whispered in my ear. I pulled away from him and looked into his face. "On the night of our dinner together, Sean gave me a letter to keep in confidence for you, if anything should happen to him. At the time, I thought he was being a little melodramatic, but maybe he knew more than any of us…" His voice trailed off.

"Where is the letter?" I asked softly.

"It's in my study, in the safe."

THE LETTER

Blake stood and offered me his hand. Taking it, I rose to follow him toward his study. Blake turned back to Blair, who had risen to follow.

"Sean's instructions were for Makayla to read his letter in private, Blair."

"But Dad," Blair argued, "surely under the circumstances I should be…"

Blake raised his hand to cut him off. "I will follow Sean's wishes, son." When Blair began to protest again, he continued, "You and I will be right outside of the study door if Makayla needs us."

Blair's face was indignant, but his father's face, although compassionate, was unyielding. Blair nodded and looked at me wordlessly.

Reaching back to take his hand, I whispered, "I'll be okay, Blair. You won't be far away." He nodded gravely.

Blake led me into his study. The walls were richly paneled in cherry, and another fireplace blazed on the west wall. In the center of the room was a large desk with two leather chairs in front of it and one behind. Blake gestured for me to sit in one of the chairs as he headed toward the east wall. I watched dazed as he pulled back a wooden panel and revealed a safe embedded in the wall.

He entered the combination, and the door swung open. Blake rummaged around, shuffling papers and small boxes out of his way. He picked up a sealed, legal-sized envelope, turned, and walked toward me. Handing me the envelope, he spoke for the first time since entering the study.

"Makayla," he said gently, "as you heard, Sean asked that you read his letter alone, and I will abide by his wishes; however, if you feel any distress, call for us immediately." His eyes were filled with a familiar compassion. "Do you understand?"

"Yes," I whispered.

Blake nodded and headed out of the study, closing the door quietly behind him.

Across the plain white envelope, in my father's unfamiliar handwriting, were written the words *For Makayla*. My hands trembled slightly as I stared at the innocuous envelope that now seemed ominous and frightening. Why would he have given the letter to Blake for me? Did he expect something to happen to him? And if so, why not leave it with my mother?

This morning's conversation with Mom cast a shadow over the letter in my hand. Dad was... What words had she used? Preoccupied, worried, and tense. In her mind, the only explanation for his uneasiness and unwillingness to discuss it with her was that he was involved in something having to do with his clairvoyance—the only topic closed to her.

Closing my eyes, I remembered the first day Blair told me about my gift. "Is my mother afraid of my gift?" I had asked him. What if she had reason to be afraid? I shook my head and opened my eyes. There was only one place to find some of these answers. I opened the seal and took out the letter.

Dear Makayla,

As I write this letter, you are almost two years old, lying in your crib sleeping soundly next to me. You are a beautiful baby, the greatest gift I have ever received. It is hard to believe that if you read this, I will not be with you, and you will almost be a grown woman.

My beautiful Makayla, it grieves me that I am not the father, the man, I should be. As my life takes what may be a very dangerous turn, I feel it necessary to pass on some important information to you.

Beyond my clairvoyant gift, I have been given empathic abilities. I can sometimes see the future and always seem to be able to feel, as well as hear, the emotions of those around me. It is the ability to see the future that I must discuss with you since it is possible, if not probable, that you will inherit the same gifts.

There are clairvoyants in the world who will try to use you and your gifts for their own evil purposes. Keep your empathic abilities a secret if possible; do not fall into the trap in which I find myself. On two occasions I have been forced to pass on information to a criminal group under threats to your mother and you. This group uses their power, mostly stemming from threats and violence, to grow rich and gain more and more influence in the realm of organized crime.

I confess my failure to you, my Makayla, to keep you from falling into similar traps. If you are so gifted, keep your empathic ability quiet; only trust your dearest friends. I should have trusted Blake; trust him. He is a good and just man.

I am leaving tomorrow for Florida, where I plan to confront my nemesis. I will not let him hurt you or your mother, but I will stop this before it goes any further. If I die to save those I love, I will have died honorably.

Be well and happy, Makayla. I wish you love and a peaceful life. I will love you forever.

Daddy

I closed my eyes and leaned my head against the back of the leather chair. The memory of my nightmare moved across my mind like a horror film. My father's agonized cries were made more painful now that I understood his sacrifice. I heard a strangled gasp and realized that it had come from me. The room shook as I opened my eyes; through the haze of tears, I tried to focus and force back the pain. But this was too much, too strong, too overwhelming.

I tried to call out for Blair, but my gasping was turning into racking sobs. There was no breath left for words. I closed my eyes again, willing myself to stay conscious.

Blair! My thoughts screamed out for him, my one true solace.

I heard the door open abruptly and tried to focus on the figures moving toward me. Lifting my arms like a child, I waited for the rescuing embrace. Blair lifted me off the chair and into his arms in one swift motion. I felt the letter slip out of my hand.

"I'm right here, Makayla," he comforted, carrying me to the other room. "Breathe slowly. It's going to be all right."

My sobbing slowed, along with my breathing, as he cradled me in his arms. Another hand stroked my face, softer and more delicate than Blair's.

"I'll get a cool cloth." Bethany's voice receded along with her footsteps.

Blair sat down with me still in his arms and kissed my forehead. He rocked me gently, whispering words of comfort in my ear. I felt cool moisture on my face and knew that Bethany was there with us. Another stronger hand wiped against my cheek.

"I'm sorry, Makayla," Blake intoned gently. "I should have stayed with you or let Blair." His regret compounded my grief, and Blair felt it.

"Close your mind, Makayla. Let yourself rest." I focused on following his directions and felt myself relax in his arms. This time, however, I didn't lose consciousness. When I had finally regained control, I lifted my head and looked into the concerned faces surrounding me.

"Where's my letter?"

"I have it," Blake answered, holding it out to me. I shook my head.

"You need to read it, Blake," I said softly. "I think you need to know what it says." Sitting up carefully to look him in the face, I added, "I have a feeling that it will be difficult for you to read, so please be prepared for that."

Blake stood up, crossed to the fireplace, and put on his reading glasses. As he read the letter, I felt a slight shift in his emotions, but he was focusing to lessen the impact. Blair looked from me to his father with anxious eyes. As Blake lowered the letter, he took off his glasses, brought his hand to his forehead, and leaned on the mantel. Bethany crossed to him at once, putting her arms around his shoulders. No one spoke, but the room swirled with emotions—pain, loss, regret, confusion.

After a few minutes, Blake lowered his hand, putting it on his wife's arm and nodding to her gently. His eyes glistened with sadness as he returned to Blair and me on the couch. Our eyes met; he knelt down and embraced me. His embrace was more than comfort; it was a father's embrace, and I was surprised by his tenderness.

Gentle tears flowed down my cheeks as Blake whispered, "I'm so sorry, Makayla. I should have done more… I should have stopped him…or…"

I pulled away from him. "You couldn't have done anything to stop my dad from following his chosen path. Please don't blame yourself; it will only make this worse for all of us."

He nodded and sat down in an easy chair, still looking regretful. "Please, Makayla," Blair implored, "please tell me what's going on!" His face was etched with worry.

I touched his cheek gently, and he turned to kiss the palm of my hand. "Blake, please give Blair the letter to read." Turning to Bethany, I added, "And then I'd like you to read it as well." She smiled gently through her distress.

Once Blair and Bethany had read the letter, I replaced it in its envelope and placed it on the coffee table. Again the room was filled with the sound of silence. Blair held me tightly to his side as his parents stared off into their individual thoughts.

An overwhelming sense of loss threatened to consume me as I considered my father's death and sacrifice. My chest felt heavy; each breath labored against the sadness, the emptiness. I had never known my father, but now I felt his loss, my loss, for the first time. It was as if he had just died and the pain seemed to be boring a hole in my chest. I concentrated on each breath, consciously listening to the whishing sound it made.

The fact that my father had committed a "crime" of sorts against the rules of clairvoyancy meant nothing to me. I would not judge him—who could? He said he had acted under threats to Mom and me. I shivered at the thought. Blair rubbed my shoulder soothingly. What kind of a person had forced my father's hand with his threats? And for what? Money? And more importantly, who was he?

All at once something extraordinary occurred to me. Could it be possible for my dad to be communicating with me from the beyond? How absurd! I really needed to reign in my imagination. And yet, if my nightmare continued to recur on a regular basis… What was I supposed to do with the information it gave me?

"Blake?" My voice shattered the silence, startling everyone a little.

"Yes, Makayla?"

"Has Blair mentioned to you that I've had a nightmare about my father's death?" If silence could become more quiet, it became so. Blake stared at me, blank shock on his face.

Blair spoke first. "No, honey, I haven't told either of them about it. It wasn't my place to share it with them."

"How long have you had the dream?" Blake asked analytically.

"I've had it two or three times since Tuesday night. Each time it gets clearer and clearer."

"Tell me about it, Makayla."

I did my best to relate the scenes from my nightmare. Explaining the fear it generated in me was hard, but I plowed on. When I got to the part about the dark shapes oozing from the walls, Blake and Bethany gasped. I froze.

"What are the 'shapes' doing as they come away from the walls?" Blake asked tensely.

"I'm not sure, but as they approach my dad, he begins to scream, or moan, I guess, as if they are hurting him. I haven't seen any weapons or anything." The memory of my father's face flew across my mind; I winced, and everyone else shuddered along with me.

Blake rose and began pacing in front of the fireplace. I looked at Bethany, but her eyes were glued to her husband; both of them looked tormented. Something I'd said had brought about their reaction, but I didn't understand. I looked at Blair, but he looked just as dismayed as I did.

"Blake?" I asked timidly. "Is something wrong?"

Blake looked from my face to his wife's before he spoke. "The phenomenon you're describing is not well known amongst most clairvoyants, but as members of the Ileesia, Bethany and I are aware of it." He paused, considering whether or not to share the information with Blair and me.

"I think they need to know, Blake," Bethany said quietly. "It directly affects her dream and Sean's death."

Blake took a deep breath. "You both have to understand that this is confidential and must not be shared with anyone else. Do you understand?" His face was severe.

I nodded, and Blair said, "Yes, Dad, we understand."

"There's only one sure way to destroy a clairvoyant's mind, ultimately causing their death," Blake began. I realized that my mouth was agape and shut it, but my eyes were wide with dread. Blair squeezed my hand.

"Only the most evil of our kind would dare to consider using it against another clairvoyant." Blake paused to gather himself. "It is possible to effectively destroy a clairvoyant's mind by overloading it with negativity." When I looked totally confused, Blake continued. "When our minds are filled with too much hate, fear, or any other negative emotion, our minds sort of short circuit, causing a severe loss of judgment. A person affected by such negativity could conceivably be coerced to walk out in front of a truck or..." Blake looked at Bethany for the strength to continue. "Or a person could step off the edge of a building."

It took me a moment to grasp his words; their horror and intensity slowly edged into my consciousness. I was too stunned to cry or speak. My head reeled with a new emotion—hate. I hated the people who did this to my father, for taking him away from my mother and from me. As this new darkness filled my mind, I felt a sharp pain wrap around my head. I grabbed my head with my hands, but the pain only grew worse. My eyes wouldn't focus; they rolled back into my head.

"Makayla!" His voice called as if from a great distance. I felt Blair's hands move me to his shoulder, and other hands encircled my head on all sides. Warmth radiated from their hands, and my mind cleared of everything but their loving presence. My body relaxed and sank into Blair's lap. The hands left my head, and Blair held me gently against him. Blake and Bethany sat close to us on the couch, each laying a hand on me. The positive energy radiating from them cleared my mind and my heart.

"I'm sorry," I whispered, embarrassed. "I didn't mean to—"

"There's nothing to be ashamed of, Makayla," Bethany's gentle voice crooned. "You've had so much, too much, to deal with this week. No one should have to emerge and cope with the possibility that their father was murdered."

Blair kissed my forehead as his father spoke. "Makayla, you must try to put the things we've discussed tonight out of your consciousness. You must promise me that you'll try to keep them out. There's nothing any of us can do to change the past. We must focus on what to do in the future."

I knew that he was right; nothing would bring back my father. I would have to find a way to live with this new information and still concentrate on living a normal life. I laughed bitterly to myself. Would life ever be normal again?

Blake cleared his throat and brought me out of my reverie. "It is important, however, for you to tell one of us if your dream becomes clearer. Do you think you could do that for me, please?"

I nodded.

"It's been a long day," Bethany interrupted. "Blair, take Makayla home soon so that she can get a good night's rest." I doubted that was possible, but I wasn't going to share that thought. "Blair told us that your mom will be away this week for work, Makayla. Will you please stay with us? I would feel more comfortable, and I know your mom would also."

"Yes, I'll stay. Thank you for inviting me." I smiled at Bethany, and she took my hand.

"We're family now. Thanksgiving is coming up in a couple of weeks. I want to meet your mother and have you two here for the holiday. Do you think that would be okay with your mom?" Bethany asked.

"I'm sure it would be. She wants to meet you too," I replied. Bethany leaned over and kissed my forehead.

Blake rose and took his wife's hand. "We'll see you tomorrow night, then. Sleep well, Makayla." He reached over and touched his hand to my cheek; a small pulse emanated from it, but it did not cause pain. In fact, it sent a wave of relaxation over me.

Blair chuckled softly, and his dad stared at him innocently. "Subtle, Dad, real subtle." I didn't understand the joke. Blair's parents left us to go to their bedroom. I watched them walk together, arms around each other, and wondered if Blair and I would be as blessed as his parents.

Blair drove me home shortly thereafter. Mom was waiting up for us and immediately saw my worn expression. Blair assured her that I was just tired after all the excitement of the past few days. He kissed me goodnight and watched as Mom led me upstairs to my room.

Mom sat at my bedside until I fell asleep, which miraculously came quickly. My mind was calm and my body relaxed. Vaguely I remembered Blake's pulsating touch and Blair's teasing words, "Subtle, Dad, real subtle." I slept dreamlessly for the first night in a long time.

THE REST OF THE FAMILY

Although I feared that my life would never be normal again, after the first few days of my emergence, life took on a certain normalcy—a routine. That first week I spent at the Davises' was a lot less awkward than I feared. Clairvoyants are easy to live with; they accepted me unconditionally and with great warmth. One of the guestrooms was designated as my room; Bethany went to great lengths to make it *my* room, even adding some movie posters and a big stuffed teddy bear on my bed.

It was impossible not to feel loved in their home, but I began worrying about what would happen if Blair and I ever broke up. It would be like losing my father all over again. They all seemed to consider me part of their family already. Although that made me feel loved and safe, it also made me anxious. My insecure nature, along with my lousy dating history, didn't leave me feeling as confident as they.

Mom and Blair's parents became fast friends, enjoying each other more than I could have dreamed. Mom confessed that she'd truly missed the company of clairvoyants, finding them sincere, loving, and deeply spiritual. In many ways, she seemed happier than I had seen her for a long time. Confident that I was going to be okay, she was able to relax and enjoy life again. This holiday season was very different for Mom and me. For the first time since the death of my grandparents, we were included in a large, traditional, family Thanksgiving. Benjamin and Holly drove up from Austin on the morning before Thanksgiving with Leila. Benjamin, who looked a lot like Blair's father but shorter and a little stockier, was in his first year of residency at Baylor Medical. It didn't take long to see that Blair loved to tease his older brother about his height.

"Ben's the runt of Mom's litter!" Blair announced brightly, putting his brother into a headlock and mussing up his hair.

"Maybe so, little brother," Ben replied, blithely twisting out of the headlock and throwing Blair over his shoulder to the floor in one swift movement, "but a black belt in Tae Kwon Do has certainly evened the odds!"

Leila giggled with glee seeing her father and uncle wrestle like kids. She clapped her little hands, jumping up and down. "Do it again, Daddy! Trow Unca Bair again!" Leila had her mother's beautiful curly brown hair, which fell in ringlets from her pigtails. They bounced up and down with her every jump.

Blair scooped Leila up in the air, much to her delight. "Uncle Blair would rather throw you in the air, Leila!" She screeched with delight as Holly and I looked on, bemused.

"Does this go on all the time?" I asked Holly, laughing.

"Yup, pretty much," she replied. "Ben and Blair have never really grown up, so they fit right in with Leila!" Holly turned her soft brown eyes to her daughter giggling in Blair's arms. "It's not so bad when you think about it," she added. "Men who never fully grow up make great fathers, and they had a great example in Blake."

I helped Holly get the pies she had prepared for Thanksgiving out of the car. "Blair tells us that you're thinking about teaching as a career," Holly said.

"It's certainly one of the things I'm thinking about," I replied, reaching for the pumpkin pies in the backseat. "I've always thought that I would enjoy teaching, but since my emergence, I've been thinking about studying to become a school counselor."

"That sounds really exciting. Of course, I'm a little biased since I teach middle school." Holly grinned, balancing a pecan pie in one hand and closing the car door with the other. Holly wasn't much taller than me, with brown wavy hair that fell to just below her shoulders. She was very straightforward and direct, probably from teaching those middle school students!

"That's a really tough age to teach, isn't it?"

Holly laughed and nodded her head. "Pretty much you either love middle schoolers or you hate them. When I tell people I teach eighth grade, they either think I'm a saint or have lost my mind!"

Bethany was waiting for us in the kitchen when we entered with the pies. The kitchen already smelled wonderful with the early preparations for our Thanksgiving dinner. The turkey giblets were boiling into broth; the intoxicating aroma filled the whole house. Bethany was busy chopping onions and celery for her stuffing.

"Girls, why don't you put the pies in the pantry so that they'll be out of our way," she said, wiping her hair out of her face. "Holly, they look beautiful, as usual. All my girls are great cooks!" Bethany bragged, pecking Holly on the cheek as she passed her. "What time does Marissa get home from San Antonio tonight, Makayla?"

"I think around seven. Hopefully her flight won't be delayed with all the holiday travelers," I said. "I know she wants to get over here early tomorrow morning to help you."

"That'll be great!" Bethany enthused. "Hey, Holly? Will you remind the boys that someone has to pick up Briana and Jonah at the airport at three?'

"Sure, Mom."

As Holly left the kitchen, I thought of a question I'd never asked Blair. "Bethany, are Holly and Jonah clairvoyants?" I asked, scooping up the chopped vegetables and putting them in a bowl for her.

"Holly is not a clairvoyant, but Jonah is," she answered in a matter-of-fact manner. "Didn't you notice her brown eyes?" I frowned in confusion. "All clairvoyants have hazel eyes."

"Really?" I asked, amazed. "I didn't know that!"

"Well, I guess you wouldn't really have a reason to."

"Does Holly ever feel, I don't know, out of the loop?"

"That's a really good question, sweetheart. I think at first it was a little difficult for her to accept that there were certain things Benjamin couldn't share with her. But as the years have gone by—they've been married for four years now—things have gotten easier for her. She understands now that it's sort of like doctor-patient confidentiality."

"I know my mother said it took her a while to accept things. Sometimes I think she kind of…blames…Dad's clairvoyance for his death," I admitted quietly, staring at the brick floor.

Bethany wiped her hands on the ever-present kitchen towel over her shoulder and put her arm around me. "I can understand that; can't you?" she asked, gazing down into my face. "Marissa doesn't know the details of Sean's death, but she suspects that it had to do with his clairvoyance. I think that's why she worries about you so much." She squeezed my shoulder gently. "She'll enjoy meeting Holly; they'll have something in common."

I nodded and tried to smile. "Don't worry, Makayla. Everything's going to be fine," Bethany added softly. She knew my thoughts were still drawn to my nightmare and the circumstances of Dad's death. Although it occurred rarely, I still had the dream and was frustrated that it hadn't become any clearer to me. Deep down, I wanted more information; I wanted to know who was responsible.

I hadn't heard Blair enter the kitchen, but I heard the disapproval in his thoughts and turned around to face him. Blair didn't like for me to think about my nightmare, especially who was responsible; he was afraid that I would freak out if I knew, do something stupid. That was ridiculous, I tried to reassure him; what the heck could little old me do anyway? But he still worried and made his disapproval clear whenever my thoughts drifted in that direction.

Makayla… I was so used to hearing his thoughts by now that his reproach was clear.

Your mom and I were just talking, Blair. Relax! It's Thanksgiving! I smiled coyly and threw my arms around him; he lifted me automatically so I could kiss him.

"Leave her alone, Blair," Bethany reprimanded. "She's got it under control." I loved it when Bethany was around because Blair always backed down faster than if we were alone. "Are you and Makayla going to pick up your sister this afternoon?"

"Yes," he said, a little shamefaced. "Do you need us to run any errands for you before we go?"

"No," she answered, turning back to start cubing her bread. "You go have a good time. Relax…and don't wrestle with your brother. He might hurt you!" Bethany smirked and winked at me.

"Very funny, Mom. You guys are a laugh a minute!" Blair reached down and tweaked my sides; I shrieked. "Serves you right for ganging up on me with Mom." Blair grinned.

"Oh really?" I asked sarcastically. "I'm not the only one who's ticklish around here!" Blair ran in mock terror as I chased him into the other room. I heard Bethany laughing behind us.

Of course, as was my intention, I never won these chases. Blair turned around and picked me up just as I approached him. He spun around in a circle until I was dizzy.

"Blair!" I shrieked again. "Stop! I'm going to be sick!"

He stopped immediately and plopped us down onto the couch in the family room. His eyes blazed as he stared into mine. I looked around surreptitiously to see if anyone was around. I wasn't worried about Bethany; she was used to us being together, but his brother and sister-in-law were another story.

"Who are you looking for?" Blair asked, grinning.

"Possible witnesses," I replied, smirking up into his handsome face.

"Were you concerned that I might commit a crime?" Blair laughed softly as his lips moved to my neck.

"No, but I didn't know how your brother might react," I admitted. "Or if Holly would think it inappropriate for us to be *affectionate* in front of Leila."

"Ben will definitely give us grief," Blair admitted, "but I don't think Holly will care. Leila might climb on top of us though."

"Well, in that case..." I broke off, pulling myself up to his face and locking my lips to his. Even after the past few weeks together, I still felt overwhelmed with joy when we were together. His hand slid down my spine, drawing me even closer to him. I shivered with pleasure, but Blair lifted my face from his.

I stuck out my lip in a pout. "Hey," I complained, "I wasn't finished yet!" I tried to move back to his face, but he held me to his chest. "Really, Blair, I'm fine."

"Why does it never occur to you that maybe I'm not fine?" he asked, smirking down at me.

"Oh..." I blushed.

Just then Leila ran into the family room, followed closely by her parents. As Blair had predicted, she immediately climbed up onto the couch with us.

"Leily want to 'nuggle too!" she whined, struggling to climb on top of us.

Blair reached down, pulling her on top of him, closely snuggled next to me. Her bright hazel eyes sparkled with excitement.

Apollo's Lights

"Leila?" I grinned at her. "Do you know what my friends and I call it when three people hug?"

"What, Kaykay?"

"A three-way hug!" I wrapped my arms around her and Blair and squeezed them tight.

Leila giggled, sat up, and began bouncing on top of us, clapping her chubby little hands. Ben and Holly laughed as Blair grimaced. "Leila, Uncle Blair's stomach is going to burst if you keep that up!"

"You big wimp!" Ben joked as he scooped Leila up into his arms. "Together they probably weigh fifty pounds!"

"Hey!" I complained.

"Stop teasing them, Benjamin." Bethany had walked in from the kitchen. "Leila, come see Nana for a while. Let's go out and play in the backyard. It's a beautiful day." Leila struggled out of Ben's arms and ran to her grandmother.

"Let me get your jacket, Leila," Holly called as she headed for their room. The Davis' large house had bedrooms for each of their children and two extra for guests. One of the guestrooms was mine now, since it was assumed that I would be staying with them a lot.

Around two, Blair and I headed to the airport to pick up his sister and brother-in-law. DFW airport was a winding puzzle of roads, five terminal buildings, and what always seemed like a million parking lots. Coming from Denver, Briana and Jonah were flying Frontier Airlines, which landed at terminal E. We parked as close as we could, racing toward the terminal. Looking at the arrival board, we searched for their baggage claim area. Their plane was miraculously on time, so we only had ten minutes to wait.

As the board announced their arrival, Blair got up and started gazing through the glass wall toward their gate. It seemed to take forever for the people to deplane, but as soon as I saw her,

I knew Briana. She stood around five feet, five inches tall with long golden-blonde hair, and as she got closer to the glass wall, I could see her hazel eyes sparkle with excitement as she waved to Blair. Briana wore comfortable jeans and a hoodie; she kind of bounced as she walked, full of excitement.

Jonah walked next to her with a backpack on his back and his hand in hers. They were still newlyweds, only having been married for a little over a year. Jonah's tall, muscular stature exuded confidence, but not in an arrogant way, in an oddly gentle way. His hazel eyes shone with obvious affection for Briana, and that love, or sense of well-being, seemed to flow out of him. Jonah's complexion was darker, almost olive, and his dark russet hair made his hazel eyes look brighter than normal.

Briana came through the security door first and ran into her brother's arms. "I'm so glad to see you, Blair!" she exclaimed. Blair reached around his sister and shook Jonah's hand.

"I'm glad to see you too," Blair said, loosening himself from her hug. "This is Makayla." He pulled me closer to him and wrapped his arm around me.

"I'm so glad to meet you, Makayla," Briana said sweetly, smiling at her brother's glowing face. "I don't believe I have ever seen Blair so happy!" My face grew hot, but I smiled.

"You're embarrassing her, Briana," Jonah chastised lightly. He reached to shake my hand. "Welcome to the family, Makayla." I took his hand and smiled up at him.

"It's great to meet you too," I said shyly.

On the drive home to Enterprise, Blair and Briana talked nonstop, catching up on each other's lives since their last visit over the summer. Briana was in graduate school at the University of Denver, getting her master's degree in social work. Jonah, three years older than she, had completed his MBA and was working for the Federal Reserve in Denver.

As we pulled into the Davis' driveway, Bethany came out to greet her daughter and son-in-law. Leila ran out the front door, her mother close on her heels.

"Aunt Brinana," she hollered, running into Briana's arms.

"How's my little pumpkin?" Briana cooed, swinging Leila around in a circle. "Have you been a good girl?"

"I been a berry dood dirl!" Leila shrieked. "Did do bring me tomting?"

"Leila!" her mother chastised. "That's not very nice. We've talked about that, remember?"

Leila pouted and buried her face in Briana's shoulder. "Torry, Aunt Brinana," she whimpered.

"That's all right, sweetheart." Briana rubbed Leila's back to comfort her. "Don't be upset or Aunt Briana will be sad."

Leila lifted her head and rubbed her eyes with her little fists. Briana made a silly frowning face at her, and Leila giggled. "That's better! Now let's all get inside. Will you help me unpack, Leila? Who knows, we might find something for you in my suitcase!"

Leila nodded her head vigorously, squirmed out of Briana's arms, and dragged her toward the house. Everyone laughed, except Holly; she sighed. "That child is going to be the most spoiled child in the state!"

Bethany put her arm around Holly. "Don't worry; there's a big difference between loving a child and spoiling one. Leila is just well loved!" Holly shook her head but looked slightly mollified.

Blake got home from his office around five, and the house exploded again with hugs and greetings. Leila threw her arms around her grandfather's legs, almost tripping him. He scooped her up and held her high above his head; Leila squealed with delight. Blake seemed to relish having his entire family together; his face was proud and full of love. The kind of chaos that reigned within the Davis house with everyone home was new to me. As an only child of a single parent, it was a little overwhelming.

Blair found me sitting in his father's study, my knees pulled up with my arms wrapped tightly around them. I was so engrossed in the fire blazing in the fireplace that I didn't hear or feel his approach. It wasn't until I felt his hand wipe the tears from my cheek that I even realized I was crying. Kneeling down in front of me, Blair searched my face and mind.

"Makayla, honey," he asked gently, "what's wrong? Why are you unhappy?"

"I don't really know," I admitted truthfully. My mind whirled with the faces of Blair's big, loving family, and I couldn't keep myself from thinking about what my life might have been like if my father had lived. Would my mother have been surrounded by several children, their spouses, and her grandchildren someday? When my father walked through the door, would his face have glowed like Blake's?

The tears flowed slowly down my face as these images broke my heart. Emptiness, loneliness, and renewed grief swelled inside of me. Blair reached for me, and I fell into his embrace. He kissed my forehead and wiped my tears.

I'm sorry, Blair. I don't know what came over me.

You have nothing to be sorry for. Do you want me to take you home now?

I nodded but hesitated to wipe my face fully and try to erase the sadness from within me. "I don't need to walk through a room of clairvoyants looking and feeling like this!" I smiled weakly and moved to the mirror on the wall to check my face. I moaned. "Why does my nose have to get so red when I cry? It's so embarrassing!"

Blair came up behind me and wrapped his arms around me. He laughed and kissed the back of my neck, making me jump and giggle. "I'll just tell Mom I'm taking you home, and then we can slip out the back door, okay?"

"Okay." I sighed as Blair walked out of the study. How did I get so lucky?

REVELATION

Thanksgiving weekend flew by in a whirl of food, family, and clamor. Mom dove into the fray headfirst, loving every minute of the time we spent with Blair's family. She loved Leila and spent most of her time over the weekend on the floor with her, building houses out of blocks or coloring princesses in Disney coloring books. Seeing her so carefree reminded me of my childhood; what a remarkable job my mother had done raising me on her own.

By Sunday evening, all of Blair's siblings had gone home, and the Davis house settled into a blissful quiet. As much as they had enjoyed the time with their entire family, Blake and Bethany seemed exhausted and in some serious need of quiet time.

Unlike her normal business trips, my mother left on Sunday to be in Los Angeles first thing Monday morning. As was the accepted procedure, I moved into my room at Blair's house. That night Blair helped me with my infinitely painful pre-calculus work. The kitchen table was spread with our books, notebooks, and homework assignments, although he had managed to finish his a while ago. I groaned and lay my head on the table.

"Really, Blair," I whined, "I can't think anymore. My brain is mush!"

Apollo's Lights

He rubbed my shoulders sympathetically. "I know you're tired, Short Stuff, but we have a test on Tuesday. We've got to keep at it."

"I can't! I'll just take a B or even a C if I have to. I'm too tired."

"Okay. Let's just stop for tonight and pick it up tomorrow."

"Okay," I said, sleepily raising my head and rubbing it; it ached and felt heavy.

Bethany walked in the kitchen. "What's wrong, Makayla?" she asked, coming over and putting her hand on my forehead. "Are you sick?"

"No, I'm just tired…I think," I replied wearily. "I think I better get to bed."

Blair walked me upstairs, stopping in front of the bedroom door and looking down at me, his hands gently on my shoulders.

Are you sure you're okay?

I'm just tired… I felt a twinge of pain and stopped the communication.

"Honey," Blair said, looking down at me warily and pulling me into his arms, "what's wrong?"

"It hurts my head to communicate clairvoyantly." I rubbed my hand over my forehead.

"Maybe you were just overwhelmed this weekend being around so many clairvoyants," he replied logically. "Get a good night's sleep, okay?" He smiled down at me.

"Okay," I replied softly.

"Let me know if you need me. Love you!"

"Me too." I stood on my tiptoes to kiss him goodnight.

I woke sometime in the night, shaky from a dream. Unlike other nights when I woke from a bad dream, I couldn't remember any of it. I only knew that I felt ill at ease. Staring at the ceiling, I tried to recall any part of it, but I couldn't. For some reason, not being able to remember the dream made it all the more frightening to me.

The clock on my bedside table read two in the morning—way too early to wake Blair. And what would I say? *I had a bad dream, but I can't remember it.* That sounded pretty bizarre and not worth disturbing his night's sleep. I tossed and turned and finally found a comfortable recess between my pillows.

My father's face was clearer, but I only saw the back of the other man's head. The voices were getting more strident with each word. My heart pounded in my chest. "This has gone far enough," *my father's calm voice spoke.* "It stops here." *The shifting dark figures wore black and moved sinuously away from the wall.* "I don't think so, my friend," *the other man's cold, majestic voice retorted. The man spoke to his lieutenant,* "Lorcan…" *and then to my father,* "The Dumaris cannot be stopped." *I shivered. The mist cleared again, and the face of the man called Lorcan looked back to his minions. The black clad men crept toward my father.* "You'll never get away with this!" *His slow, agonized moans pierced the night.*

Screaming…flailing…thrashing…struggling. Someone called my name. I had to get away. Someone grabbed me. *Who's screaming?* The scream was mine.

"Makayla!" Blair's voice broke through the fog.

Finally released from the twisted bedding, my eyes flew open. Blair tried to restrain me, but in my frightened half-sleep, I continued to struggle.

"It's me, Makayla; it's Blair!" My eyes tried to focus on him, but I was shaking too violently. His arms enveloped me while softer hands gently rubbed my back.

"Makayla." Blake's voice was clear and strong. "Focus on your breathing; you're hyperventilating." I tried to obey him, but I couldn't slow down. My heart pounded in my chest, and my head grew dizzy. I was falling…falling…

"Dad!" Blair called anxiously as my back arched toward the bed.

Two strong hands grabbed my head and held me still; soothing warmth radiated from them and traveled through me. My eyes were still unfocused, but my heart and breathing rates began to drop toward normal rhythms. As the shaking slowed, I could focus my eyes and found Blair's frightened face.

"Blair…" I choked, my voice raspy. Blake released my face and allowed his son to pull me into his arms. Someone put a cool cloth on the back of my neck. I shivered; my body was clammy, my top drenched. Bethany brought a towel and wrapped it over my back. No one spoke as Blair held me, and my body relaxed.

"Makayla," Blair whispered, "was it the same nightmare?"

I buried my face in his chest; recalling the nightmare was too painful. The lieutenant had turned. I had seen his malignant face, grinning evilly at my father's fate. My body began to shake again as the memories penetrated me. I tried to block them but could not. The men dressed in black followed the unspoken directions of their leader, attacking my father with unseen negativity, strong enough to bring him to his knees. And there had been more. The leader had said something new this time. *The Dumaris cannot be stopped.*

Someone gasped. Blair stopped rocking me. I raised my head. Bethany's face was tortured, her hand raised to her mouth in shock. Blake, who looked like he had been pacing, was frozen in horror, looking down at me in Blair's arms. Their loving faces, now sculpted in anguish, scared me. I shivered as fear slithered down my spine. I burrowed further into Blair's chest as my tears began to fall again.

"Makayla," Blake whispered hoarsely, "please show me your dream."

I shook my head slowly, afraid to relive the nightmare again. How many times would I have to be assaulted by the abhorrent images? It was too much to ask, too much to handle. My breaths came in jagged, short bursts; pain stabbed my chest.

I can't do it. Please don't ask me to...

"Makayla, I know it's hard, but—" Blake began, but Blair cut him off.

"Dad! Please," he begged angrily, tightening his arms around me protectively. "She can't take any more tonight. Look at her!"

"Blair, you don't understand how important this may be," Blake answered sharply. "I must see what she is seeing!"

I felt Blair's body tense as if for a fight. Raising my hand to his lips, I stopped his bitter retort before it was spoken. He kissed my hand and began rocking me again but did not continue arguing. The tension was electric, making it difficult for me to compose myself. I wanted to answer Blake. I, more than anyone, knew it must be important, but I couldn't make myself face it again. *Not now...not tonight...*

"Blake," Bethany said softly, "it can wait until tomorrow." I heard Blake inhale sharply, but Bethany moved to his side and placed her hand on his face. "Not tonight, honey. Blair, I'll stay with Makayla tonight. You can go back to bed."

No! my thoughts shrieked. My arms tightened around Blair's neck as if my life depended on his presence, and at the moment, it felt like it did. *Blair, please don't leave me!* A strangled sob tore through my chest.

Bethany stroked my head softly. *Okay, sweetheart, Blair will stay with you.* "Let's go back to bed, Blake. Call me if you need me, Blair." I felt her kiss my head and heard their footsteps leaving the room.

It occurred to me somewhere in the deep recesses of my mind that only in a clairvoyant home would parents leave their son with his girlfriend in her bedroom, but I was grateful for their ability to see the necessity. This had nothing to do with physical or sexual attraction; I needed Blair to shore up my eroding soul—something only he could do for me. He lay down gently on the bed and pulled me close to his side, encircling me in the safety of his arms, where I slept dreamlessly for the rest of the night.

Early in the morning, I felt Blair awaken as his thoughts began sifting through last night's events. My body was nestled tightly against his, and my muscles felt stiff and achy. I stretched and opened my eyes. Blair tried to smile, but worry was carved too deeply into his face. I wanted to reassure him that I was okay, but I couldn't find the words. Undoubtedly, he wouldn't have believed me anyway.

When I began to get out of bed, Blair stopped me. "Makayla," he said softly, "are you going to be able to handle school today?"

Sometime during the night, I had made my decision. "Sure," I answered casually. "There's no reason why I shouldn't go to school." I got out of bed and headed toward the door.

"We need to talk about it," Blair said softly, obviously not wanting to upset me.

"There's nothing to talk about. I'm going to take a shower," I replied evenly as I left the room. Behind me, I heard Blair sigh.

Today was going to be a good day—a day free of pain and anxiety. I was determined to make it so; I would bury the nightmare in the depths of my mind and never revisit it. I couldn't adequately express the overwhelming pain that bored through me every time I had to relive it. Never again, I told myself; how could I live happily having to witness my dad's murder on a regular basis?

I knew that my decision would frustrate Blair, maybe even anger him, but it was my choice, my dream, my horror. It wasn't anyone else's problem; it was mine.

I may have made the decision, but it didn't mean that it was going to be easy. In reality, I knew that escaping the dream was going to be nearly impossible. It would take all my strength to push my newest revelation deep enough for it to be lost—maybe impossible. Maybe my infamous tenacity would finally be useful.

When I got downstairs, I could hear Blake and Bethany's soft voices in the kitchen. They would be waiting to talk to me, wanting the information I refused to share last night. I took a deep breath and steeled myself against the coming battle.

"Good morning," I chimed, entering the kitchen.

Blair's parents shared a quick glance at each other. "Good morning, Makayla," Bethany said warily. "How are you feeling this morning?"

"Great, couldn't be better." I wondered how long I could stall them with this charade, knowing that my attempts would probably be futile.

"That's good," Blake replied uneasily. I concentrated on blocking every thought in my head.

Blair entered the kitchen looking as uneasy as his parents. He shook his head slightly in response to his father's unspoken thought. Blake wanted to know if I had spoken to Blair about the dream.

I poured myself a glass of orange juice and reached for a cereal bowl. No one spoke; the kitchen was eerily quiet. I went to the pantry and found the Cheerios. "Do you want some, Blair?" I asked brightly, holding up the box.

"Yeah, thanks." Blair's response was already tinged with frustration. The ride to school was going to be difficult, to say the least. I handed him a bowl and went to the refrigerator for the milk. Blair sat down with his parents as I handed him the milk.

"Makayla," Blake began gently, "we really need to talk about what happened last night." His voice was apprehensive.

"Oh, excuse me. I forgot something upstairs," I responded, totally ignoring his statement. "I'll be ready for school in a minute, Blair."

As I left the kitchen, a little too quickly, Blair's exasperated voice called after me, "Makayla…" I ignored him and ran up the stairs. At the top of the staircase, I stopped, grabbing the banister for support, and took in a deep breath. If I was honest with myself, I was terrified, but there was no way I was going to succumb; I had to do this on my own. I had to find a way to be happy again.

Fifteen minutes later, Blair and I headed to school. In my attempt to avoid the family, I'd never eaten breakfast; my stomach rumbled. Blair handed me a granola bar without a word.

"Thanks," I said, taking it gratefully.

"You're welcome," he replied stiffly. Taking in a deep breath, Blair brought up the subject again. "You do realize, don't you, that you can't just ignore this? It won't simply vanish by some miracle of 'non-communication'." I could hear his aggravation turning into anger now.

"Everything will be fine, Blair. Don't worry," I said between bites of my granola bar, refusing to look into his face.

"Makayla." The strain in his voice was beginning to break through. "I know it's frightening, but not dealing with it will end up making it worse for you. Don't you understand? This dream will not stop recurring simply because you won't discuss it." His argument sounded reasonable, but I refused to consider it.

When I didn't respond, Blair's anger finally broke through. "You are being so freaking stubborn, Makayla!" he bellowed. I flinched inwardly but tried to keep my face composed. Still, I refused to answer him; he sighed.

Makayla, honey, please talk to me. It only took a second for him to realize that I was blocking him. "Great! So now we're going to play games, is that it?" Blair's angry words bore into me.

I could feel the tears beginning to well up in my eyes. Turning my face to the window, I concentrated on controlling them. I wasn't sure whether I was upset because Blair was yelling at me or because I was really hurting him—both probably. It went against my nature to cause conflict or pain.

"Maybe I should stay at my house tonight," I whispered through tight lips.

Blair drew in a deep breath, trying to rein in his anger. "I'm sorry, Makayla. Please don't stay over there alone. I won't bring it up again until you're ready to talk about it." He reached over and took my hand. "Okay?"

I nodded. Blair pulled into the school parking lot and into his parking space. I turned to open my door quickly, but he stopped me. Feeling the tears beginning to fall, I refused to look at him. He reached over and turned my face to his.

"I love you, Makayla." Blair's voice was soft and gentle. "Please don't shut me out." His supplication was shaky with emotion.

The frigid disposition I was so desperately trying to maintain melted away. I touched his cheek softly and leaned over to kiss him. "I love you too. This doesn't change that."

INESCAPABLE

Blair took my hand as we walked into the school. I looked up at him, but he kept his eyes forward. I knew that he was still annoyed with me but that he would keep his promise and not mention the nightmare. I began to wonder if my decision would create an irreversible chasm between us. Would it be worth losing the man I loved? Was my inability to face this horrific vision from the past going to destroy my future as well?

"Kayla!" I turned to see Amy and Rob coming up behind us. "How was your Thanksgiving?" Amy asked brightly.

"It was great. How about yours?" I asked, hoping that my despair hadn't broken through my voice.

"It was crazy. Dad's whole family came from all over." Amy smiled. "There were thirty people crammed into our house for dinner!"

"Wow, and I thought we had a lot of people at Blair's house with only ten." I smiled awkwardly at Blair, who returned it with a tight grin. Amy registered the tension immediately.

"Oh well," she said uncomfortably. "I guess we'll see you later." She looked at me, but I didn't meet her worried gaze.

We parted company to go to our respective math classes. Outside the door, I paused. Blair looked down at me, his face still mask-like. Moving off to the side of the door to allow the other students to pass us, I pulled Blair toward me.

"I'm sorry, Blair," I said sheepishly. "Please don't be mad at me because I don't think I can deal with that on top of everything else." As usual, my eyes began brimming with tears.

"Makayla," he responded gently, "I'm not angry with you." He brushed the lone tear from my eye, pulling me into his arms. "I'm just frustrated because you won't let us help you through this."

"I don't really know how to explain this, Blair," I began, keeping my eyes on the floor. "Just give me some time to sort through my tangled thoughts and then…maybe…I'll be able to." My voice broke.

Blair kissed the top of my head. "Take as long as you need, honey," he said softly. "Just don't forget that we're here to help you, okay?" I smiled up at him and nodded. He gave me a little squeeze and then led us into class.

With the distraction of schoolwork and friends, I was able to push last night's terror to the back of my mind. I worked hard to reassure Amy that I was fine by acting as normally as possible. By lunch, her thoughts were relaxed and seemingly unworried about Blair and me.

"Is anyone going anywhere special for Christmas this year?" Jesse asked at the lunch table. Rob barely stopped eating long enough to shake his head.

"No, Mom and I don't usually travel over the holidays since she travels so much for her job," I commented. "It's more of a vacation for her to stay home."

"That makes sense," Jesse answered, knocking Rick's hand away from her potato chips. "How about you, Amy? Blair?"

Amy replied excitedly, "Actually, my parents are taking us to Disney World for the Christmas break. I'm really excited since I've never been there." She looked at us a little embarrassed. "Is that weird? I'm kind of old to want to go to Disney World, aren't I?'

"Of course not, Amy," I asserted. Jesse enthusiastically nodded in agreement. "I think it's great that your family is taking a vacation together before you graduate and go to college." I smiled at her and added conspiratorially, "Bring me back something, okay?"

Jesse turned to Blair. "How about your family, Blair?" She picked up her sandwich and took a bite, waiting for his answer.

Blair's face was serene, but I couldn't help but notice the slight tightening of his eyes. "Well, I'm not actually sure," he said offhandedly. "My parents mentioned going to the Florida Gulf coast, but we don't have any firm plans."

Florida Gulf coast? Blair hadn't mentioned anything to me about his family going away at Christmas. I turned to look at him, but he picked up his hamburger and began eating. His thoughts were not helpful, either.

Jesse began telling us about her family's plans to go to the Bahamas for the Christmas break, including with glee that Rick was going with them. I tried to concentrate on her words, but my attention was drawn back to what Blair had said. He had never told me where the Ileesia was located in Florida, but I didn't need my gift to guess that it was located on the Gulf coast.

"Kayla!" Jesse's voice broke into my reverie. "Are you listening to me?"

"I'm sorry, Jesse. My mind just wandered for a second. Go on, I really do want to hear about your plans."

On our way to his car, Blair talked about the pre-cal test the next day, pointing out all the equations we needed to study that evening. He opened the car door for me and waited for me to get in. Once he got into the driver's seat, I looked at him, curiosity finally getting the better of me.

"Blair," I asked, casually, I hoped, "Why didn't you tell me that you were going to Florida for Christmas?"

"It's not definite." He started the car and put it in reverse. "Dad just mentioned it this morning at breakfast."

"Oh," I answered blandly. My thoughts drifted to the Ileesia, and Blair heard them. He sighed heavily.

"Makayla," Blair began, "I didn't want to upset you after this morning. I was going to tell you if the plans got firmer." I nodded, looking out the front windshield. "Could we just not talk about it right now? It's been a long day." He reached and took my hand. Blair sighed. "Hey, has anyone told you that I love you?" He grinned impishly. I giggled and nodded my head.

Opening the front door to the house, Blair stood back and let me enter first. I put my backpack at the foot of the stairs and headed for the family room. Before I took more than three steps, Blair swept me up from behind and cradled me in his arms.

How about some time just for us? he mused, his eyes alight with excitement.

His mood was infectious. *What did you have in mind?*

I tightened my arms around him, nuzzling my lips into his neck. Blair laughed and turned toward me, pressing his lips against mine. I laced my fingers into his hair, pulling myself closer to him. He climbed the stairs two at a time, kicking the door of my bedroom open.

Lowering us onto the bed, Blair moved his lips to my neck, making me giggle as usual. He chuckled and moved his mouth down my shoulder, pushing my blouse aside to kiss my skin. I shivered and reached down to bring his lips back to mine. Blair pushed back to look into my eyes. He took a deep breath.

"Do you have any idea how much I love you, Makayla?" he asked, his voice rich and beautiful. I blushed as he caressed my face. "Every day my love for you grows stronger and deeper." Blair's voice rang with emotion.

I couldn't speak; the words of the English language were not adequate to explain the effect his avowal had on me. My soul sang for joy; my mind danced with images of love and exultation.

You are the source of my hope and dreams—my everything. My heart wanted to burst for joy; my body shivered. Taking his face in my hands, I returned his lips to mine and reveled in our passion.

Blair rolled on top of me, his lips moving slowly down my neck to my chest. My heart thudded as he kissed me just below my collarbone. I gasped, and he rolled over, pulling me onto his chest, his breathing as irregular as mine. As I lay safely in his arms, my eyes got heavy and closed, the stress of the previous night finally releasing me from its grasp. I slept in blissful relief.

When I awoke, Blair wasn't next to me. I stretched and yawned, feeling more rested than I had all day. The clock on the bedside table read six o'clock; I'd slept for three hours. Knowing that Blair's parents were probably home by now and that I should be helping Bethany in the kitchen, I hurried down the stairs.

Bethany was standing at the stove, with Blair and his dad seated at the table. A delicious aroma of garlic and rosemary wafted in the air. They looked up when I entered the room.

"Sorry, Bethany," I apologized. "I didn't realize that I'd slept for so long."

"That's okay, sweetie," she said gently. "You needed to catch up on some sleep."

I moved to stand behind Blair's chair and wrapped my arms around his neck. He picked up my hand and kissed it.

"Is there anything I can do to help now?" I asked.

"Sure," Bethany answered. "Why don't you start making the salad? Blair, please set the table."

Moving to the refrigerator, I took out the lettuce, spinach, cucumber, carrots, and radishes, piling them into my arms and depositing them on the counter. Blair was taking the plates out of the cabinet when Blake finally spoke.

"How was your day, Makayla?" he asked kindly.

"It was fine. How was yours?" I asked, smiling at him. I was feeling a little guilty about my behavior that morning and hoped that he would have forgiven me. Deep down, I knew that Blake was trying to fulfill his unofficial duty as my father figure; he wanted to help, somehow, to relieve my pain.

"Busy," he said, smiling back at me. I was forgiven. I began tearing the lettuce and spinach leaves for the salad, putting them into Bethany's favorite teak salad bowl.

"Blake, will you please check the roast in the oven with the meat thermometer? I can't stop stirring the risotto right now," Bethany asked, stirring her delicate side dish conscientiously.

Blake dutifully donned oven mitts and opened the oven door. "What temperature is it supposed to be? I can never remember."

"About one hundred fifty is perfect."

"It's ready then. Do you want me to take it out or just turn off the oven?"

Bethany rolled her eyes at him. "How many times do I have to tell you that leaving it in the oven, even if it is off, will continue to cook the meat?"

Blake laughed, taking the roasting pan out gingerly so as to not spill the juices. "I guess at least one more time!" He winked at me and shook his head playfully.

I was relieved that the conversation had not turned to my dream, but I wondered how long that would last. Why did I react so stubbornly this morning anyway? They all had insisted that sharing the information would help ease the pain it caused me, and yet, besides being horrific, the dream felt somehow personal. It was like the pain was meant only for me—that my dad was sending me this message.

Throughout dinner, we talked animatedly about our respective days' exploits. Blair shared that our friends were talking about Christmas travel plans, but Blake didn't say anything about Florida. After dinner, Blair and I loaded the dishwasher and cleaned up the kitchen while his parents retired to the family room for coffee.

When we were finished, Blair said, "Well, Short Stuff, we better get cracking on that pre-cal test." I groaned, and he feigned a stern disposition. "Makayla…"

"I know, I know! I hate math—have I ever told you that?" I crossed my arms across my chest and scowled.

"One or two… hundred times!" Blair laughed, picking me up and swinging me around in a circle.

We retrieved our backpacks and spread everything out on the kitchen table, as was usual for these ordeals. It wouldn't be long before my head was laying on the table and the whining and pouting would begin. Tonight, however, it didn't turn out that way; this time I actually started to understand the study guide problems. I was ecstatic; understanding mathematical equations was so rare for me. It was an odd sort of high. Blair was happy that I was catching on, thinking I would be in a better mood after tomorrow's test than was usual. I was just happy that we wouldn't have to spend the whole freaking evening studying for it; it was only nine thirty!

"Finished!" I shouted after completing the study guide.

Blair laughed as I slammed my math book shut and shoved it into my bag. "You'd think you'd just run a marathon or something."

"Hey! Math is like running a marathon for those of us who are math challenged," I complained. "Unlike you smartie pants math nerds!" I stuck my tongue out at him, turned with my nose in the air, and started to strut away from him.

"You asked for it!" he bellowed, pushing his chair away from the table.

I shrieked and ran toward the kitchen door, knowing that it was futile. Blair caught me, threw me over his shoulder, and marched proudly into the family room to parade his quarry.

Bethany was reading in the easy chair but was already looking up when we entered. We were making quite a racket. She laughed at Blair swaggering around the room with me over his shoulder while I screamed and pounded on his back.

"Blair," she chided. "For heaven's sake, put her down before you hurt her."

So swiftly that I didn't feel it coming, Blair swung me forward into his cradling arms. I was breathless and somewhat embarrassed; he had never acted quite like this in front of his parents before. When I finally stopped feeling dizzy, I looked up to see Blake standing in the doorway of his study, with his reading glasses in his hand, grinning at us.

"Put her down, Blair," his father commanded. "You're embarrassing the poor girl." Blair stood me up on my feet and held on until I was steady from all the swaying. Blake laughed, shaking his head, and walked back into his study.

"Is he always this big of a brat?" Bethany asked me, smirking.

"Not always," I replied, and then with a evil grin toward Blair, I added, "Sometimes he's worse."

"Hey!" Blair complained. "You women need to stop ganging up on me."

Bethany and I laughed. I hugged Blair around his waist and smiled up at him. "Love you!" I cooed.

"Uh-huh," he grumbled, rolling his eyes at me. "Do you want to watch a movie or something before bed?"

"Believe it or not, I'm actually a little tired," I answered. "I think I'll just get ready to go to bed, okay?"

"Sure, honey." Blair leaned down and kissed the top of my head. "Call me if you need me," he whispered softly. I nodded.

"Goodnight, Bethany. See you in the morning!" I tried to sound as cheery as possible; I knew they were worried about the night ahead and the terrors it might hold for me. She smiled and nodded. "Goodnight, Blake," I yelled as I headed toward the stairs.

"Goodnight, Makayla. Sleep well," he called from his study.

I slept dreamlessly for most of the night, but sometime in the early morning, I had a different dream—or was it a memory?

My dad was standing in what seemed to be a park. At first, I saw him from a great distance, but as the picture zoomed in, I saw that he was pushing a swing. It was a baby swing, the kind with a molded seat and a crossbar to secure the baby. A little girl sat in the swing, giggling as my dad pushed the swing to and fro. Was it possible? Could it be me?

Dad stopped the swing and removed the child. He held her—me—close to him and kissed my cheek. I threw my arms around his neck, still giggling with glee.

"Daddy loves you, Kayla. Don't ever forget that," my dad said soothingly into my ear.

The baby—I—yawned, and Dad moved me up onto his shoulder and patted my back. As if he knew I would be watching this scene, he looked up and spoke right to me. "Tell them, Makayla. Don't be afraid…" His voice faded along with the vision.

As I opened my eyes, I lifted my hand to wipe the tears from my face. The message was clear—it was time to face the nightmare.

COMMUNICATING

I lay in bed until five thirty, the earliest time I could deem acceptable to wake Blair. I tiptoed down the hall, knocked gently on his door, and opened it. Blair was sleeping soundly and didn't hear my entrance, so I called softly to him.

"Blair," I whispered, walking closer to his bed. He started, as if I had yelled his name, and sat bolt upright.

"Makayla?" His voice was alarmed as he swung his legs over the edge of the bed and reached for me. "Are you all right?"

Nodding, I climbed onto his bed and hugged him around his neck. "I had another dream." His arms tightened around me, assuming that it had also been a nightmare. "It wasn't a nightmare this time," I assured him, pulling away so he could see my face.

"What did you dream?"

Suddenly I felt a little foolish. How was I going to explain this without sounding like I'd lost my mind? My hesitation made Blair nervous. "This might sound a little bizarre, Blair. I've never had a dream…or vision…or memory like this before. I don't even know what it was."

"Just tell me what you saw and don't worry about it making sense," Blair reassured me. "You're a new clairvoyant; sometimes we have strange dreams in the first few months, especially if we have experienced traumatic events in our lives or possess certain gifts. Tell me what you saw."

"I saw my father in a park…" I began telling the dream, trying to describe every aspect of it. The pictures in my mind were so clear: the trees and bushes in full greenery, the playground equipment, the baby swing, my dad…me. When I finished, I looked into Blair's eyes to see if he thought I was nuts. He hugged me and kissed my forehead.

"Makayla," he said tenderly, smiling down at me, "I believe that your father was communicating with you." I stared up at him, astonished. "It's not common but also not unheard of in our world. It's sort of a mix of a memory and a message combined."

I thought about that for a minute. "So you think it was real?"

"Yes, I do," Blair stated in a matter-of-fact manner. "I think he wants you to share your nightmare for several reasons. First of all, I'm sure that he wants you to be relieved of the pain and stress that it awakens in you, as we all do." He looked at me sternly, reminding me of his parents' and his failed attempts at just that. I grimaced and bit my lip guiltily. "Also, if there is information about his death that can bring the perpetrator to justice, I believe that his soul awaits that resolution." When I looked perplexed, he added, "Your dad's soul will not be at rest until justice is served."

I stared at him, wide-eyed. The thought that my dad had been waiting all these years for me to be old enough and gifted enough to pass on this information was overwhelming. Shame flooded my face, and my eyes blurred with moisture. Blair tightened his arms around me.

There's nothing to be ashamed of, Makayla. Sometimes it takes a while for us to understand what we are supposed to do with our gifts.

I'm so obstinate, Blair! I could have—might have—blown this whole thing. My father's soul…

Tears glided silently down my cheeks as Blair held me to his chest. He stroked my face, soothing me. One thing was certain: I needed to tell Blake and Bethany everything I could about the nightmare, and I needed to do it immediately. I wiped my eyes fiercely and looked at the clock on Blair's nightstand; it was six o'clock.

"Is it too early to talk to your parents?"

"No, honey." Blair laughed. "They've been waiting for two nights for you to finally agree to tell them!" I lowered my head, ashamed. Blair lifted my chin and kissed me gently. "I'll go wake them," he said, standing up.

Suddenly I was nervous. "Blair," I blurted out. He stopped and turned toward me. "Are they,"—I swallowed—"disappointed in me?" Loving them as I already did, the thought of having disappointed Blake and Bethany in any way was painful. I twisted my fingers absentmindedly in front of me.

No, we are not! I heard a clear thought coming from outside Blair's door.

Blair grinned and opened his door. "Welcome to a clairvoyant home, Makayla!" He rolled his eyes and shook his head playfully. Blake and Bethany stood on the threshold of his door, in their bathrobes, smiling at me. Blake opened his arms, and I rushed into them; Bethany put her arm around me as well.

"Let's go downstairs and have some breakfast while we talk," she suggested brightly. "I'll pop some cinnamon rolls into the oven, and we can talk while they bake."

"When did you make dough, Mom?" Blair asked. "I didn't see you making it yesterday."

Bethany grinned at her youngest son. "Only the Dough Boy and your mother know for sure!" We laughed as she and Blake headed downstairs to the kitchen; Blair and I followed behind them.

Everyone sat around the kitchen table; the aroma of cinnamon and coffee filled the air. I looked at the glass of orange juice

I was holding in between my hands, wondering where to begin. This morning's dream seemed to be the place to start, since it was that dream that convinced me to talk about it at all.

"This morning," I began, "I had a dream, or vision, about my dad and me when I was a little girl." I looked up to see Blake's expression, but he just smiled at me gently and nodded his encouragement. "We were in a park, and at first it was like I was watching a movie—Dad was pushing me in a baby swing, and I was giggling, as usual." Everyone laughed. "When he took me out of the swing, he held me close to him and whispered, 'Daddy loves you, Kayla. Don't ever forget that.'"

I paused, gathering courage for the last part of the dream. Blair reached over and took my hand. "At that point, the picture changed. It was no longer like watching a movie but as if I were standing a little ways from them. Dad looked at me, the me standing apart from him, and said, 'Tell them, Makayla. Don't be afraid...' and then the picture faded and I woke up."

Blake's and Bethany's eyes glistened with tears, but not tears of sadness, tears of joy. Blake looked down for a moment and cleared his throat. "Well, I knew that Sean was a powerful clairvoyant, but I didn't know he was that strong," he asserted. "It's only the most powerful among us who can still communicate after we have passed on."

"How do you feel about your dream, Makayla?" Bethany asked, looking directly into my eyes.

"At first, I thought I was going crazy," I admitted. "But after Blair explained that this form of communication was possible, I..." A lump rose in my throat, but I pushed it away. "Now I think I understand that Dad wants me to share the information in my nightmare so that he can rest." I looked over at Blair, and he winked at me.

"There's only one thing I'm kind of worried about," I admitted.

Blake leaned forward, resting his elbows on the table. "What's that, Makayla?"

"It's really painful to think about the nightmare; I'm not sure I can talk about it." I grimaced sheepishly. "I'm afraid to talk about it," I confessed, looking down at the table.

Out of the corner of my eye, I saw Blair look over at his father. I raised my eyes in time to see Blake nodding at him. My forehead furrowed in confusion as I looked at Blair for an explanation.

Blair began stroking my face to reassure me. "Makayla, Dad has gifts beyond simple clairvoyance, as you do." He smiled at me and turned his eyes to his father; I looked at Blake.

"You won't have to repeat the dream verbally or even relive it fully in your mind, Makayla," Blake explained. "If you'll allow it, I can pull the dream from your memory without much effort on your part." He stopped to gauge my reaction.

At first I didn't understand, but then I remembered something Blake had said the night of my last nightmare. When I didn't want to talk about it, he had asked me to show him my dream—not tell him, *show* him.

"How?" I asked quietly.

"We will sit quietly together until you are relaxed and comfortable; then I will place my hands on your head. You will fall into a shallow, painless trance, and I will be able to find your dream in your subconscious and see it." Again he paused, waiting for my reaction. It didn't sound too terrible to me; in fact, it sounded pretty painless.

Bethany broke into the silence. "There is something you need to understand, sweetie." I turned my attention to her as she continued. "As Blake is searching for your dream, he will also see *all* the other things in your subconscious." She enunciated every word, emphasizing *all*.

My face grew hot as comprehension dawned within me. I stared at Blair; he was smiling serenely, but he knew what I was anxious about. Blair's father would see—know—all the emotions and desires of my heart, including my love for his son. As my embarrassment grew, Blair stood and held his hand out to me.

"Excuse us for just a minute," he said politely. His parents nodded their understanding. I got up, took his hand, and allowed him to steer me blindly into the family room.

"Makayla," he said softly, drawing me into his arms, "this is one of those occasions that I've told you about where having clairvoyant parents changes some aspects of your relationship with them." I didn't speak; I was still too mortified. "There's nothing in your subconscious that they don't already know from being in close proximity to me. Do you understand?"

I looked up into his brilliant hazel eyes and nodded slightly. "It's just…I don't know…*weird* to think that your father, and then through him your mother, will know my most intimate thoughts and feelings." I blew out a gust of air. "Are you sure about this, Blair?"

"Honey, I promise that Dad and Mom have heard much more lurid thoughts than yours! They have to deal with all sorts of different thoughts and emotions sitting on the council." He paused, and his voice was gentle. "And you know what? They already know how committed we are to each other; otherwise, they wouldn't have left us together two nights ago, would they?"

"I guess not," I admitted hesitantly. "Do you think that's the best way to tell them?"

"It's the most painless way to tell them," he explained. "When you and Dad are finished, he can relay the information to us without the emotional distress it causes you. I don't want you to suffer any more than is necessary."

Fifteen minutes later, I sat with Blake in his study, our two chairs facing each other. I was nervous and worried that I wouldn't be able to relax enough for this to work, but I had to try. How much bravery did it take to just relax, for heaven's sake!

Blake could feel my tension. "Makayla, just lay your head against the back of the chair. I can help you relax, so don't worry." He hesitated and whispered reassuringly, "Everything we share, besides the dream, will be kept between us forever; I promise." I nodded my understanding. "Close your eyes, honey."

Laying my head back, I closed my eyes and felt Blake's hands grasping the sides of my head gently. Immediately the stress and anxiety left my body, and I drifted off. Images sailed across my mind, dreamlike and peaceful, too rapid for total understanding or an emotional response. Colors washed together, forming pictures reminiscent of the Impressionist era; an image of a father and mother pushing a stroller...a brightly lit Christmas tree...a park in full bloom...a couple in full embrace...an evil face grinning gleefully...a room of dark figures.

When I opened my eyes, Blair was kneeling next to me. He smiled at me. Blake was standing against the wall opposite me, his mind obviously elsewhere. I felt great—relaxed and refreshed. Looking at Blake's troubled face, however, brought some of the harsh reality back to me.

"Blake," I called quietly, "are you okay?"

He turned slowly to face me. "Yes, Makayla. I'm fine. Why don't you two go get some of those cinnamon rolls while they're hot?" He tried to smile, but his eyes were tight, and his forehead creased with worry.

I stood and crossed to him, steeling myself for his judgment. "It's bad, isn't it?" My voice trembled slightly as I spoke, but I didn't turn away from him.

Blair came up behind me and wrapped his arms around me. I hugged his arms but did not take my eyes off his father.

"Yes, Makayla," he admitted quietly. "Your vision corroborates information brought before the Ileesia in recent years, which in itself is good and bad. It's important to know what crimes are being committed by clairvoyants, but it's unfortunate that our fears have been confirmed."

Seeing alarm in my eyes, Blake backtracked quickly. "There is nothing for you to worry about right now, Makayla. Thank you for allowing me to see into your memory." He kissed my forehead and crossed to his desk.

Blair guided me out of the study just as Bethany entered carrying two cups of coffee and cinnamon rolls. Her eyes were wary, but she too smiled at me as we passed. Just before Blair shut the study door, I turned back.

"Blake, did you recognize the man called Lorcan in the dream?" I asked quietly. Blake shook his head sadly. "Will you explain the rest of it to me later? I'd really like to understand."

Blair's parents looked at each other. "Yes, Makayla, I'll explain what I can to you both tonight. Don't worry, honey. Everything will be fine," Blake assured me.

THE DUMARIS

We had to rush to make it to school on time. Once there, it was easier to forget the pained expression on Blake's face and his confirmation of my fears. Something about the words the man had spoken during the nightmare two nights ago had alarmed Blake and Bethany; tonight, maybe I would finally understand all the implications of that.

The pre-cal test went pretty well, and luckily we didn't get a large load of homework. When Blair and I got to his house, his parents' BMWs were in the driveway; they had obviously come home early from work or not gone at all. My stomach tightened. I wrapped my arms tightly around myself and sighed.

"You okay, Makayla?" Blair asked as we pulled into the driveway.

"Yeah, I'm just a little worried," I admitted.

Blair turned off the engine and turned to face me. "My parents will know how to deal with whatever this is. Let's just take it one step at a time." Blair got out of the car and came around to open my door for me. "Makayla, are you coming?" he asked, holding his hand out to me.

I smirked, remembering the first time he had asked me that question, the day we had to tell my mother she couldn't stay home with me during my emergence. I had been pretty nervous that day also. When she came home on Thursday, would there be some other crisis she'd have to face?

Blake and Bethany were waiting for us in the family room when we got inside. We dropped our backpacks by the stairs and headed in to see them. I searched their faces and minds for signs of distress but found none there. Either they were just as relaxed as they looked, or they were highly skilled at hiding their emotions—probably the latter.

"How was your pre-cal test, Makayla?" Bethany asked.

"I think I did well actually," I responded happily. "How about your day? Is everything all right?" I shifted my focus to Blake, awaiting his response.

"I've spent most of the day on the phone with Zandria, the Most Blessed of the Ileesia," Blake began. "The vision that your father has been communicating to you not only concerns his murder but the resurgence of an old threat within our community." He paused to consider his words and my emotional state. Blair and I sat on the couch, my hands in tight fists.

"It appears that an organized crime family has reappeared within the clairvoyant community. The name of the Dumaris has not been heard for nearly a century. Let me try to explain this from the beginning," he said, rubbing his hand over his eyes wearily. "The Dumaris are a clairvoyant family dating back centuries. World history is replete with their exploits without completely understanding who was responsible for them.

"Makayla, the majority of the people gifted with clairvoyance are honestly committed to using their gifts for the benefit of humanity, which is, of course, our obligation. Unfortunately, however, there are those who take advantage of their gifts and use them for their own gain, both in wealth and power. The Dumaris are such a group, an organized crime syndicate."

I raised my shaking hand to my mouth. Blair put his arm around me and pulled me closer to him, his face frozen. The idea that my father had been murdered was difficult enough to cope with, but to think about it as a mob hit was revolting. I closed my eyes and leaned against Blair's shoulder. The image of my father falling to the floor in agony flashed across my mind—Blake had said that there was only one sure way to destroy a clairvoyant's mind, and I had witnessed it over and over again in my nightmare.

Not sure that I wanted to know, I asked, "What crimes do they commit, besides murder, I mean?"

"In recent years, there have been reports of international drug smuggling and weapon sales that the FBI and ATF can never seem to solve. When they get close to connecting anyone to the crimes, either someone investigating it disappears, or the evidence shifts in another direction. If the Dumaris are behind these crimes, they can use their gifts to alter the perceptions of the agents involved, using their own members who have infiltrated the bureau, or they simply make them vanish."

I shuddered involuntarily and shook my head to clear it. "Do you think my dad knew something about the Dumaris' activities and that's why they killed him?"

"It seems to me," Blake began, leaning forward, "that Sean had been forced into using his empathic abilities to aid the Dumaris in some way and then decided that he wouldn't do it anymore." He sighed and whispered, "No one betrays the Dumaris and lives to tell about it."

My mind was spinning with conflicting emotions—anger, fear, revulsion. If they were impossible to stop, why did my dad send me the vision? What was I, or anyone else I loved, supposed to do about it? Suddenly it occurred to me that there was more to this than I had originally thought. I sat bolt upright, my eyes wary.

"Blake, Zandria doesn't expect you or your family,"—I swallowed hard, looking from his face to Bethany's and then up into Blair's—"to act on this information, does she?" Panic began to rise in my chest as I considered losing anyone else to the Dumaris.

Blake crossed to me and knelt in front of me, his hands reaching for my head. I leaned away from him. "No!" I shouted. "I need to know!"

Bethany crossed to the couch and sat next to me. "Makayla," she soothed, "Blake wasn't trying to keep anything from you. He just wanted to keep your anxiety down so we can continue discussing this calmly." She reached over and placed her hand on my shoulder, rubbing it.

I closed my eyes and forced myself to calm down. *Sorry, Blake. It's all right, honey. Let me know when you're ready to continue.* Blake returned to his chair and waited for me to calm down.

As my breathing settled into its normal rhythm, I opened my eyes. "Please tell me that none of you are going to do anything that would endanger your lives with this information." I shuddered again.

Blake looked at me intensely. "Makayla, the Ileesia would like us all, you included, to come to Florida over the Christmas break to talk to them about your vision." When my eyes widened in terror, he continued gently, "They are not expecting any of us to risk our lives, honey. They just want to get the information firsthand so that the council can discuss the issue. Zandria and Andreas, the heir to her seat and one of your father's best friends from college, are especially anxious to meet you."

He waited for a minute then added, "Zandria was very fond of your father. She wants to meet you and express her condolences in person, but at eighty-two years old, she can no longer travel. It would mean a great deal to her to see Sean's child before she joins him." Blake smiled tenderly; his eyes shone with renewed emotion.

"I can't leave my mother at Christmas," I whispered. "I'm the only family she has left." My voice cracked on the last words. Blair leaned down and laid his head on mine.

"We don't have to leave until after Christmas Day, Makayla," Bethany assured me. "I would never leave your mother alone on a holiday, and besides, I have a granddaughter to spoil." She grinned at me and winked.

I smiled back at her wistfully. "How will we explain the trip to her? I don't want to alarm her in any way."

Blair answered first. "Can't we just say that we are going on a vacation for a few days and that we want Makayla to come with us?" He looked to his parents for their agreement.

"I think that's a great idea," Bethany agreed. "We'll leave around the twenty-seventh of December and get back for New Year's Day. Is that okay with you, sweetheart?" she asked, patting my knee and smiling at me.

"I guess so," I mumbled, rubbing my head with my hands. "Do we have to decide right now, or can I have a little time to sort this all out?"

"Take some time, Makayla," Blake answered, "but it is our responsibility to report this information to the Ileesia. Ultimately, we *will* do so." His eyes were kind, but his voice was stern and unyielding. "Do you understand?" I flinched; his tone was almost reproachful. The full weight of a clairvoyant's responsibility to and for others fell on me with his words. Blair wrapped his arms tighter around me as he heard my fears begin to rise.

"Yes, sir," I whispered, swallowing the lump in my throat, afraid to argue or look at him. Blake heard the formality of my response and came over to me. My eyes were moist; I shifted my eyes down to the floor, trying to hide them from him. He came closer and lifted my chin.

"I'm sorry, honey," he said tenderly. "Sometimes it's a father's job to insist his children face unpleasant things. If I could spare you from it, I would. You know that I love you like my own, don't you?" Blake smiled warmly and waited for my response.

"Yes," I whispered, smiling through my tears. Blake opened his arms to me, and I hugged him. "I will not let anything happen to you, Makayla. I give you my word."

"Now," he said, "you guys go get a snack and relax for a while. It's been a stressful afternoon." Turning to take Bethany's hand, he added, "Let's go do those errands you needed to run, and then we'll come back and take the kids to dinner. Take the night off, chef!"

"Thanks a heap!" She smirked, kissing him before they headed out the door to the garage.

Blair and I sat in silence for several long minutes. I was tired of feeling scared and anxious; it wasn't my normal disposition, and it felt like an ill-fitting shirt. I took a deep breath and looked up at Blair. He smiled down at me, and I grinned impishly. Jumping up and grabbing his hand, I bounded toward the stairs.

Hey! What about a snack? Blair teased, following close behind me. *Aren't you hungry?*

Halfway up the stairs, he swept me up and took the rest two at a time. He opened the bedroom door and tossed me playfully onto the bed.

"I'm not sure this is the kind of snack my dad was talking about!" Blair said, smiling devilishly at me.

"Shut up and kiss me, Blair!" I laughed as he bounded onto the bed next to me. He growled playfully and pulled me onto his chest, locking his fingers into my hair and kissing me fiercely.

I was so tired of the unrelenting bombardment my mind had been receiving lately, so emotionally drained from the fear and pain. Losing myself in Blair's love was all I could think about now. I pressed my body to his as his hand slid down my back. My every nerve tingled with desire. He responded willingly to my advances, rolling on top of me and moving his lips down my neck.

"Makayla…" he whispered, breathing unevenly against my neck. Without thinking, I reached down and unbuttoned my blouse, encouraging him to move down my chest. His lips moved gently across my collarbone and then brushed against the top of my bra, kissing my breast. I gasped softly as his touch pulsed through me. A swell of emotions rushed my mind, making me dizzy. Blair froze, sensing my distress.

We lay together, our breathing irregular, as my mind refocused and unwound. Blair rolled to his side and reached to rebutton my blouse; I stopped him and did it myself.

"I'm sorry, Blair," I whispered.

Blair leaned in and kissed me gently. "It's my fault. I lost focus; I should know better than to put you in that position." He frowned, disappointed with himself.

"It'll get better, won't it, Blair? I mean, I'll eventually be able to…" My face flushed with embarrassment.

"Yes, honey. Of course you'll be able to…eventually." He smirked at me.

"It's like built-in birth control!" We laughed, and I snuggled into his side.

As I lay in his arms, my thoughts returned to the trip to Florida and its implications in my life. My poor mother…what would she think if she knew where we would be going? I knew exactly how she would feel—terrified. By Thursday, when she returned home, I would have to have a firm grip on myself. She must not see anything but excitement over a trip with Blair's family.

Also, if I was honest with myself, I was kind of unnerved about appearing before the Ileesia. Ever since Blair first explained about the Ileesia, when he confessed his "illicit" love for me, thinking about the council filled my stomach with butterflies. My connection between the rules that I often found unjust and the Ileesia made it difficult to think of the group as a just and proper governing council. Now that I knew and loved Blake and Bethany, I felt somewhat better, but still…

"Blair, have you ever been to the Ileesia before?" I asked, curious.

"Yes, shortly after my emergence," he answered offhandedly.

"Why did you go then?"

Blair hesitated slightly. I raised my head off his chest and looked at him. "What's wrong?" I asked.

"Nothing," Blair commented casually.

"Then answer my question."

"The Ileesia asked my parents to bring me because of my early emergence."

"And?" I encouraged, frowning at him.

Blair seemed almost embarrassed to continue, but my frustration was growing by the minute.

I thought we shared everything with each other, I thought petulantly. *Every time your emergence comes up, you clam up. Why?*

Because my emergence is the one thing I'm not certain about, Blair confessed, looking up at the ceiling.

"I don't understand, Blair," I admitted, softening my voice. "What is it that you are uncertain about?" I reached over and turned his face back to me. "Please talk to me."

Blair tightened his arms around me, pulling me back onto his chest. "Everyone thought when I emerged at sixteen that I would possess additional gifts, strengths beyond the ordinary, but…" His voice trailed off, and he sighed.

"But what, baby?" I asked softly, my hand on his cheek.

Blair's voice rang with frustration. "It's been two years, Makayla! Two years and nothing has surfaced. It's humiliating to think that even my dad's extra gift has passed over me." He paused to gather his thoughts. "I know it shouldn't bother me; I should be grateful for the gift I have and be satisfied. Sometimes I just…"

I tried to lift my head to comfort him, but Blair's arms tightened around me, keeping me from seeing his expression.

Blair, you are the most important thing in my world. I'm so lucky to be able to share my life with you just the way you are. I wouldn't have survived the last weeks without you. Tears for his pain spilled over my eyes and onto his shirt. *You are everything I desire and more than I could have dreamed or hoped to receive.*

Blair's arms loosened; he pulled me up to his face and kissed me gently. *As you are to me...*

TARPON SPRINGS

I lay my head against the headrest of my seat; the flight was smooth, but my nerves were ragged. The last few weeks had soared past at an alarming speed, as time does when you are dreading something. Between all the preparations for Christmas and final exams, the time flew by in a haze of busyness. Even spending Christmas with my mother and Blair's family did little to soften my anxiety over our trip to the Ileesia.

Blake had explained that the Ileesia was located in a small town twenty-three miles northwest of Tampa called Tarpon Springs. Somehow I had expected it to be located in one of the big cities, at least a city the size of Tampa. The explanation made more sense when Blake connected the little town to its comparatively large Greek population. Apparently, Tarpon Springs had one of the largest Greek communities in the country, especially considering its small population of twenty-three thousand people.

Years ago, Greeks found the Gulf waters off of Tarpon Springs to be rich in sponges, an important industry in their culture. Over the years, the population grew, and founding members of the US Ileesia decided to headquarter there. All of the Ileesia headquarters around the world were located in cities and towns with strong Greek heritage, all in keeping with its ancient beginnings at Delphi. Only in such a place would a replica of a temple to Apollo appear comfortable across town from a large Greek Orthodox cathedral. The "temple" was opened as a museum, a fitting cover for its real purpose below the street-level edifice.

Blair reached over and stroked my face, soothing me as he had so often in the past days. Although I wished that I could, it was impossible for me to hide all my nervousness from him. When I had been distracted with school, family, or the holiday, I could lose myself in the activities around me, but when it was quiet… My stomach performed another somersault.

Adding to my anxiety was the memory of our conversation with my mom. Blair insisted on being with me to explain our trip to her, knowing that I would need help hiding the full truth from her. It was essential that Mom feel at ease about my leaving; I wouldn't leave her worrying that somehow I wouldn't come home.

"Mom." I began shifting nervously next to Blair on the couch. He placed his hand on my knee to stem the bouncing.

"What is it, baby?" she asked, barely looking up from her book.

"Would it be okay with you if I went away with Blair's family for a few days after Christmas?" I tried to make my voice steadier than my nerves. "They invited me to join them."

Mom looked up, smiling. "How lovely! Where are you all going, Blair?"

"My family has a condo near the beach just twenty miles or so from Tampa. We like to go for a few days when we have an extended break from school and work," Blair explained calmly, smiling at her.

I thought I saw Mom's expression change minutely but couldn't be sure if it was my imagination or not. "When would you leave?" Mom asked serenely. Her thoughts were not quite so serene. *Lots of people go to Tampa...calm down. Nothing will happen to Kayla.*

"Blake said we would leave around the twenty-seventh of December and get back on the first of January. I wouldn't even consider leaving before Christmas," I added quickly. "If you don't want me to go, I'll stay home, Mom." *Please, Mom, need me to stay home.* Blair squeezed my hand.

Mom took a deep breath. "Well, that sounds like a very nice trip. If you want to go, you should, Kayla. I have to work the week between Christmas and New Year's anyway. We'll celebrate the New Year when you all get back."

And that was that. My one last hope for escape faded with her resigned agreement. I rubbed my temples slowly, trying to relax.

"Makayla," Blair whispered softly, "everything is going to be fine. We're even going to have time to go to the beach and do some sightseeing." His feigned enthusiasm didn't sway me much.

"I'm sorry." I apologized for what seemed like the millionth time in the last week. "I really am trying, Blair. I just can't seem to relax. So many thoughts and emotions are fighting each other in my head."

"Close your eyes, honey." Blair reached over with his other hand and subtly cupped my face against his shoulder. The release of tension was immediate and comforting; I felt myself drift off.

We landed at Tampa International Airport around six; the winter sun was low in the western sky over the Gulf of Mexico as I looked out the plane's window. The beauty of the pink-streaked sky reflected off the windowpane and lit the cabin with soft, filtered light.

The drive to Tarpon Springs didn't take long, and we soon arrived at the Davis' condo—a four-bedroom, three-bath unit with a balcony facing the Gulf. Like their home in Enterprise, the condo was decorated in an eclectic mix of antique and more modern furniture; pictures of the family plastered the walls and tabletops. The view was exquisite, and the white sandy beach stretched as far as the eye could see. Blair promised a moonlit walk after we had dinner in town.

Within the relatively small town, there were ten or more Greek restaurants; some were lit with strands of white lights, and the sound of vibrant stringed instruments filled the surrounding streets. Blake and Bethany chose a restaurant and introduced me to some incredible food. By the end of the two-hour meal, I was truly ready to burst!

The dinner and the atmosphere of the restaurant had much improved my mood, and I felt lighter, happier than I had in weeks. Around ten, Blair and I headed for our walk along the beach, the moon high overhead and a soft breeze flowing in off the water. For a long time, we didn't speak at all—we strolled together with Blair's arm wrapped securely around my shoulder.

"Hmmm." I sighed. "This is one of the most beautiful places I've ever seen."

"I'm glad you like it." Blair grinned. "It does have a special quality about it." He leaned down and kissed the top of my head. "What would you like to do tomorrow?"

Tension seeped in through my bliss. "When do we have to go to the Ileesia?" I asked, casually looking down at the white sand under our feet.

"Not until the day after tomorrow," Blair answered, rubbing my shoulder. "Mom and Dad will go tomorrow and talk to Zandria and Andreas, but we won't have to go with them, so I thought we could do a little sightseeing."

"Whatever you want to do is fine with me," I said. "As long as I'm with you, I'll be just fine." I stretched up on my toes to kiss him. His arms wound around me and pulled me tighter to him.

"Well, we can tour the sponge docks, go visit St. Nicholas's Greek Orthodox Cathedral, eat, stroll around the shops in town, go to the aquarium, eat again, walk along the beach, eat some more…" He trailed off, grinning impishly down at me.

"How can you even think about eating any more?" I groaned, clutching my stomach. "I ate enough tonight for a week or two!"

"Tarpon Springs is one of the only places I get to eat really authentic Greek food. I have to fill up while I'm here!"

"You really are guided by your stomach, aren't you, Blair?" I laughed.

"Not always," he teased. "Sometimes I can be distracted away from the table."

"Hmm." I sighed. "I have no idea what you're talking about." I turned and ran back the way we had come, giggling. Blair's longer strides caught up to me almost immediately.

He grabbed me around my waist and pulled me down onto the sand with him; it still retained some of the day's heat and felt warm on my back. His hands grabbed my face urgently, and his lips crushed against mine. My fingers laced into his hair, and my lips parted, feeling his tongue tracing them. Rolling on top of me, Blair's body pressed against mine gently. My muscles tightened spasmodically under him. Rolling over again, Blair pulled me onto his chest.

My face flushed; I had forgotten we were on a public beach. Lifting my head toward a soft sound, I saw several couples passing us on the sand. One girl was giggling into her boyfriend's shoulder. Blair sat up, hearing my embarrassment. I buried my face in his chest.

"Sorry, Makayla. I didn't mean to embarrass you, but don't worry too much," he added, lifting my face up to his. "Anyone on the beach at this hour is here for exactly the same reason!" Blair laughed and hugged me to him. "Let's head back before we get into real trouble out here."

"Blair!" I squealed as I got up. "We're covered in sand. We can't go back into the condo like this!" Frantically I began brushing the sand off my clothes, as did he—well, not quite as frantically. Blair was apparently highly amused by the whole situation.

I leaned over and flipped my hair in front of me, brushing the sand from it as best I could. Blair laughed. I scowled up at him through my hair. "What are you laughing at? This is not funny!"

Sensing my less than sunny disposition, Blair explained, backtracking, "It's just that both my brother and sister came back to the condo with their prospective spouses covered in sand when I was younger, and I never understood why!" He laughed loudly again, and I couldn't help laughing with him.

The day of travel, along with all the food I'd eaten, the walk on the beach, and the stress I was under, had worn me out. I slept soundly through the night, listening to the gentle waves of the Gulf lapping the sand through my open window as I fell asleep. I woke to sunlight streaming into my bedroom window, rested and relaxed.

Blake and Bethany had already left for the Ileesia by the time I was showered and dressed. Blair was on the balcony with a book. I joined him with my toast and juice.

"Morning, sleepy head," Blair teased, leaning over and kissing me on the cheek. "Did you sleep well?"

"Actually, I slept great," I said, smiling at him. "I really loved listening to the water. It was very relaxing." Looking out over the beach while eating breakfast was glorious—not to mention sharing the view with the handsome boy sitting next to me.

"Have you decided what you want to do today, Short Stuff?"

"Not anything definite, but I understand there will be a lot of eating involved!" I rolled my eyes at him, and he laughed. "Wherever you want to take me will be great, but I would like to see the cathedral. I've never seen a Greek Orthodox church before."

"I'll call and see when they might be open for a tour; they're very proud of their cathedral and have volunteers almost every day to lead guided tours," Blair explained, getting up and heading for the phone book.

As I finished breakfast, my thoughts drifted to Blake and Bethany. I wondered if everything was going okay, not even sure why I was so concerned. What could possibly happen? If I was just telling them about my visions, surely I couldn't upset the proverbial apple cart too much.

Blair called to me from inside, "Makayla, there's a tour beginning in an hour or so. Do you want to aim for that?"

"Sure," I answered, taking my dish and glass inside. "Let me just brush my teeth and put on my sandals. Should I bring a sweater?"

"It might be chilly on the beach, so bring it just in case."

Our day in Tarpon Springs was amazing. The St. Nicholas Greek Orthodox Cathedral was exquisite, with its soaring domes, icons, and mystical aura. Next Blair took me to the sponge docks, the so-called heart of Greek culture—in Tarpon Springs at least. The streets were lined with over a hundred stores, restaurants, and bakeries, each radiating tantalizing aromas; even I was tempted to stop at more than one of them. Blair introduced me to *souvlaki*, a lamb kabob served in pita bread, for lunch and then insisted on hitting one of the bakeries for baklava.

Around six, Blair's cell phone rang; Blake and Bethany had returned to the condo and wanted us to meet them for dinner. My stomach did its usual flip contemplating the news they would bring. Blair wound his arm around me, towing me toward our next eating adventure—Mama's Greek Cuisine. Rounding the corner onto Athens Street, we saw Blake and Bethany waiting outside for us. Bethany waved and smiled.

"How was your day, Makayla?" She beamed, hugging me.

"Great!" I exclaimed. "We got to tour the cathedral, which was amazing, and then the sponge docks. I bought my mother a mother-of-pearl bracelet and had *souvlaki* for lunch and baklava for a snack…" I broke off, embarrassed; I was rambling.

Bethany squeezed my shoulder. "I'm glad you had a good time."

My eyes sought Blake's; he read the worry in them easily. "Everything went just fine with Zandria and Andreas," he explained, trying to soothe me. "We'll talk about it at dinner, okay?" He smiled warmly and held his hand toward the door for Bethany and me.

As the evening progressed, multiple courses arrived and disappeared from our table. The owner at Mama's knew Blake and Bethany well and stopped by every so often to make sure that our table was full and our appetites satisfied. After the third course, Bethany and I surrendered to our full stomachs, but the men ate through two more.

When the dishes were cleared and coffee served, Blake turned to us and began explaining about their visit to the Ileesia and what the schedule and procedure would be for the next day. Blair scooted his chair closer to me and draped his arm around my shoulder.

"Both Zandria and Andreas are looking forward to meeting you, Makayla. Zandria sort of adopted Sean after his mother died, so she wants to meet her 'grandchild.' Zandria is one of the only Greek nationals on the Ileesia; she is still old world—very loving and motherly. Don't be fooled by her grandmotherly appearance, however." Blake laughed softly. "You don't become the Most Blessed of the Ileesia without extraordinary gifts and powers."

My curiosity outweighed my fear at his comments; I leaned onto the table, my eyes wide. "What kind of gifts and powers does she have?"

"That is for her to share with you in her own time." He smiled at me to show that my breach of etiquette was forgiven.

"Sorry," I said, grimacing. "I still have a lot to learn, I guess."

"No harm done, honey," Blake assured me. "Andreas went to college with your dad. They discovered their shared gifts during their freshman year." When I looked confused, he added, "Apparently they were each trying to answer a question on a test and heard each other's thoughts." We all laughed, imagining how weird that would be.

"He too wants to meet you. I know that he misses Sean a great deal and will take comfort in the fact that you share his gift."

Thinking about the warning in my dad's letter, I wondered silently if he would approve of Andreas knowing about my additional gift.

Your father trusted Andreas fully, Makayla, Blake thought.

I nodded my understanding. "So what do we do tomorrow?" I asked quietly. "Do I have to go in front of the entire council, or can I just meet the others first?"

Bethany spoke for the first time. "Zandria would like to meet with you privately first." She paused and exchanged a glance with her husband. "Andreas wanted to be in on the meeting, but she felt like you would be more comfortable if it was just the two of you."

I was already appreciative of Zandria's sensitivity. She obviously understood how difficult this was for me.

"Will Blair be allowed to be with me?" My question came out as a supplication. Instinctively I tightened my hold on his hand; he leaned down and lay his head on the top of mine.

"We'll all go into Zandria's office with you at first," Blake explained, "but she will wish to speak with you alone at some point. I'm sure you'll feel totally comfortable with her, honey."

"What about in front of the council? Can he be with me then?" I realized that my voice had risen in pitch along with my butterflies. I shouldn't have eaten so much.

"Blair can sit beside you, sweetie," Bethany assured me. "You know, the council won't bite you or anything." She smiled at me and added, "Let's face it, you already have two members wrapped around your little finger." She winked at me; I giggled.

A thought occurred to me: "How many members are on the council, Blake?"

"There are twenty voting members. In the event of a tie vote, Zandria's vote breaks the tie."

We sat in silence for a while; the bouzouki music swelled from inside the restaurant. I yawned and stretched.

"Let's get you home to bed, Short Stuff," Blair teased, mussing my hair.

I must have fallen asleep leaning against Blair's shoulder in the backseat of the rental car. The last thing I remember was him lowering me to my bed, covering me with the blanket, and kissing me on the forehead as the sound of the gentle waves soared through my window.

ZANDRIA

I woke early but lay quietly in my bed trying to gather my thoughts and courage for the day ahead. A soft tap on my door brought me out of my reverie.

"Come in, Blair," I called softly, sitting up on my elbows.

"How'd you know it was me?" he teased, sitting next to me on the bed. "Are you feeling all right?" Blair asked more seriously.

"I think I'm okay. I'll just be glad to get this over with. Then I can just stop worrying about it."

"Sounds good to me." Blair pulled me into his lap and cradled me against him. "I'll be glad when you stop worrying about it too!"

"It's not my fault you can read my mind," I whined, burying my head in his chest.

"That's all part of the job description, ma'am." Blair lifted my chin and kissed me gently. "I'm going to shower. See you in a bit."

This morning, Blake and Bethany were waiting for us on the balcony. We ate a quick breakfast, brushed our teeth, and headed straight for the Ileesia headquarters. As usual, my legs bounced up and down in the backseat, but Blair didn't bother to try to stop them this time.

As we approached our destination, Blair pointed toward a white-columned edifice. It sort of glowed in the morning sun, its radiance creating a halo around it. Blake drove behind the building and parked in the lot. There were only two other cars parked there; the museum didn't open for an hour.

Blake used a key pad and opened the door for us to enter through the back. Inside the door was a lobby with a marble counter at the far end; a young woman sat behind it with a welcoming smile.

"Good morning, Blake, Bethany," she greeted them as she stood.

"Good morning, Erica," Bethany answered. "We have an appointment with Zandria at nine."

"Certainly," Erica replied. "She is waiting for you in her office. I'll let her know you are on your way down. Have a blessed day!"

"You as well, Erica," Blake added genially as he guided us to the elevator.

In the elevator, Blake used another key pad and entered a code. A panel slid aside, revealing two buttons: L1 and L2. He pushed L1. As the door closed, I shuddered slightly; I felt claustrophobic, but I was sure it was just my nerves.

When the door opened on level L1, an elaborately decorated hall stretched in front of us. The walls were decorated with paintings from Greek mythology, and statues of the Greek gods stood at attention along the corridor. Blair's parents walked past several offices, finally stopping in front of a large, intricately carved mahogany door.

Bethany reached for my hand and squeezed it. "Remember that within these walls, we never enter another clairvoyant's thoughts without permission." I nodded and tried to smile up at her.

"Are you ready, Makayla?" Blake asked, studying my face.

"I think so," I mouthed—the words just wouldn't come out.

"I love you," Blair whispered in my ear. All I could do was nod.

Blake knocked on the door and waited. A melodious voice, heavily accented, called, "Come in, blessed ones." Blake opened the door.

Zandria's office was less stark than the hallway. It was decorated in soft pastel tones, the furniture plush and comfortable looking. A desk stood against the opposite wall, but Zandria was seated on a chintz wingback chair in an area obviously set up for visits with guests. A tray strewn with pastries and a coffee set were on the table in front of her.

When my eyes found Zandria, I was surprised by her appearance. She was white-haired and small-boned, almost fragile looking; she was clothed in a stylish black pantsuit. Her age-lined face was gentle and her hazel eyes warm. Zandria met my eyes, and a joyful smile brightened her already friendly face. I smiled back at her shyly.

"Good morning, Zandria," Blake said, taking her outstretched hand and shaking it gently. "You are looking well this morning."

"Such a flatterer, you are, Blake!" she replied in her broken English. With her other hand, Zandria reached out to Bethany. "How lucky you are to have such a man, my dear."

"Thank you, Zandria," Bethany answered softly, reverently. "May I reintroduce my son Blair?"

Blair approached Zandria's open arms and embraced her gently. "How blessed I am to see you again, my son," she intoned. "You have grown into an even more handsome man than I imagined."

"Thank you, Most Blessed One," Blair replied. "I'm glad to see you looking so well."

Zandria's eyes turned toward me. Blair stepped aside as she opened her arms to me. "Come to me, my child." Her voice quavered with emotion, and her hazel eyes shone blue in the soft light.

I moved toward her without speaking but felt no hesitation to approach her. Leaning down so she could see me better, I wrapped my arms around her fragile frame.

"What a blessing God has given this old woman," she said softly, "to see the child of one of my lost children." Zandria held me at arm's distance to look at me. "You have your father's eyes, of course, but also his smile. Your size you must get from your mother!" Everyone laughed gently as she pulled me closer to her again.

"Where are my manners? Eat something, please; eat something! Make yourselves comfortable—sit wherever you like," Zandria invited, but she pulled me down on the arm of her chair. Bethany passed the small glass plates to everyone and then passed the pastries.

"Would you like a *kourambiedes*, Makayla?" Zandria inquired hospitably.

"I'm sorry, Most Blessed One," I apologized softly. "I don't know which one that is."

A delighted laugh escaped from her lips. "Of course you don't! My apologies. This is a *kourambiedes*; it's a butter cookie from my country. I think you will like it," she added proudly.

"Thank you," I said, taking the delicate cookie dredged in powdered sugar. It tasted delicious, but sugar sprinkled all down my blouse.

"Not to worry," Zandria said quickly, wiping my blouse with her napkin. "These cookies are notoriously messy. It's part of their charm!" She winked at me, and I giggled.

After fifteen or twenty minutes of friendly banter, Zandria addressed Blake, Bethany, and Blair. "Would you mind excusing Makayla and myself for a short while? I would like very much to get to know her better." She smiled warmly at the three of them as they rose immediately to leave the room.

Blair hesitated, looking at me nervously. I smiled and nodded at him to reassure him that I was fine. He turned and joined his parents, who were waiting for him by the door.

When the door closed, Zandria gestured for me to sit on the couch. "Blair loves you deeply, my child," she said tenderly. "He will be a blessing in your life, as you will be in his."

"Thank you, Most Blessed One," I answered, blushing. "He has already been a great blessing."

"Will you do this old woman a favor, Makayla?"

"Yes, of course. What can I do for you?" I added without hesitation.

"I was never blessed with children of my own. Blake has told you, I am sure, that your father was very special to me." I nodded. She paused, looking down, almost embarrassed. "It is a vanity, a foolish request."

Seeing this powerful woman look so vulnerable upset me. I knelt down in front of her. "Please ask me, Most Blessed One."

Zandria took both of my hands in hers. "When we are alone, Makayla, would you please call me *YaYa*? It is Greek for *grandmother*." She smiled shyly at me.

"I would be honored to call you my grandmother, YaYa." Zandria's face lit up with joy at this simple favor. She hugged me again.

"Now we must get down to business, my child." Her tone became businesslike and strong; it was easy to hear the authority in her voice. "Blake and Bethany have told me about your father's letter, without details, of course," she inserted quickly, "and of your nightmare and vision. First I must ask, how do you interpret your visions?"

I stared in blank confusion into her eyes. No one had ever asked me to interpret them myself; I didn't feel capable of such a task. "I'm not sure, YaYa," I admitted. "I have relied on those more experienced with our gifts to help me interpret them. I'm not sure I would know where to begin."

"Listen to me, Makayla." Zandria leaned toward me for emphasis. "It is imperative that you learn to interpret your visions as well as to call them to you at will." When she beheld my staggered expression, she reached for my hand. "There is nothing to be afraid of, my child. As a priestess of Apollo, you have been gifted with great abilities, but they are worthless to humanity or to you without the ability to focus them."

"A priestess of Apollo? I don't understand, YaYa."

"The very few of us who are gifted with visions of the future, and, in your case, the past, are called priests and priestesses of Apollo. Do you know the story of the oracle at Delphi, the priestess Pythia?" I nodded. "You, as was your father, are gifted as she was—with the ability to foretell the future and receive messages from the past as needed." She waited for me to take a breath.

"Don't worry, Makayla," she added gently. "I can teach you to focus and control your visions, but first we must deal with the present problem. Will you allow me to see your nightmare as Blake did?"

Knowing now that this process was totally painless for me, I was about to agree, but something about Blake's reaction to it made me hesitate. "YaYa, the nightmare was disturbing to Blake." I paused to think before I spoke. "I don't want it to upset you." What I was really afraid of was that somehow the nightmare would weaken or hurt Zandria; she looked so fragile.

She patted my cheek. "You sweet child. Just like your father, always worried about everyone else but yourself." I smiled to know that I was like my dad in more "normal" ways also.

"I promise," Zandria assured me, "I will be able to process it without distress. May I?"

Zandria rose more agilely than I thought she could and sat beside me on the couch. I lay my head back and closed my eyes;

her aged but surprisingly strong hands grasped both sides of my head. I began to dream. An image of a father pushing a toddler in a swing…a moonlit beach…a park in bloom…a couple in full embrace…a restaurant terrace with lights hung from its beams… an evil face grinning malevolently…a room of dark figures.

I opened my eyes to find Zandria sipping her coffee serenely in her chair. She smiled at me and offered me another sweet from the tray. I shook my head and waited for her to speak.

"Now," Zandria began, "we will begin your training. It will not take as long as you might think. Once your mind adjusts, it will be natural for you. At times you will still be gifted with unexpected visions, for those are the ones that usually need immediate attention, but by focusing, you will be able to control most of them.

"If you concentrate on a specific event, person, or impending concern, your mind will isolate your foresight and give you the vision you desire. For instance, if you wanted to be sure that a loved one would arrive safely at a destination, you would close your eyes and concentrate on the individual and their destination. Your gift will provide the vision without any further exertion on your part."

As was usual since my emergence, I realized that my mouth was agape; I closed it and shook my head. "Are you sure it's that easy, YaYa?" And then realizing who I was speaking to, I added quickly, "No disrespect intended, Most Blessed One." I lowered my eyes in shame.

"Never be afraid to ask the questions on your mind, my child," Zandria chided, lifting my chin with her hand. "It is by asking questions that we learn. Now where were we? Ah yes, your question. I share your gift, Makayla. I assure you that you will be able to focus it."

Zandria smiled warmly at me. I realized that she had just shared an intimate detail of her life with me. I was honored.

She continued her lesson. "Close your eyes, Makayla, and focus on what will happen when you speak before the council." My eyes grew wide in surprise. "Trust me, child. Close your eyes." I obeyed. "Now envision sitting around a large oval conference table with Blair and the Ileesia. In your mind, tell your story. What happens?"

Suddenly I could see it all, even the faces of those around the table. Blair sat beside me and Zandria across from me. Blake and Bethany sat to her left and smiled at me. And the vision unfolded.

I became so excited that I ended the vision before it was complete. I threw open my eyes and looked at Zandria. "That was amazing, YaYa!" I exclaimed, unable to control my enthusiasm and throwing my arms around her neck.

She laughed softly and continued as I sat back on the couch. "Now as for the visions from the past, these might be a little more erratic in nature. A great deal depends on who is sending you the message."

Her tone was so casual that it was hard to believe what she was really saying. "Who…is…sending?" I stuttered, staring into her wise and gentle eyes.

"Yes, my child. It may not only be your father who sends you visions from the beyond. Sometimes it is possible that the message will be sent to you by someone you never met." I stared at her aghast. "The important thing to remember is that these messages are always sent for a specific reason, whether it be to find someone or something that has been lost or," Zandria paused for a moment and continued, "to right a wrong."

I raised my head a little higher. "That's what my vision is about, YaYa," I said with conviction. "My father was murdered by a group still amongst us, wasn't he?"

Zandria nodded her head gravely. "This afternoon, I will convene the council to hear of your vision. Tell it confidently—for your father."

BEFORE THE COUNCIL

Around noon, Zandria called for Blair and his parents to return; she informed them that the council would convene at three and dismissed us for lunch.

"Until later, blessed ones," she said, lifting her hand in farewell. Blake and Bethany inclined their heads to her as Blair walked to my side. He wrapped his arm protectively around my waist. Zandria's face glowed with joy; she winked at me, and I giggled silently.

As was par for the course, my appetite returned with a vengeance now that my nervousness had abated. Once again, we feasted on Greek delicacies, sitting on the restaurant's terrace overlooking the Gulf. I knew that they were bursting to hear of my meeting with Zandria, but following proper clairvoyant etiquette, they waited for me to begin.

"Zandria shared her gift of foretelling the future with me," I began simply. Blake nodded his approval. "She explained how the phenomenon occurs and how to cope with it."

"What does that mean?" Blair looked confused and concerned.

"Zandria taught me to focus and call upon my visions at will."

Blair was flabbergasted, but his parents had expected this. "You can call them up out of your mind, Makayla?" Blair asked, amazed.

"Yes, although Zandria explained that some of the visions will come without warning, like the visions of the little boy at Panera and Jesse's 'almost' accident. Those visions, she said, were the ones that would need the most immediate attention."

"That's unbelievable!" Blair exclaimed. "Did you expect that Makayla would be able to learn to do that, Dad?"

"Your mother and I discussed it with Zandria yesterday," he admitted. "We hoped that she would be able to teach her while we were here."

"Neither your father or myself are gifted with visions, so we didn't know how to help Makayla," Bethany added. "We were pretty sure that Zandria would love to help her. How did you like her, Makayla?"

"I love her! She was warm, loving, and so grandmotherly." I smiled to myself about my shared secret with Zandria. "I felt totally comfortable with her."

Blake grinned and shook his head slightly. "What's so funny?" I asked.

"Zandria is all of those things, Makayla, but as I mentioned before, never be fooled by her appearance. She is a formidable woman." Bethany nodded her assent.

Blair was not finished with his questions. "What did she say about the visions from the past?"

"Well..." I hesitated a moment, deciding how to word it correctly. "She said that I may not only receive messages from my dad. It's possible—at least Zandria thinks so—that others may send me messages."

Apparently this news was a surprise to them all. Even Blake and Bethany seemed stunned into silence. Blair blew a gust of air out through his mouth and rubbed his hands through his hair. I was embarrassed by their response; my face flushed, and I couldn't meet their eyes.

"Did I say something wrong?" I whispered, my voice breaking a little.

Blair wrapped his arms around me immediately. "No, honey. Of course you didn't say anything wrong," he assured me; his parents were shaking their heads in agreement. "We're just amazed by the extent of your gift." He leaned down and kissed me gently. I smiled shyly at him.

"Well, let's get back to the condo for a while so you can rest up before the meeting convenes," Bethany suggested.

Having already seen that my appearance in front of the Ileesia would go well, I was able to rest. Blair sat with me on the balcony as I slept contentedly in his arms. Shortly after two, Bethany told us that it was time to get ready to leave.

Approaching the museum, I noticed that there were quite a few cars in the parking lot. Tourists were going in and out of the front door, some carrying bags from the museum store emblazoned with the Greek flag.

Erica greeted us again in the lobby and handed Blake and Bethany an agenda for the meeting. In the elevator, Blake entered the code and pushed L2. When the door opened, I saw a small crowd of people milling around a spacious lobby, beyond which a set of carved double doors stood closed.

Blair and I followed his parents. His arm wrapped securely around my waist again. Several members of the Ileesia extended their hands in greeting to Blake and Bethany, who then introduced Blair and me. They were all very hospitable, aware even without using their gifts that I must be nervous.

From across the room, a deep voice called to Blake. "Blake! Ah, finally!" Striding toward us was a man around Blake's age extending his hand as he neared us.

"Andreas," Blake called, "how good to see you!" Andreas shook hands with him and Blair and turned to Bethany, embracing her.

Andreas turned his hazel eyes toward me. He was shorter than Blake, a little stockier, with dark brown curly hair that was receding slightly from his forehead. He smiled, but something in his gaze unnerved me. Was he evaluating me?

"You must be Makayla," Andreas said, extending his hand to me. I shook it and smiled but said nothing. "I have wanted to meet you for some time, my dear. Sean spoke of little else once you arrived on the scene. Have you enjoyed your visit so far?" he asked politely.

"Yes, thank you," I replied formally. Noticing the stiff set of my voice, Andreas's eyes grew sad.

"I do hope that we'll become good friends, Makayla," he said gently. "I miss your father, and I see so much of him in you." Andreas rested his hand on my shoulder.

"I'm sure you'll have time to visit before we leave, Andreas," Blake assured him. Just then, the double doors opened, and silence fell in the lobby. The members of the Ileesia began filing into the room.

Bethany turned toward Blair and me. "Wait here in the lobby until you're called. It won't be long; Zandria just wants to call the meeting to order before you come in, okay?" She placed her hands on my shoulders and smiled down at me.

"Okay," I whispered, more nervous than I realized. Bethany pulled me into her arms.

"Don't be afraid, sweetie," she whispered in my ear. "Everything will be fine. Love you!"

"Love you too."

Blake winked at me as he led Bethany into the meeting room. The doors shut firmly behind them.

Blair wrapped his arms around me, pulling me close to him. "There's nothing to be nervous about," he assured me, smirking. "You've probably already seen that, haven't you?" He looked down at me, waiting for an answer.

"Yes, but…"

"But what, honey?"

"Nothing," I said nonchalantly. "I'm just having trouble giving up my worrying habit." I stood on my toes to kiss him.

The double doors opened, and Blair released me except for my hand. Andreas stood at the door and invited us into the room. I experienced déjà vu as we entered the room and took the two empty chairs directly in front of us. Zandria sat opposite me, with Blair's parents on her left. Andreas returned to his seat on her right.

"Welcome, blessed ones," Zandria said kindly. "We are so glad to have you join us today." She then addressed the room at large, her voice strong and commanding.

"Today we have convened to hear the visions of our lost brother Sean Taylor's child. Makayla is eighteen years old and a fairly new emergent. Shortly before she emerged, Makayla began having visions, along with hearing the thoughts of those around her. Blair was her guide and can attest to that, can you not, my son?"

"Yes, Most Blessed One," Blair agreed. My fingers grasped his hand tighter, worried that some chastisement might follow due to our relationship. It did not.

"In the days and weeks since she fully emerged, Makayla's visions have become more defined and repetitive. I have asked her to come today to share her most recurrent vision, which I believe Sean is sending her from beyond." Zandria paused, allowing for the gasps and shock to subside. Andreas leaned forward in his chair.

Zandria continued, "When our brother Sean was found dead, there were many of us who questioned the official police reports, which stated that Sean had accidently fallen from the rooftop garden to his death. Unfortunately, we had no other evidence to present, so the case was closed." Zandria drew in a deep breath.

"Today his child will present evidence as to the cause of her father's death." Zandria's voice boomed through the silent, awestruck assembly. Several members shifted uncomfortably in their seats; Andreas locked his eyes on mine.

"Makayla, are you ready to proceed?" Zandria asked formally.

"Yes, Most Blessed One," I replied. Blair squeezed my hand.

"Proceed, my child." Zandria gestured with her hand and smiled at me across the oval table.

The members of the Ileesia all looked at me, waiting patiently for me to begin. I took a deep breath and began the story. As it had happened when I first told Blake and Bethany about the shapes moving away from the wall, several members gasped upon hearing it. I paused and looked up; Andreas had his head in his hands. Zandria nodded for me to continue.

I tried to describe the voice of the leader—majestic, deep, commanding. No one seemed to react to the name Lorcan; when I mentioned the Dumaris, however, there were audible groans and signs of distress among the members. My voice broke when I described my father's last words and the sound of his painful cries.

Blair leaned closer, comforting and reassuring me of his presence. Soft sniffing noises occasionally broke the still silence. Zandria sat unmoving in her chair, allowing the members time to process my words. I looked at Blake; his face was grave, but he inclined his head to me.

"Most Blessed One," a man on my left spoke.

"Yes, Ethan."

"Forgive me, but I am concerned with the accuracy of this emergent's story." Blair stiffened next to me. "Is it not possible that in the throes of her emergence she might have misunderstood her vision?" The man called Ethan leaned forward. "The Dumaris have not been heard from in fifty years or more. Why would they resurface now?" Murmurings of agreement could be heard around the room.

Andreas spoke angrily, "Are you such a fool to believe that such a reappearance is not possible? What other explanation could there be for Sean's death?"

"Peace, Andreas." Zandria's voice was gentle but absolutely authoritative. Andreas sat back in his chair in obvious disgust. Zandria turned her attention to Ethan. "Thank you for raising your concerns, my son. It is possible for a young emergent to misunderstand many aspects of his or her new gift."

Andreas sighed loudly and began to interrupt; Zandria's raised hand silenced him. She continued, "That is not the case here, however." Ethan sat back, and the murmuring stopped. "Two members of this hallowed body have seen the vision for themselves, myself being one of them."

It was obvious that no one was prepared to dispute Zandria's gift; the majority of the Ileesia were immediately convinced of the validity of my vision. Andreas relaxed, but his eyes were troubled. Watching him, I could see the pain and grief he felt for my father's loss. New affection and trust rose in my heart for him.

"The issue at hand," Zandria continued, "is how to deal with the return of the Dumaris. Without a doubt, Sean Taylor was murdered by the Dumaris, and to assume that they disappeared thereafter is ludicrous." Every face was riveted on Zandria, their eyes apprehensive but determined.

Zandria turned to face Blair. "Blair, would you please escort Makayla to the museum? I believe she would enjoy seeing it.

We'll be finished here within the hour, and your parents will join you."

"Yes, Most Blessed One," Blair replied.

"Thank you, Makayla, for sharing your vision so bravely." Zandria inclined her head to us. Blair rose and held my chair out for me. Together, we left the room and closed the doors behind us.

In the lobby, I finally succumbed to the tension wound so tightly within my body. Blair knew that I was losing control; he half-carried me to a couch at the far end of the lobby. The walls seemed to be trembling; I closed my eyes and realized that I was shaking violently. Tears began to flow gently down my cheeks and then grew into racking sobs.

"It's okay, honey. Breathe slowly," Blair crooned. "I'm right here with you."

I obeyed as best I could, but recalling the nightmare out loud had brought it back to the surface in a much more violent way than it had when Blake and Zandria had retrieved it from my mind. The grief swelled anew within me, cutting through me like a knife.

When it was obvious to him that I needed more help to control myself, Blair moved me onto his lap and pulled my head gently onto his shoulder. Slowly the pain abated, the tears slowed, and I relaxed into his chest. Blair patiently held me until I was in control again.

"Are you feeling better?" he asked, kissing my forehead. I nodded as he wiped the tears from my face. "We should probably go upstairs to wait for Mom and Dad. Do you think you'll be all right?"

"I think so," I answered softly. "Do we have to go through the museum, though? I don't really feel like being around a lot of people right now."

"We can just wait outside. There's a small park behind the parking lot. I'm sure we could find a bench to sit on."

We took the elevator to the lobby. Erica smiled gently at me, obviously noticing my distress. It was cool and breezy outside; the air felt good against my face. Blair led me across the parking lot into the park, where we found a bench under the shade of a palm tree.

After a short time, Blair pointed back toward the building. Blake, Bethany, and Andreas were crossing the parking lot, coming toward us. Bethany sat down next to me and hugged me tightly. Blake lay his hand on my shoulder.

"Are you doing all right, Makayla?" he asked tenderly, examining my face.

"I'm okay, Blake. Don't worry," I replied, smiling up at him.

Andreas shifted uncomfortably; I looked up at him. "Thank you for defending me, Andreas. It meant a lot to me."

He smiled ruefully down at me. "I'm sorry that you had to hear such stupidity within the walls of the Ileesia, Makayla." Andreas's voice was tinged with disgust. "Some people would rather hide from the truth than face reality."

"It's okay. I won't hold it against all of you," I teased. Andreas finally smiled.

"Makayla, would you join me for dinner tomorrow evening?" he asked kindly and then added quickly, "If that is all right with you, Blake."

Blake looked at me; I nodded. "That's fine with me, Andreas. I'm sure that Sean would want you to know his daughter better."

"Then I'll pick you up around seven tomorrow evening." Andreas smiled.

"That will be great, Andreas. Thanks."

Andreas bid us all good-bye and headed back toward the parking lot. Blake turned toward Blair and me. "Let's go home. We could all use a quiet evening, don't you think?"

"Sounds good to me!" I agreed, standing up and pulling Blair toward the car. Everyone laughed. I was just glad the day was over.

LOSS

I slept late the next morning, waking around ten; dust danced luminously within the sunbeams streaming through my window. Gulls called to one another on the beach, and the smell of saltwater filtered into the room. Laying in bed, I reviewed yesterday's events in my mind—meeting Zandria and Andreas, speaking before the Ileesia.

So much had changed in my life since my birthday a little over a month ago. A new world had been introduced to me, some aspects of which only seemed feasible in science fiction, as my mom had once said. Discovering my dad had opened up this world to me but also led me down paths of sadness and pain. No longer was my life my own; I had responsibilities never before imagined—visions of the future, the past, and the beyond to interpret and use for the betterment of humanity.

Above everything else, however, was the greatest gift—Blair. Seemingly, the fates had intertwined our souls through my emergence—given us each other to comfort, support, and love. The weight of my newly discovered gifts and the resultant responsibilities were lightened by Blair's presence, his very existence.

Blair knocked on my door and bounded into the room. "What do you want to do today, Short Stuff?" Before I could even open my mouth, he blurted out, "How about just hanging out at the beach?" He rumpled my hair, his face alight with excitement.

"You're certainly in a good mood. What's that all about anyway?"

"Just happy that everything went well yesterday and we can spend a couple days relaxing before we go home."

"The beach sounds good to me. Are your parents busy with the Ileesia today?" I asked, curious.

"Yup, they're leaving in an hour or so and will be gone most of the afternoon," Blair explained. "The temperature will be pretty warm today, so I thought you could actually go to the beach without your 'parka'."

"Not funny!" I glared. "It's not my fault I get cold easily; I don't have a lot of insulation, you know."

Blair laughed and stood up. "Let's get ready, have some breakfast, and then head out. Okay?"

"All right. Now get out of here so I can get ready," I teased. He leaned over and kissed me before loping out the door.

By eleven, Blake and Bethany left for the Ileesia, telling us they would be home around four. Blair and I headed down to the beach with our towels and sunscreen. The beach wasn't too crowded, so it was a quiet, peaceful oasis to relax and soak up some sun.

Mid-afternoon arrived, and Blair's stomach started growling, as usual. Actually, it was about time for me to eat too, so we headed back up to the condo to eat lunch. Afterwards, we lay together in the double chaise lounge on the balcony. The sun always left me exhausted; I fell asleep, content in Blair's arms.

He was shielding me. The man stood in front of me with his arms outstretched, protecting me. We were backed against a wall in a dark alley. Peering under his arm, I saw several people creeping slowly toward us. "Stay away from her!" the man shouted. Laughter echoed in the alley. "I just want to talk to her," a man jeered. "I want her to tell my fortune!" More laughter…evil…malicious. As my back hit the wall with a thud, my mind screamed out for Blair. The man trying to shield me was thrown aside by an unseen force. My screams stabbed the night as the men drew closer; the leader extended his hand to stroke my face. I shuddered and collapsed to the ground. My last thought was of Blair…

"No!" I shrieked, wrenching myself awake.

"Makayla! What is it?" Blair's anxious hands grabbed my shoulders to steady me.

"A dream," I panted, "a horrible dream!" Tears flooded from my eyes; I buried my face in Blair's chest.

"It's okay, honey. Calm down now," Blair soothed. "It was just a dream; you're safe. I'm right here."

"But you weren't there!" I sobbed. "I couldn't see or hear you!"

Blair lifted me off the chaise and carried me inside. He sat down on the couch with me and held me close. "I'm here. It was just a dream."

"Was it?" I asked, my eyes wide with terror. "Will I ever know if what I dream is *just* a dream? What if…" My breath came in short gasps. "What if it wasn't just a dream?"

"Makayla, look at me," Blair ordered, guiding my face to his. "Even clairvoyants can have regular dreams—good and bad. We probably spent too long in the sun this morning; you just got overheated. Slow down your breathing and keep looking at me."

He held my face gently so that I could focus on him. Slowly my breathing and heart rates decelerated back to normal. Blair lay my head on his chest. The door to the condo opened. Blake and Bethany stopped short when they saw us on the couch.

"What's wrong, Blair?" Blake's voice sounded alarmed as they crossed to us.

"Makayla and I spent most of the late morning and early afternoon on the beach. After lunch, we lay down on the balcony and fell asleep. Makayla had a bad dream," Blair explained calmly. "I think we just spent too much time in the sun."

"Makayla, sweetie?" Bethany soothed, brushing my hair out of my face. "Do you want to talk about it?" I shook my head.

"Honey," Blake asked quietly, "was it another vision of your father?"

"No," I whispered. "It didn't make sense at all really. Just a scary dream. Blair wasn't with me, and I couldn't hear him." Blair tightened his arms around me.

Bethany smiled down at me. "You know, even you can have dreams, simple dreams, normal human dreams."

"All bad dreams tend to center around things we inwardly fear," Blake explained gently. "It's been a stressful time for you; it's natural that you might have a bad dream or two." He smiled at me; I nodded.

"Andreas is really looking forward to spending the evening with you," Blake said then hesitated. "Do you think you're still up to going?"

"I'll be fine. I don't want to disappoint him," I answered. "I'll go take a shower and get ready." Blair helped me up.

Andreas arrived promptly at seven to find me dressed and ready to go. He told Blake that we would be down on the sponge docks and that he'd bring me home around ten. Blair kissed me good-bye, and I followed Andreas to his car. The feeling of uneasiness I'd felt the first time I met Andreas was gone. He was my father's friend, and through Andreas, I would learn more about my father.

"You look so much like your father, Makayla," Andreas said. "I can't get over the similarities. Every time you smile, I see Sean!" He beamed over at me from the driver's seat.

"Blake told me that you went to college with my dad."

"Yes, that's right. We met in our freshman economics class." Andreas grinned. "Did Blake tell you how Sean and I discovered that we were both clairvoyant?"

"He said something about hearing each other's minds during a test. Is that right?" I asked, smiling at him.

Andreas's laugh thundered in the car. "That's exactly right. Of course, once we made the connection, we were inseparable."

Parking at the end of the docks, Andreas said, "I thought it was a nice evening for a walk. Do you mind?"

"No, sounds great," I replied, getting out of the car, eager to know my father's friend better.

As we strolled down the street, Andreas asked about my mother, how she was doing with work and if she was happy. I told him that she and I were very close and that our lives were full, but I had to admit that Mom missed my dad a lot.

"Your father's death was a terrible blow to us all," Andreas said sadly. "I can't imagine how much harder it was for Marissa." Sorrow billowed out through his eyes.

Andreas greeted the hostess at the restaurant, and we were seated by a windowed wall overlooking the Gulf. As we ate dinner, the conversation shifted to me. Andreas wanted to know all about my hobbies, academic interests, and friends. I felt like I was dominating the discussion for most of the evening, but he kept encouraging me to continue.

Something had been nagging at me since yesterday. "Andreas, why didn't you keep in touch with Mom after Dad died?" I smiled, hoping that he would not be offended by my question.

Andreas met my eyes, obviously considering his words. "I tried, Makayla." He sighed. "Marissa didn't want to stay in contact with any of us. It was too painful for her, I guess." He took a sip from his wine glass. "That's why I'm so happy to get to meet you. I was afraid we might never get the chance, especially if you hadn't inherited Sean's gift."

"Makayla," he asked after we had finished dinner, "how was your emergence? Did everything progress normally?" Andreas lifted his coffee cup to his lips, but his eyes were riveted on me.

"I think so," I answered honestly. "Since I don't have anything to compare it to, it's hard for me to say. I guess that Blair could answer that question for you more accurately."

"Besides the vision of your father, have you had any other visions?" His tone was casual, but concern nudged me. My father's letter, his warning, shot through my mind like a arrow. I was instinctively wary.

"Not really," I lied, concentrating on blocking my mind from intrusion. I was probably overreacting, but I wasn't going to take the chance. After all, I really didn't know Andreas well at all, and suddenly, I recalled that Dad's letter did not mention *him* as one to be trusted.

"That's interesting," Andreas mused. "Sean had so many extraordinary abilities, I just assumed that you had inherited them all."

"I guess not," I said casually. Discomfort edged its way into my mind—I didn't like the direction of our discussion. "Would it be okay with you if we headed back to the condo?" I asked, stretching for emphasis. "I'm getting sort of sleepy."

"Certainly," Andreas agreed jovially. "Let me just pay the check, and we'll be off."

The night was darker than it had been for the past several nights; clouds obscured the moon, veiling its light from us. We walked past the shops, bakeries, and restaurants still busy with tourists. Andreas stiffened as we approached a corner; he put his arm on the small of my back and drew me in from the curb.

"What's wrong, Andreas?" I asked quietly, sensing the tension in his body.

"We're being followed, Makayla," he answered tersely. "No, don't turn around. Let's just get to my car as quickly as possible."

He picked up the pace of his strides with me half running alongside to keep up.

In his anxiety, Andreas turned at the next corner only to find a dead end—an alley. I gasped. The scene was not totally unfamiliar to me. Andreas spun around. Three men were standing at the opening to the street. Protectively, he placed me behind him before he spoke.

"What do you want?" his voice rang out. Andreas threw his wallet to the ground in front of the men.

They snorted, grinning darkly as they continued to approach us. My heart pounded in my ears; my hands were ice as I clutched onto the back of Andreas's jacket. Fear like I had never known in my life held me in its iron grip; every breath I took seared my chest.

"We don't want your money," one of the men jeered. "We just want to talk to the girl."

"Stay away from her!" Andreas warned.

"I just want her to tell my fortune!" The men's sonorous laughter echoed off the walls. How could they not be heard on the street?

My throat constricted as the contents of my stomach struggled to remain there. From behind me, I heard more footsteps. I wheeled to see three more men emerging from behind some large packing crates at the end of the alley. We were surrounded. Trapped.

In my terror, my mind called out to Blair—hoping that through some miracle, I would see him again. I thought of my mother, Blake and Bethany, and Zandria, who in her old age was going to lose more people she loved. Andreas heard the men behind me and twisted so that my body was against the brick wall.

"She's of no use to you," Andreas tried to bargain. "Take me instead."

From the entrance of the alley, another voice rose. "What use could you possibly be to us, Andreas Pappas?" Andreas and I froze. The glare of the overhead light blurred the man's features.

"Who are you?" Andreas asked. "How do you know me?" His trembling belied his calm voice.

"We know everything, Andreas." The man sneered. "It is our *business* to know everything."

As the sneering man grew closer, he raised his hand. Fear was dulling my senses. As if in slow motion, Andreas flew through the air and crashed into a crate, shattering it. He landed with a thud and didn't move.

"Andreas!" I screamed, too paralyzed to move. I heard their jeers and taunts; they enjoyed my anguish. The man moved closer to me, his face no longer obscured by the glare. My nightmare awakened.

"Lorcan…" I whispered. The mediocrity of his stature surprised me. He was neither tall nor particularly muscular, yet he embodied evil. He sauntered closer to me, arrogance seeping out of every pore. His olive complexion and prominent nose pointed to a Mediterranean background. I couldn't help but wonder how hazel eyes could be so black.

"Ah, Makayla." Lorcan sighed, his voice silky and dangerous. "You are as talented as your dear father. How useful you will be to the Dumaris." Lorcan nodded to the man closest to me; he grabbed my arms and locked them in his vise grip against my sides. It hurt. I struggled uselessly—anger and loathing fused with my terror.

Lorcan advanced on me until he stood offensively close. I turned my head from his malevolent eyes, calling out to Blair once more. Lorcan stroked my face with his hand, pulling it slowly along my cheek and jaw. I flinched. Revulsion shook me.

"So small to be so gifted. What a convenient little package you are, my dear."

"Don't touch me, you murderer!" I shouted, outrage in my voice. Lorcan's hand flashed. He backhanded me across my face. The pain was stunning. My head slammed into my captor's shoulder. The sting of tears mingled with fear.

"You must learn respect, Makayla. Respect for the family is our number one rule." Lorcan touched my face, gently this time, but his caress made me shudder. "Release her, Nicholas," he ordered, and my arms were immediately loosed from their bonds.

I staggered and gripped the wall for support. Enraged tears poured down my face. I was not going to help the Dumaris. I was going to die, like my father. *Blair…*

Once again Lorcan moved toward me. My body pressed against the brick wall, but I continued to move back, as if into my mother's protecting arms. Lorcan placed his hands on either side of my head, trapping me within his stare.

"Such a fiery spirit you possess, Makayla." Lorcan sighed. "I like my women passionate." He moved one of his hands to the back of my neck and jerked me toward him; the smell of stale liquor twisted my stomach. With his other hand, he raised my chin. His mouth crushed against mine. I groaned in revulsion, bile rising in my throat. Lorcan smiled. "I imagine you will be much more entertaining than your father!"

A sudden movement behind him forced Lorcan to release me. My trembling body slid to the ground; pain and terror sucked at my consciousness.

"No!" someone shouted. There was an ear-splitting crash, followed by grunting and cursing. Lorcan turned away from my crumpled body to face the tumult. It was then that I saw them—my two angels—standing in the circle of light just beyond me.

"Zandria! Blair! " Lorcan yelled. "Get them! They must not escape!" Lorcan barked the order, and his minions lurched forward.

No, not Zandria! She's old and weak! Blair! I wailed in my head.

Zandria's face was fierce with anger, her body erect and commanding. She casually raised her hands to the two men closest to her. They soared across the alley, smashing into the wall. Their bodies lay motionless, contorted, and broken. Zandria turned to meet her next opponents fearlessly. She dispensed with them similarly and continued toward me.

Blair's eyes sought mine, their fury only matched by the pain. He advanced on the next two men, his hands fisted at his sides. Thinking him easily handled, the men jeered as he approached them. Eyes blazing with determination, Blair swept his right hand across his body. The men strutted forward into an invisible wall, their bodies thrown back by the impact.

My eyes widened in shock. I looked at Blair's face. Its potency and conviction was strangely striking.

Stunned, the men looked to Lorcan for direction. Antipathy seethed under Lorcan's cool disposition. His eyes narrowed as he scrutinized Blair's potential. Lorcan nodded his head toward Blair. The men were poised to advance, adrenaline surging visibly in their bodies, sneers repositioned on their faces. Blair stood unmoved and focused.

The men split their formation, coming at Blair from two sides; he raised his hands as if beckoning them forward. From the back of the alley, a creaking of wood drew Lorcan's attention. Two crates raced each other forward, crushing the men under their weight. The splintering cacophony concealed Blair's movements; stealthily, he moved closer to me.

Lorcan, still astounded by the rapid turn of events, stood motionless in front of me. Terror seized his face. He reached down, picked me up roughly, and shielded himself with my body. Weary of the struggle, I hung limp in his arms. Zandria restrained Blair's arm, her face stoic and circumspect.

Makayla... Blair's soul cried out to me.

"So, Strong One, is this your *love*?" Lorcan jeered. Blair glowered daggers at him, straining against Zandria's surprising grip. Lorcan placed one of his hands on my head. "One more step and her mind will be inundated with more negativity than her little head can withstand," he threatened.

Zandria took a step forward, still gripping Blair's arm. Lorcan pressed his hand against my head. My eyes rolled back into my head, my body slumping further into Lorcan's arms. Hate…raw violence…agony…cruelty…lust. Darkness threatened to engulf me. And then it was gone.

My body slid with finality to the ground. Lifting my head slightly, I saw Lorcan stumble away from me dazedly. In the next moment, Zandria and Lorcan were locked in a wordless battle, each one's hands raised and trembling in front of the other. Zandria's eyes, dark with fury, bore into Lorcan's face. His hands quaked under the force of her power.

Blair grabbed me in his arms and carried me farther down the alley, away from the rising pitch of the battle. It was then that I noticed other members of the Ileesia running into the alley, with Blake in the lead. They headed for the members of the Dumaris, who were slowly regaining consciousness. Blake ran to Andreas's side as Bethany leaned down next to us, her face ashen.

"Makayla…" Blair whispered my name over and over again, holding me close and kissing me. I lay limp in his arms, trying to break through the darkness. It was so deep, so heavy.

"Makayla, can you hear me, honey?" Blair's voice strained against his panic. I followed his voice up, up out of the murky black. My hand reached up and stroked his face. He buried his face in my hand.

A sudden loud oath rent the air. Lorcan flew twenty feet into the air. He landed with a crushing blow against the wall and crumpled in a heap on the ground. Blood gushed from the side of his face.

"Zandria!" Blair cried. He placed me quickly but carefully into Bethany's arms and raced to her side. Zandria was leaning against the wall, her face pale. Blair caught her as she slid to the ground, her head lolling over his arm.

"Zandria!" I cried, trying to get to her. Bethany lifted me up and helped me move toward her.

Blair cradled Zandria in his arms like a small child. She called to me, her voice quivering. "Makayla…"

Bethany lowered me by Zandria's head. "I'm right here, YaYa," I said, tears streaming down my face. She looked so frail, so tired. I stroked her head softly.

"Don't cry, Makayla," Zandria said, her voice weak with exhaustion. "It is time. The prophecy…has been…fulfilled." She gasped as my hands fluttered helplessly over her face.

Blake supported Andreas, who looked stunned but otherwise unhurt. The small circle of my clairvoyant family surrounded Zandria, comforting her in her last moments.

"I love you, YaYa." I sobbed, laying my head on her chest.

"As I…love you, my child." Zandria looked up into my face and then into Blair's. "Most…Blessed…One…" she muttered. She gasped, and she was gone.

THE PROPHECY

Chaos. Confusion. Despair. Eddies of emotion swirled through the alley in the immediate aftermath of Zandria's death. One moment she was there—alive—and the next she was gone, snuffed out, leaving nothing but darkness. To have only known her for such a short time was an injustice too painful to endure.

I lay across Zandria's shell, my heart shattered and fearful. I could hear the whirring conversation around me. Someone sobbed. Someone sent questions up to God. Someone moaned. Someone called my name.

Blair attempted to gently pry me off Zandria, but I couldn't bear to leave her cold and alone. I wailed and struggled and clung to her. Loving hands caressed my hair and back, endeavoring in vain to console me.

The police were summoned to the scene. Andreas reported that we were attacked without provocation and that Lorcan's death occurred in self-defense. Of course, the police assumed that Zandria had been killed by Lorcan or one of his men and not the other way around. The surviving members of the Dumaris were hospitalized under police surveillance and charged with attempted kidnapping, assault, and manslaughter.

Finally it was time to move Zandria's body.

"Makayla," Blair whispered, "we have to go, honey. The coroner's office is here."

My arms reflexively tightened around the body, no longer the home for Zandria's soul. It was already cold. I lifted my drowning eyes to look into her face. It was peaceful, strangely beautiful in death. I kissed her forehead and turned away into Blair's waiting arms.

We sat up for hours that night; there were so many unanswered questions, so many mysteries. Blake and Bethany questioned Blair about the details of the attack, from the time he and Zandria arrived. I understood. They needed to make sense out of senselessness. But I was numb—in a surreal fog of sights and sounds. Their words floated around me but could not penetrate my grief. My eyes were dry, cried out, stinging and swollen. They closed, weary of grief.

Vivid memories tormented my sleep.

Lorcan advanced on me. He stood offensively close, stroked my face with his hand. I flinched...revulsion...moved toward me...placed his hands on either side of my head...trapping me...one of his hands to the back of my neck...jerked me toward him... He raised my chin. His mouth crushed against mine.

"No!" I screamed. I pushed against him. "Let me go! You're too close! Move away!"

"Makayla!" Blair shouted over my ranting as I pushed against him. Arms tightened around me. I struggled and kicked. "It's Blair, Makayla. Open your eyes!"

A door burst open. Strong hands grasped my head. I fought but was sucked into semi-consciousness. New thoughts danced through my mind. Blair's smile...Mom's arms outstretched...Amy blushing shyly...Leila giggling in my arms...Blair...Blair...

"Blair?" My voice was hoarse and raw. I opened my eyes and searched for my strength, my love, my soul.

"I'm right here, honey." Blair cautiously wrapped his arms around me, meeting my eyes, communicating his intentions. Blake and Bethany sat on the sides of the bed, their hands resting softly on me.

Sobs burst from the depths of my sorrow, my fear, my loneliness. "I'm so scared, Blair. I felt his body pressed against me, his mouth suffocating me!"

Hysteria threatened to swallow me. All the progress I had made over the past month was thrown asunder. The nightmares were back, different, but still haunting. Would I ever sleep peacefully again?

"Makayla, Lorcan will never touch you again," Blair pledged. "Please let us take away your pain. Let us help you get through this. We'll cope with it—together."

I looked into his eyes, so passionate, and nodded. All three of them placed their hands on my head. My eyes closed as warmth coursed through me. A quiet peace drifted over me. I floated, strengthened by their love.

When I opened my eyes again, it was morning. Light poured into the window—a new day, a new beginning. My head lay on Blair's chest, and as he felt me stir, he rubbed my back slowly.

"Hi," I said, looking up into his concerned face.

"How are you this morning, Makayla?" Blair's voice was tight with suppressed emotion.

"I'm okay. Kind of tired, like I haven't slept in a week," I answered, stretching my arms. They ached.

Blair stroked my arm gently, pausing at distinct intervals. I looked down then. Purple bruises stained my upper arms. Abrasions covered my palms and elbows. The visible scars of the attack were obvious and painful to Blair, but deep in his thoughts, I heard his concern for the invisible ones. Anger and... was it guilt?

I sat up on my elbow to look into his eyes. "Why on earth are you feeling guilty?"

He closed his eyes and drew in a deep breath. *I should have gotten to you sooner, Makayla. I should have been able to stop him from hurting you.*

No, Blair. Look at me. Blair opened his eyes and turned to me. *You saved my life. Please don't do this to yourself. It will only make it harder for me.*

Blair pulled me tight against his chest. "Hearing and seeing you in pain,"—he winced—"was the most terrifying thing I've ever experienced." He sucked in another slow breath. I tightened my arms around him. "I feel guilty,"—he swallowed hard—"because you had to endure such agony and I couldn't protect you from it."

I started to answer him, but he lifted his finger to my mouth. "Rationally," he continued, "I know there was nothing more I could have done, but emotionally…" Blair's words faded away. Despair choked them off.

Words that my mother spoke the day after my birthday party returned to me. When I asked her why my dad told her about his mother's bitter feelings toward their relationship, she had said, "We shared everything, Kayla, the good and the bad. That's what love and marriage are about." Blair heard my mother's words as they repeated in my head.

"I guess moms really do know best sometimes," I whispered, smiling up at him.

"Makayla, last night taught me that I can't imagine life without you." Blair's arms tightened around me. "I love you more than words can express."

My heart leapt despite its grief. Blair's words etched themselves into my soul and washed away any doubt. "You are everything to me. I will love you forever."

Blair brought his lips to mine and kissed them. *Today... tomorrow...forever.*

Later that morning, we sat together in the living room. Blake and Bethany had been up for hours but didn't disturb us, hoping that we had found some relief from the pain in sleep.

They shared the details about Zandria's funeral, which she had preplanned months before. Guests from all over the world would be attending. Andreas was now the acting head of the Ileesia until his appointment could be voted upon, which was only a formality.

My own questions fought their way through the haze in my brain. So many things to think about. How did Lorcan know where to find me? Would his death put an end to the family's activities? The most important questions were for Blair.

"Blair, how did you know that I was in trouble?" I asked, wrapped securely in his arms.

"I heard you calling my name," he said softly. "At first it was just a subtle cry and then..." Blair closed his eyes to regain his composure. "Mom, Dad, and I were taking a walk with Zandria in the park behind the Ileesia. She called after you left with Andreas and asked us to meet her," Blair explained.

"We were just talking about everyday things; Zandria wanted to know about our school and what activities we were involved in, things like that. Suddenly your voice screamed in my head." Blair shuddered, remembering the sound. "I didn't know where you were exactly, but Zandria closed her eyes, and when she opened them, she said she knew exactly where you were.

"She told Mom and Dad to gather other members of the Ileesia while she and I raced toward the docks in her car. The whole time I was listening to your terror, and I was afraid we would be too…" Blair's voice broke; he lay his head on mine.

When Blair had regained his control, I asked him about his newly emerged powers. Beyond his ability to hear me call for him from so far away, for the first time, he had used his hands telekinetically. Along with Zandria, Blair had thrown the crates—blasted them, really—into the air and slammed them into his would-be attackers. And he had created an invisible wall.

"I don't know how that happened," Blair admitted sheepishly. "Instinctively I wanted to get to you, and they were blocking us. My hands did what seemed natural to them." He shrugged at my amazed expression.

"What about Lorcan? How did you get him to release me?" A shiver ran down my spine at the memory.

"When Lorcan was hurting you"—his eyes filled with rage—"all I wanted to do was stop him, to remove the negativity he was forcing on you." Blair took a deep breath and continued. "I'm definitely not sure how I did it though." He looked over at his father for his opinion.

Blake sat with Bethany, silent and grief-stricken. He had not spoken for quite a while. "What you did, Blair, was counter Lorcan's negativity by projecting positive thoughts and energy," he explained. "It's a very rare gift but exceptionally useful against the Dumaris' tricks."

Bethany reached over and placed her hand gently on her son's shoulder. "I'm so proud of you, Blair," she whispered. "What you did last night was far beyond what anyone would have asked of you."

I felt Blair's body tremble with emotion and raised my head to look at him. A tear escaped from his eye; Blair gazed down at me.

I couldn't save Zandria, he thought, his emotions releasing themselves from their tight bonds. *Maybe if I had been stronger, quicker, she wouldn't have…*

"No, son," Blake said firmly. "You did everything humanly possible to keep Makayla and Zandria safe. She was old, and even though she was powerful, the exertion was too much for her heart. It was not your fault."

"Blair, Zandria wouldn't want you to blame yourself for any of this," his mother soothed. "She was proud of you. She said…" Bethany broke off and stared at her husband.

"She said, 'The prophecy has been fulfilled.'" I finished Zandria's words for her. "But what does *that* mean, Blake?" Both Blair and I looked at his father for the explanation.

Blake closed his eyes and breathed deeply, steeling himself, it seemed to me. He kissed Bethany on the forehead and squeezed her shoulder. A tear flowed gently down her cheek.

"There was a prophecy told many years ago, probably eighty years ago or more, that foretold the coming of a powerful young leader rising to the chair of the Most Blessed One. This powerful leader would show him or herself to have powers similar to those of his or her predecessor.

"Of course, for the past eighty years, clairvoyants have waited for such a leader to emerge, but to no avail. Zandria rose to the position at the age of sixty, after the death of Gregory. His powers, although formidable, were not nearly as strong as Zandria's. So the prophecy went unfulfilled.

"Zandria, in the past few years, as her health steadily failed, has been hoping that such a leader would present him or herself. Of course, it was not necessary because Andreas had been named the heir to her position three years ago by a council vote. Still, Zandria hoped with all her heart that the prophecy would be fulfilled within or shortly after her life."

Silence rang through the room. Blake's words hung thickly in the air, too surprising to comprehend.

"Are you saying that Zandria thought that Blair…" My voice died out in awe and fear. I looked at Blair, but he stared forward, stunned beyond reason.

Leaning forward in his chair, Blake said, "Yes, Makayla, I believe that Zandria thought that Blair was the prophecy's fulfillment." I looked at Bethany; she nodded gravely. Blake waited for Blair to look at him, but he was still frozen in disbelief. "Blair, look at me, son." Slowly Blair turned his head toward his father.

"There is no reason for you to be concerned with this right now. By the codes of the Ileesia, you cannot be considered as leader until you are at least twenty-one and then only if you accept and are approved by the council."

Blair's eyes widened as though he thought his dad had lost his mind. "Not be concerned?" he blurted out. "I can't be… I don't want to be… I don't know how to be…" Blair stammered incoherently. I could feel the fear and panic rising with each utterance; I tightened my arms around his waist.

"Blair, hold on to your focus," Blake's voice commanded. I'd never seen Blair lose control, but this news would make anyone lose it. He was visibly shaking now, even as his father rose to calm him.

Blake grasped Blair's head in his hands and closed his eyes. Slowly I felt the tension leave Blair's body; his eyes closed, and he leaned his head back. We sat quietly for a few moments. Blake returned to the couch with Bethany while I held Blair in my arms.

I moved up to kiss Blair's cheek. He turned his eyes to me and shook his head sadly, still greatly disturbed by his possible destiny.

We'll face whatever comes together, Blair. Nothing has really changed. Blair nodded and leaned down to kiss me softly.

"I'm sorry, Dad," Blair apologized. "I didn't mean to lose it."

"Blair," Blake said gently, "you have nothing to be ashamed of. I'm more proud of you than you could ever imagine." He sighed.

"Makayla, you need to call your mother and explain that we'll be delayed here for another few days. Tell her a close family friend died. I'm sure she will understand."

"Of course. She won't mind, and I wouldn't want to miss…" My voice cracked and broke. Blake rose and held his hand out for Bethany, who turned to us.

"Try to relax your minds as well as your bodies today. Dad and I will be at the Ileesia for most of the day. Tomorrow is the funeral. You'll need your strength for that." Bethany leaned down and kissed us both before they left.

Zandria's Greek Orthodox funeral took place at three in the afternoon the next day. St. Nicholas's Cathedral was packed with friends and admirers from all over the clairvoyant world. Blair and I sat with his parents and Andreas on the front row, in the seats reserved for Zandria's family. The service passed in a blur of traditional liturgy, incense, and chant.

People rose to expound on Zandria's attributes: her love, service, and devotion to all those around her. Zandria had confessed to me her sadness over not having children and grandchildren of her own, but here within the confines of this holy shrine, her true children praised and remembered her.

Andreas called the Ileesia into special session at six o'clock on the evening of the funeral, knowing that every member, as well as guests from around the world, would be in town. Blair and I were invited to attend as Andreas's special guests.

Due to the larger crowd, the great hall of the museum itself was turned into a meeting hall. Rows of chairs lined the rotunda, which was draped in black in deference to Zandria. When Blair and I entered, the area was swarming with people, many of whom were speaking different languages. Several people approached us to shake our hands and express their happiness that we were safe.

Andreas entered and stood behind the podium with the members of the Ileesia standing on either side of him. Each one wore a black armband around their right sleeve. The guests took their seats, waiting for his comments. Blair and I sat directly in front of Andreas in the front row. He smiled down at us.

"Good evening, blessed ones," Andreas began. "On behalf of the US Ileesia, I would like to welcome you and thank you for supporting us in our time of grief. The tragic loss of our beloved Zandria has darkened our lives; we will miss her wisdom, grace, and beauty." Murmurings of assent floated over the audience.

"The circumstances of our beloved leader's death are most disturbing. To lose our Most Blessed One to a insurrectionist group of our own people is shocking beyond comprehension." Again muttering and whispers could be heard from the audience. "The resurfacing of the Dumaris is an issue that should concern us all," Andreas continued. "There can be no doubt that their poisonous tactics are contrary to the clairvoyant mission on earth. As a world group, we must stand together against them." The room erupted into applause; Andreas waited before he spoke again.

"If anything positive has come from this tragedy, it is the death of the Dumaris' leader Lorcan Stamos and the arrest of several of their members." Applause, again.

I leaned over to Blair and whispered in his ear, "But Lorcan was not the leader…" Blair raised his finger to his lips and shook his head slightly. I frowned in confusion.

"It is my belief, blessed ones," Andreas continued, "that a serious blow has been dealt to the Dumaris, one that may well crush them from our existence. Let us commit ourselves, on this most sad night, to one another's safety and the safety of humanity by continuing to keep alert for signs of the Dumaris' return." The audience rose to their feet, applauding wildly and enthusiastically.

Andreas raised his hands for silence. "Let us never forget our Most Blessed Zandria. She sacrificed her life to save the lives of myself and an emergent clairvoyant." Andreas's voice broke with emotion. "May her memory be eternal." With those words, the meeting was adjourned.

Groups of people approached Andreas to shake his hand and offer their condolences. As the crowd grew around the dais, I became claustrophobic; the events of two days ago pressed in on me along with the crowd. My hands became icy, but my body burned as my head spun. The image of Lorcan's face close to mine, his mouth assaulting mine…trapped. Blair was shaking someone's hand as the room began to spin. As if they were underwater, the crowd swirled around me. Blair caught me before I hit the floor.

Somewhere, a great distance away, someone gasped. Hands brushed over me as Blair carried me through the worried crowd, catching his parents' and Andreas's eyes on the way out of the rotunda. He kicked open the door to an empty sitting room, followed closely by the others.

"Makayla, stay with me, honey," Blair called softly as he sat down, supporting me in his arms. I felt dizzy but was able to push back the wave of unconsciousness threatening me.

"What happened?" Andreas asked, his voice anxious.

Bethany sat beside us and laid her hand on my forehead. "She's a little warm. Maybe she just got overheated in the crowd."

My eyes fluttered open and found them all around me. Embarrassed, I tried to sit up, but Blair held me still. "Just wait a minute, Makayla; lay still."

"Are you okay, honey?" Blake asked as he touched my check.

I nodded and muttered, "I'm sorry. The crowd was bumping into me…" I shuddered and buried my head in Blair's chest. *It was pressing against me…like him.* Tears flowed silently down my face.

"Damn that Lorcan to hell for doing this to her!" Andreas spluttered angrily.

"Peace, Andreas," Blake said. "Anger won't help anyone, especially not Makayla."

"I'm sorry, Blake," Andreas apologized. "Of course you're right. I just hate to see her so torn up."

"We all do," Bethany assured him. "Let's take Makayla back to the condo. It's been a traumatic and exhausting time for all of us."

Blair stood without speaking and cradled me against his chest. Andreas moved closer to us. "Blair, thank you for all you did the other night. I will be forever grateful to you. I look forward to your future. We'll all be watching."

Andreas leaned forward. "Makayla, may I keep in touch with you?" he asked gently. "I would like to hear how everything is going for you back home, if you don't mind."

I lifted my head. "Of course. I'm sorry that our evening ended so badly the other night. Next time will be better." I smiled feebly; Andreas lay his hand on mine and nodded.

Andreas turned to speak to Blake and Bethany. "Well, it has certainly been a trying few days." Andreas rubbed his hand wearily over his eyes.

"Everything will be fine," Blake assured him. "The Ileesia has gone through transitions before. We're all here for you, Andreas."

Andreas smiled weakly and shook Blake's hand. Bethany embraced him.

"Oh, will you need us to convene again before next month, Andreas?" Blake asked as we headed for the door.

"I don't think so, my friend," Andreas's voice rang. "I think we all need some time to gather our thoughts for the future."

"Let us know if you need something, Andreas," Bethany said.

"Thank you. Have a safe trip home, blessed ones."

Fatigue wrestled with me and made it difficult to concentrate on their conversation; weights pulled against my eyelids. *Wait. What did Andreas say?* There was something in his voice…or was it his words? I shook my head to free myself from my confusion.

"Are you all right, honey?" Blair asked as he carried me out the door.

"I'll be fine, Blair," I assured him. "As long as we're together."

Blair leaned down and kissed me tenderly. I lay my head against his shoulder and closed my eyes. My dad stood in front of me and spoke.

Makayla, they're still out there.

And then he was gone.